The Second Term Trilogy

THE DAY

A Novel of America
in the Last Days

John Price
Christian House Publishing, Inc.

The Day is Book Three of a trilogy of novels arising from
events which may occur in the second term of an
American President based on Biblical prophecy.

THE DAY

A NOVEL OF AMERICA
IN THE LAST DAYS

www.endofamericabook.com

Price, John
THE DAY
A Novel of America in the Last Days
ISBN-13: 978-0-9840771-7-5 (Amazon)
ISBN-13: 978-0-9840771-8-2 (Kindle)

Printed in the United States of America

TABLE OF CONTENTS

Chapter 1   Chapter 2   Chapter 3
Chapter 4   Chapter 5   Chapter 6
Chapter 7   Chapter 8   Chapter 9
Chapter 10   Chapter 11   Chapter 12
Chapter 13   Chapter 14   Chapter 15
Chapter 16   Chapter 17   Chapter 18
Chapter 19   Chapter 20   Chapter 21
Chapter 22   Chapter 23   Chapter 24
Chapter 25   Chapter 26   Chapter 27
Chapter 28   Chapter 29   Chapter 30
Chapter 31   Chapter 32   Chapter 33
Chapter 34   Chapter 35   Chapter 36
Chapter 37   Chapter 38   Chapter 39
Chapter 40   Chapter 41   Chapter 42
Chapter 43   Chapter 44   Chapter 45
Chapter 46   Chapter 47   Chapter 48
Chapter 49   Chapter 50   Chapter 51
Chapter 52   Chapter 53   Chapter 54
Chapter 55   Chapter 56   Chapter 57
Chapter 58   Chapter 59   Chapter 60
Chapter 61   Chapter 62   Chapter 63
Chapter 64   Chapter 65   Chapter 66
Chapter 67   Chapter 68   Chapter 69
Chapter 70   Chapter 71   Author's Note to Reader
Excerpt-The End of   Seven Things to Do If   About the Author
America   Moving Offshore

"Alas for the day."

(Joel 1:15)

"The day of your watchmen, of your punishment, has come"

(Micah 7:4)

"Behold, it is coming and it will be brought about, declares the Lord. That is the day of which I have spoken."

(Ezekiel 39:8)

I

BEFORE

THE

DAY

"The word of the LORD came to me: "Son of man, set your face toward Gog, of the land of Magog, the chief prince of Meshech and Tubal (currently known as Russia), *and prophesy against him and say, Thus says the Lord GOD: Behold, I am against you, O Gog, chief prince of Meshech and Tubal.....Persia* (currently known as Iran), *Cush* (Currently known as Ethipia and Sudan), *and Put* (currently known as Libya) *are with them, all of them with shield and helmet; Gomer and all his hordes; Beth-togarmah* (currently Turkey and parts of Eastern Europe previously under Soviet domination - Muslim population) *from the uttermost parts of the north with all his hordes—many peoples are with you....*

"After many days you will be called to arms. In the latter years you will go against the land that is restored from war, the land whose people were gathered from many peoples upon the mountains of Israel, which had been a continual waste. Its people were brought out from the peoples and now dwell securely, all of them. You will advance, coming on like a storm. You will be like a cloud covering the land, you and all your hordes, and many peoples with you. (Ezekiel 38:1-3, 5-6, 8-9)

1

Russian/Iranian Coalition Headquarters

Damascus, Syria

The time to annihilate Israel must surely be near. Russian Colonel Nikolaevich carefully read each day's digital flash traffic from Moscow. What he had not yet seen, but was anxious to read, was the message – *PREPARE TO INVADE ISRAEL.* For the last several weeks thousands of troops from Russia, Iran, Libya and Turkey poured into Damascus, chosen as the staging area for the upcoming invasion of Israel. The only thing needed now was the joint final attack order from Moscow and Tehran.

Colonel Nikolaevich's view was that he had been stationed in Damascus too long. He missed the tasty borscht and other food and drink which he previously enjoyed in Moscow. He was tired of eating mostly Syrian food for the last fourteen months, during which his assignment from the Coalition was to assemble and store thousands of armored military vehicles. Twenty acres of warehouses at Mazah Highway (Route 7) and Hafez Al Asad Road sheltered Russian and Iranian tanks, assault vehicles, troop carriers, mobile rocket launchers and other instruments of war.

From the warehouses the assault force would travel thirty miles southwest along Mazah Highway to reach the border with Israel. Once in Israel, the distance to Tel Aviv was just over a hundred miles. The Colonel's review of terrain maps showed that the average driving time from Damascus to Tel Aviv was five hours and twenty-two

1

minutes. He multiplied the projected travel time by ten, given that the average speed of the armored vehicles in his warehouses was ten percent of that of a highway motor vehicle. Traveling by day only, Colonel Nikolaevich calculated that he could enter Tel Aviv within four days of his departure from Damascus. He also was painfully aware of the fact that his standing order was to immediately halt the Coalition assault force should the United States militarily oppose the invasion. Should America intervene by force of arms Colonel Nikolaevich was to make a one hundred and eighty degree turn back to Damascus. Moscow, though, rated the odds that the US would come to Israel's defense at less than 10%.

Right on time, the Colonel's aide brought his noon lunch, the only meal of the day he enjoyed, as it usually consisted of food as close as possible to that of Mother Russia. Dark bread, sliced tongue, stone ground mustard and a carafé of Stolichnaya vodka. The aide knocked, then entered into the Colonel's makeshift command center on the second floor of the expansive warehouse. From his office the Colonel looked out at the sea of Russian and Iranian armored vehicles. He wondered how soon it would be before the Coalition launched the attack, He doubted that the over one hundred fifty thousand soldiers now scattered in Damascus would be staying in the Syrian city very much longer. The cost alone of doing so militated against a substantial delay. As he finished the last of his lunch, swallowing the final gulp of Stolichnaya, the satellite phone on his desk commenced loudly buzzing, crawling slightly across his desk as it sounded.

He quickly grabbed the satellite phone, saying in his Ukrainian accented Russian, "Colonel Nikolaevich. Coalition Command Center. Damascus."

"Colonel, this is Vladimir. I have *very good* news for you. You have been patient in waiting....but it is now *finally* time....Time to launch our joint invasion of Israel. Your command orders will be digitally flashed to you on the secure communications system, of course, but I wanted to give you an advance call. Expect your orders within the hour. As the Attack Commander you are expected to be in Tel Aviv within no more than five days, less if possible. Your attack is to begin prior to dawn tomorrow morning. Understood?"

"*Fully* understood, sir. Thank you, Mister President, for this call. We *won't* let you down. We won't let *Mother Russia* down."

2

Press Briefing Room – White House West Wing

Washington, DC

Normally when a President plans to address the media in the Press Briefing Room a media advisory goes out with at least two hours' notice. The advance notice allows the most visible talking heads to be in the press room so they can appear on camera. Today the President's Press Secretary broke the informal rule. Media in the area had ten minutes' notice that the President would be doing a no question 'presser'. Some speculated that the President was not anxious to have maximum coverage, but nevertheless felt it necessary to address the media in person.

The President strode briskly into the Press Briefing Room on the lower level of the west wing of the White House. He stepped behind the podium on which was hung his Presidential seal. Reporters noticed that there were no teleprompters in use, which was not the norm for this President. He had what appeared to be a three by five card in his hand. During his brief statement the President's eyes only looked up briefly, returning to the prepared text on the card which he held with both hands.

The text was read by the President in what one Fox reporter called a "somewhat low mumble". The President read, "Thanks for coming. I have a brief statement....*No questions*....It now appears that the joint Russian, Iranian and Libyan military training exercises north of Israel may have taken a different turn. We have intelligence sources reporting that these troops may be under orders to enter into Israel. If true, the United States does not favor this incursion. We call on the nations involved to stand down their men and equipment before violence commences.

"I have just finished a conversation with the Secretary General of the United Nations. I requested that he convene an emergency meeting of the Security Council to discuss this potential threat to world peace. I have also been in communication with the Prime Minister of Israel. He has demanded that the United States enter this potential armed conflict on the side of Israel. I have thoroughly discussed this request with our nation's Secretary of Defense, who is in complete agreement with my decision. I have decided that honoring Israel's request would not be advisable. Let me be clear, the United States will *not* honor Israel's request. Our entry into any military conflict could be de-stabilizing in this inter-regional disagreement. Again, we urge these nations to work out their differences for the best of all concerned. That's all I have. Thanks again for coming."

The Fox reporter turned to the CBS reporter and said, "*Good bye, Israel.* Your only true friend in the world just kissed you adios, suggesting that you should *just get along* with your attacking enemies....the Rodney King School of International Diplomacy. Since when did an armed invasion become an *inter-regional disagreement?* The SecDef hates Israel, so his lack of support for a military response comes as no surprise. What about our treaty to defend Israel if it's attacked? Julie, CBS better get ready to start airing video of dead bodies, *lots of dead bodies.* What a *betrayal* of our ally!"

3

Office of the President, The Kremlin, Moscow, Russia

Office of the President, Sepah Square, Tehran, Iran

Sheba and Dedan (Saudi Arabia today)...will say to you, 'Have you come to seize spoil? Have you assembled your hosts to carry off plunder...to seize great spoil?'(Ezekiel 38:3)

"Mahmoud? Vladimir here. Did you just *hear* the President?"

"Yes, Vladimir, Allah be praised. You were *right* about him all along. You said you had looked into his soul....you knew he would *flinch.* His weak reaction to your takeover of Crimea also proved it. There'll be *no* American involvement in our, what did he call it....our *inter-regional disagreement?* If the American President only knew that we would have stopped, *instantly*, had he just said the word – just one word that his country would fight us. We couldn't continue this invasion of Israel without either America's consent or its cowardly refusal to oppose our Coalition forces. Vladimir, we're *finally* on the brink of *getting rid* of the Zionist pigs and apes."

"I told you. It's in his background and his beliefs that America is the world's problem maker. In his heart he looks at America the same way we do.....And don't forget, Mahmoud, we're also on the brink of grabbing the Middle East's *largest supply* of natural gas just off Israel's coast. What a *coup.* The only push back worthy of our attention is the protest by the Saudi King. Can you believe that the King seriously asked us if we're coming into Israel to take

7

a great spoil? What kind of question is that? Why else would we invade...."

"To *push Israel into the sea,* of course, and to get rid of *the Little Satan.* Don't neglect that goal, Vladimir. Are your people in the *Great Satan* ready for our signal?"

"Yes. *More* than ready, Mahmoud. As you know, we've had our special gifts to America in the ten cities we discussed in place for some time. My secure lines are ready to transmit, when you are ready to do the same."

"*Let's do it,* Vladimir, as soon as we *capture Tel Aviv.* As we discussed, *before* America is destroyed I want the Great Satan to *watch* as we push Israel into the sea. Let them watch *Jewish blood* flowing in the streets of Israel on their large screen TVs. Then we'll light up our special gifts for the American fools. Allah be praised. *Death to Israel* now....and then....soon....*very* soon....*Death to America.*"

4

Israel Defense Force War Room
(Tzva Hahagana LeYisra'el)
HaKirya Compound, Tel Aviv, Israel

Israel's Prime Minister was sick at his stomach. He had just watched a televised US President reading from a small card in the White House press room, announcing that America would not come to Israel's military assistance. The PM was incredulous that the President described the recent invasion of Israel by Russia, Iran, Libya and other Nations, most of which were Muslim, as 'an inter-regional disagreement'. The leader of the western world at least acknowledged, the PM bitterly thought, that Israel had demanded that the United States come to Israel's aid. But the President revealed that he had decided not to do so, facetiously arguing, the PM angrily reflected, that to do so might 'destabilize the region'.

Shaking his head, the PM said to no one in particular of the twenty military advisors gathered in Israel's war room, "Did you hear what he just suggested? That we *'work out our differences'*? *How* exactly do we work out our *differences* with what looks like well over a hundred thousand land-based invading troops? *Differences?* I should take advice from a man who extorted me into signing a peace treaty with our enemies? How did *that* work out for us? Look....look at our drone video feeds....we're staring at our extinction as a people. *Differences?"*

Lieutenant General Abraham 'Benny' Walzer responded to the Israel's leader's outburst, "Sir....do *not* forget that we have the big stick. We can selectively target *our nukes* on the invaders, as we can....."

"Benny....Benny....*listen* to yourself. *We can't nuke* the invading forces....they're on *our own* soil. Selectively target? Are you suggesting we nuke Moscow....or Tehran? Do we want to bring Russia's many nuclear weapons down on our heads? Face it, Benny, *we're stuck*....We have only one move....now that America *has betrayed us*. We have to throw everything we can at the invading forces. We're about to be in a straight up conventional war against a huge armed force. Our odds are no better than 50/50. *Damn* the Americans....damn them....*damn them.*"

"Sir, if the evangelicals and some of our own people are right, that's exactly what's about to happen."

5

The Moshe and Sophia Guttman Home

Petah Tikva, Israel

Moshe loved Sophia and vice-versa. Moshe and Sophia originally met as students at Tel Aviv University, where Moshe was pre-med, leading eventually to dentistry school. Sophia loved children, leading her to obtain her degree in elementary education. Moshe was described to friends by Sophia as "tall, dark and handsome". This always caused Moshe to smile, as he was under five feet seven inches tall, slightly portly and prematurely bald. Moshe referred to Sophia as his "beautiful Jewish jewel of a woman", which she was internally, though her looks were quite a bit shy of movie star level.

Soon after Moshe and Sophia were married, the Guttmans moved to Petah Tikva, a comfortable suburb located east of Tel Aviv. They liked the fact that the name of the Israeli city was chosen by its founders from the prophecy of Hosea 2:15, which referred to "an opening of hope" in the Valley of Achor, with vineyards and singing. Once they moved, Moshe launched his dentistry practice, which prospered due to Moshe's friendly and caring demeanor with his patients. Some even told Dr. Guttman that they didn't mind going to the dentist because he was so kind when he worked on their teeth. Sophia was soon hired at an elementary school not far from their small apartment in Petah Tikva. Within a year of their marriage Sophie conceived their first child, a beautiful girl whom they named Golda, in honor of Israel's only female Prime Minister. Within another two years the Guttmans

11

welcomed into their family a second child, whom they named Yitzhak, after Israel's martyred Prime Minister.

Once the Guttman family had grown to four, Moshe and Sophia decided that it was time to move into a larger living space. After carefully calculating how much they could afford, Moshe and Sophia made an offer on a four bedroom flat in a new development on the far eastern edge of Petah Tikva. The apartment tower was located at the edge of the Milkhemet Sheshet HaYamin Garden and looked across at the Shilo River wadi. From their flat east they had a great view of the open fertile plains of central Israel, south of the Sea of Galilee, with hundreds of acres of citrus trees. Residents of Petah Tikva knew well its history, that in the late 1800s the area was a malarial swamp, which was drained by early Jewish settlers, with funds supplied by Baron Edmond de Rothschild. In 1886 the first recorded attack on Jewish residents by Arabs took place in Petah Tikva.

Over time, Moshe, Sophia, Golda and Yitzhak grew and prospered in their community. Golda entered high school, with Yitzak two years behind in the local middle school. Both youngsters were athletically inclined, a fact that never ceased to amaze their parents, who were definitely not. Golda and Yitzhak, though, were skilled at soccer and spent many hours a week at the Pais Sports facility just north of their flat. The Guttman children were playing soccer at the facility when they first heard reports from a late-arriving teammate that he had just heard on his car radio that Russia might be invading Israel. Yitzhak found Golda on an adjoining soccer field, breathlessly suggesting that they needed to get home, immediately.

6

Our Redeemer Baptist Church

Richmond, Virginia

In his twenty three years in the pulpit of one of America's leading evangelical churches Pastor Harold "Hap" Atkinson had never been so stressed. As a believer he was well aware that he was to cast all of his worries on the Lord. How many times had he preached to his four weekend services and through his television ministry that God's people need not worry, only trust? How often had he counseled with members of his congregation in his office, advising them against stress arising from doubting that God would work out the problem, no matter how serious? Knowing what he was supposed to do with his worry-induced stress, though, just made his worry all the more difficult.

His best friend in seminary, Jack Madison, had warned him almost two years ago to flee the country and re-locate his family outside of the United States. How often had he replayed Jack's final words which he left on Hap's voicemail as he was leaving America, saying *"Hap, my brother, just a final word before we leave the country. I know you want to stay. I know you think you're supposed to stay here and minister to the sick and dying. All I ask is that you re-read God's ten warnings to flee the Daughter of Babylon, pray as hard as you've ever prayed and then let me know what you've decided. Believe me, I know what it's like to give up a growing church and a thriving ministry. But, Hap, God's commands are God's commands. I'm so hard-headed he had to almost put me in federal prison to convince me to give it all up, grab my family and get out while we still could. But, a final word before we depart. I know that God's blessings are no longer on this land, the culture war is over, and we lost. I believe without any doubt that America will betray Israel, and when it does it will be destroyed as a result. When the US turns its back on Israel someday, stabbing it in the back and refusing to come to its defense, millions will die. Don't be here when it happens. God bless you Hap, my dear brother."*

Pastor Hap's problem was not that he didn't believe his friend Jack's warnings. He now knew that everything Jack had said would happen had either already taken place, was happening right now or was about to happen. The Pastor had warned his congregation, in the sanctuary and nation-wide by television, that America was almost certainly the nation that the prophets described when they foresaw what would happen to the Daughter of Babylon, also named in prophecy as Babylon the Great. Many had accepted what he said, researched what scripture said, prayed about it and fled offshore. Most had said they appreciated what he had to say and that they would think and pray about it, but then stayed in the U.S.

Pastor Hap's stress was not caused by refusing to warn his flock. No, he was in intense anxiety because he was about to confront the most important and powerful man in the world, let alone the most famous public figure on the planet. As a leader among evangelical pastors Hap had come to the attention of the President of the United States. When the nation's Chief Executive had attempted to force religious organizations to issue insurance policies to the employees including abortion coverage, Hap had publicly called on the President to re-consider, to back

14

down. The President had refused to do so, resulting in numerous law suits by religious groups. Following the fracas, Hap was called by a White House staffer tasked with trying to put out the fires caused by the President's attacks on First Amendment guarantees of freedom of religion. He was asked to be a member of an informal group of religious leaders of all faiths to advise the White House on religious issues.

Hap's first reaction was to refuse, to turn down the flattering offer. But after the fourth call back, and much prayer, along with his wife's nudging, Hap reluctantly agreed. As he expected, though, the President's Religious Leaders Advisory Group, as it was labeled by the' media, was largely window dressing. The group had no power, only that of persuasion, which it could only offer when the President called them together to meet in the Cabinet Room, which was increasingly infrequent. Because Pastor Hap was better known than most of the twelve leaders, the mainstream media usually contacted him for public comments when religious issues hit the nation's news rooms. Hap had gone out of his way to appear fair in his reported comments, so as not to unduly embarrass the man who had asked him to serve on the advisory group.

Hap's diplomacy, however, had caused many of his evangelical peers in the pulpit to suspect that Hap had trimmed his sails a bit, in order to go along and get along. Hap didn't think of it that way. He knew if he kicked the President too hard, he would most likely not be asked back to the Cabinet Room, thus terminating any chance he had to influence the President. So, Hap bit his tongue on occasion, choosing to stay in his advisory role instead of lashing the nation's leader when Hap thought he was wrong.

By what some in the advisory group said was a coincidence, but Hap saw as God's providential timing, the group had been scheduled a month previously for a Cabinet Room meeting the day after Israel was invaded. As the day for the meeting approached and as events heated up in the Middle East Hap was certain that the White House would cancel the meeting. He waited for the cancellation call that never came. Before driving to DC the night before the Cabinet Room meeting his staff confirmed with the President's staff that the meeting was still on the schedule, the White House not wanting it to appear that it was operating under a siege mentality.

Hap enjoyed coming to the White House's Cabinet Room, recalling the newsreels, newscasts and newspaper photos of the nation's top leaders assembled in this historic room. Today was no different. Hap looked around the room as he sipped the diet drink that he preferred, provided by the Navy Mess one floor below. Only one member of the group was missing, due to a death in his church. The President was late, which was normal. When he walked quickly into the room he looked like a man who was dealing with a crisis. His Chief of Staff, who came in with him, apologized to the assembled leaders and told them that due to the crisis in the Middle East the President's time would be limited to twelve minutes. Strictly enforced. A short three point agenda had been placed in front of each member of the group, but Hap noticed as he looked it over that there was no mention at all of Israel and its invasion yesterday.

One of the longer-winded members consumed the first six minutes filibustering on an arcane issue limited only to his denomination and of little interest or application to others in the room. Hap watched the President during the monologue and decided that he was purposely giving body language that he was about to cut the meeting short. Hap couldn't blame him as he would have done the same. When the windy speaker took a sip of coffee, Hap saw his chance, and jumped in, saying, "Reverend, that's all quite interesting, but with all due respect, and in light of the President's tight time schedule, I'd like to change the subject, if we may."

The President looked slightly relieved and took his arms off of his chair where they had been poised to bolt the meeting. He glanced at his watch, saying, "Pastor you've got two, maybe three minutes. What's on your mind? Another *abortion issue* got you cranked up?", he asked with a sardonic half grin.

Hap said a quick silent prayer, smiled back and said, "No, Mister President, though it is a matter of life and death. Israel is under attack. America must come to her aid. If we don't help, *millions* may die and they...."

Now starting to rise from his chair, the President snarled, "Deaths in Israel are *their* problem. I'm *not* the President of Israel, I'm the Pres...."

"Mister President," Hap interrupted, "I'm not talking about the deaths of millions of people in Israel, as sad as that would be, I'm talking about deaths of many, many *Americans* if you don't intervene and *keep our word* to support Israel militarily if it's attacked. Genesis 12:3 promises that we are cursed if we curse Isra.....”

“We're *done* here. I don't need a Bible lesson, Pastor. I have a lot of....”

Hap would not be intimidated, raising his voice, and responding, “*Sir*. With *all due respect* you apparently could use a lesson from the Bible. If we betray Israel, we will be *destroyed* as a nation. Prophecy says in one day, one hour, *one minute*. Please, sir, *re-consider....*”

At the mention of prophecy the President was out the door to the adjoining Oval Office, as Pastor Hap threw out his last words of advice. Most in the room were looking at Hap with distinct disdain.

Outside of the entry to the West Wing the religious leaders met with the media. Though the media occasionally covered what was given them, they normally stuck the brief article on the last page and usually only quoted the most liberal of the spokesmen. Today was different. Pastor Hap and three other evangelicals approached the microphones, the others having slipped away to Executive Avenue to their cars.

Pastor Hap stepped up to the bank of microphones, swallowed hard and said, “Ladies and gentlemen of America's media, today, on behalf of American Christians we formally called on the President of the United States to militarily intervene and *save Israel* from being destroyed by the invading armies storming into Israel. I cited God's promise that he will curse a nation that curses His chosen people, Israel. If we betray Israel and the people of Israel shed their blood, what will happen here will be similar to, but much worse than, what happened when we forced the Jewish settlers of Gaza from *their homes*. The next day America was struck, forcing many tens of thousands from *their* homes. God is a God of Justice who keeps His promises. If we fail Israel in this her hour of greatest need, God will remove His hand of protection and we will be *gone*, finished as the greatest nation on the globe.....That's essentially what I told our nation's leader just minutes ago....Any questions?"

As most of the media walked away, murmuring to each other about what they had just heard, the AP White House reporter said, "Yeah, Pastor. Just *one* question. Did the President *change* his mind? Are we going into Israel?"

Pastor Hap considered his answer. Was it time for diplomacy....or truth? He chose the latter. "The President walked out of our meeting *without* committing to support Israel. He may change his mind later, but it appears that America is about to *betray* God's chosen nation. *May God have mercy on us all.*"

7

The Moshe and Sophia Guttman Home

Petah Tikva, Israel

Virtually every Jewish family, by necessity, had a family panic plan. The Guttmans' plan was simple. If any family member heard anything about any possible trouble, an invasion, rockets launched, bus explosions, anything, they were to immediately return to the Guttman flat in east Petah Tikva. Like most every housing unit built since 1990, the Guttman flat included a 'safe room'. The room was built in the interior space of the four bedroom flat and included a steel locked door and doubled hardened wallboard to hopefully lessen any explosion effects. The room was large enough for the four residents to sleep on cots and was wired to the outside world with a telephone landline. The family had stocked the room with several cases of dried fruit and packaged water in plastic bottles.

Sophia's school was closest to their flat, so she was the first to arrive when Israeli news media reported that Russian and Iranian troops had been detected by satellite leaving southwest Damascus on Iran's Highway 7 towards Israel. Next were Golda and Yitzhak, who ran into the flat, asking their mother what she had heard? Before she could answer them, her cell phone rang. The phone showed an incoming call from Moshe's dentist office, which was a ten minute drive towards Tel Aviv.

"Yes, Moshe, *why aren't you here*? Don't you know about the...."

Moshe, generally the calmer of the two, responded, "Calm down *Sophie*, I'm calling to let you know it's going to be at least a half hour, maybe more, before I can get home. I have two patients, both in their chairs, both in mid-procedure. One is a root canal and the other is a large filling. I can't just run out and leave them, of course. So, we're accelerating the work. It could be longer than a half hour, come to think....more like an hour. Turn on the TV. I have ours on. Let's just keep our eyes open and see what's happening. It may be *nothing*. We just heard a patient here say, supposedly quoting the White House, that the Russians and Iranians are just doing a military exercise. Not an invasion. Just trying to *scare us*, I guess."

"Moshe", Sophie replied, "listen to yourself. *Scare us?* Well, Its working, *I'm scared*. We signed a peace treaty that was supposed to guarantee us peace and security. No more violence, no more rockets and bombs. America, if you have forgotten, Moshe, *forced us* to sign it....threats of U.S. and European boycotts....'delegitimizing Israel' and all that....remember? I don't buy what you just heard....Finish your patients, quick, Moshe....who knows how long it will take them to start firing rockets and bombs, *or worse*? We're vulnerable, Moshe....We're on the eastern edge of the Tel Aviv metropolitan area. Where do you think they'll hit *first?* Please, Moshe, get home....*OK?*"

Moshe checked his pulse. Sophie's words accelerated his weakened heart. During IDF reserve forces training Moshe suffered cardiac injuries which exempted him from further service, otherwise he would have been called up with the IDF reserve forces, now on heightened alert. It was definitely time to get home to his family.

8

Hannah and Gary's Family Room

Birmingham, Alabama

"*What was I thinking?*" Scott was visibly upset. "Liz and Max saw what was coming, and they moved to Central America at the end of last year. Tom and Marty were a little slower, but they've been in Panama now for almost two months. We should have left when our friends did. I can't *believe...*"

Sally interrupted her husband, "Scott. Don't be so hard on yourself. *I* was the one who kept dragging my feet. I studied the prophecies, like all of us in this small group, but I just couldn't do....that is....I couldn't build my faith strong enough to believe what God was trying to tell us with all those *warnings*. I'm *so* sorry, honey....I just feel so.......Hannah and Gary, and Audrey and Beau, I'm afraid that my glaring reluctance may have held you guys back from moving....while we all still could. It's *my* fault....Can you ever...."

Audrey, the member of the small group with the most obvious gift of compassion, couldn't let Sally go on, "Sally, my dear sister in Christ, *please don't* blame yourself. We're all adults, we *all* studied the Word. We understood that God was using those two hundred and some verses to warn us."

Gary, Hannah's husband, looking terrible, said, "Look, guys, if anyone is to blame it should *be me*. Hannah and I have been active in this county's tea party for over four years. We followed the news. We went to the

23

rallies. We read everything coming out of Washington, and look. Here we are in central Alabama, facing the potential destruction of this country we love. Well....that is....we *used* to love it a lot more before all these things starting happening."

Hannah dabbing her moist eyes, said, "Gary, sweetie, I *never* supported the idea of moving out of the country. Not even when we were pretty sure that the US was going to pressure and force Israel into giving up its land and signing the peace treaty. When the ink was drying on the document we should have been packing our bags. It might have been too late to sell the house and our accumulated stuff....make that treasures....," she smiled grimly, trying to lighten the mood a bit...."but we could have made it out of the country and into safety. We could have hooked up with Marty and Tom or Liz and Max. Both couples offered to let us stay with them until we could get settled. Your question is right, Scott, *what were we thinking?*"

Beau, Audrey's husband, finally spoke up, "It doesn't do any of us any good to wring our hands and cry over what we *should* have done. I'm the first to admit that I knew the truth, the Daughter of Babylon prophecies, but, like you all, I kept putting the decision off. When Liz and Max moved I was privately *very* skeptical. Were they over-reacting, I wondered? Then Tom and Marty adiosed. That should have done it. I should have figured that if four bright students of the Bible, Max was a professor at UAB, after all, decided to move offshore I should get serious myself....but, of course, *I didn't.*"

Scott observed, "Beau, you starting out by saying that wringing our hands won't do any good. Then you started *wringing* your hands. The question is *what* do we do now?"

"OK, yeah, Scott, you're right, sorry....went down a rabbit trail there. Your question is what do we do *now*? You saw the news last night, same as this morning. The President is continuing to refuse to come to Israel's assistance. The Israeli Prime Minister....I always say his name wrong....you know who I mean....has been all over the news, begging, even *pleading* for the US to keep our word and come to Israel's defense. So the White House says that the President doesn't want to increase tensions in a regional conflict. *Say what?* How could you increase tensions when Russia and Iran and those other Muslim countries are obviously headed to Tel Aviv? One guy, some retired general type, said on Fox that Israel only has a *limited* time, maybe just a few days, before they are overwhelmed by the invading troops."

Hannah, trying to stop the flow of her tears, asked, "Guys, you do know what this means if America *betrays* Israel....if we *don't* come to their defense?"

"Yeah, Hannah....it's in the Bible. In Genesis If we curse Israel, we will be....cursed. God is deadly serious about Israel. He repeatedly says that He *loves* Israel and He will be its shield and protector."

Hannah responded, "So....Israel won't be totally destroyed, though the news out of Israel, and the prophecies in the Bible, both say that there will be *a lot* of blood that will be shed, before God himself intervenes and destroys the invading armies."

"Max studied this deeper than the rest us," Beau added, "he concluded that the destruction of the Daughter of Babylon will happen soon....*very soon*....after America stabs Israel in the back and breaks its word that we gave in the Camp David Accords to come to Israel's defense militarily if Israel is invaded."

Audrey stood up and embraced Beau, asking, "Darling, that can only mean *one thing*. Right? *How soon?*"

Beau hugged his wife, took his time and then said, "Audrey, my dear, eventually the US is going to get hit....hard....cataclysmically. God hasn't thrown back the invaders of Israel *yet*....so we only have a short time. Once it's too late for the U.S. to intervene....which quite obviously the White House doesn't intend to do....then what the five Prophets wrote about *will happen*."

Weeping almost uncontrollably, Sally gasped out, "We studied what happens next, *didn't we*? Remember? The Daughter of Babylon *will fall in one day*....*in one hour*....*and in one moment*. We may be with the Lord....soon....right?"

Beau was retired military so he had some idea how the destruction of the nation prophesied in the Bible would take place. "When we looked at those verses we quickly concluded the obvious - that the only way to destroy an entire country in such a short time is with nuclear weapons. You'll recall that we also read that the fall of this rich, influential and powerful nation will happen like Sodom and Gomorrah. The Bible records what happened to the land around those two destroyed cities, that is, no vegetation would grow. The limbs of the people who died were like blackened sticks. Those are signs of *a nuclear event*. A big tip-off to what happened was the description of smoke coming up as from a furnace. Cities burning fill the whole sky with smoke, but a mushroom cloud looks like smoke coming up from a furnace."

Sally, her voice breaking, asked, "Will we be *nuked?*"

"Sally," Beau responded, "only God and America's enemies know what cities will be taken out with nuclear devices, but I *seriously doubt* if Birmingham, Alabama is high on the Jihadists' list. Instant incineration, though, in a nuclear blast would be a quick and relatively painless death. If they do what that Congressional study committee concluded, and use ten nukes in America's major cities, that will kill fifty or sixty million people in a moment. About the same number of infants we've aborted since Roe v. Wade. Sally, I know this isn't a new thought, we've talked about it here in small group, but those who survive the detonations will be short-termers. That same study said that *90% of all Americans would be dead* within a year of a nuclear attack on some of its cities."

Scott decided to steer the discussion back to less frightening grounds, "OK, guys, we can't change any of that at this point. It's way too late to move offshore, so let's discuss what we *can* do, what we *will do* if the next few days result in the nuking of America."

9

The Moshe and Sophia Guttman Home

Petah Tikva, Israel

Moshe Guttman finally made it home, though the streets filled with Israelites doing the same delayed him by an additional hour. Sophia embraced him with tears as soon as he entered their flat. After a family group hug, Moshe gathered the four Guttmans around the kitchen table. Moshe had been listening to Israeli radio on the way home, so he had a good idea as to what was happening 150 miles northeast just outside of Damascus. Nevertheless, Moshe asked his wife and children what they had heard and seen on television.

Yitzhak, who did not resemble either parent, being almost six feet tall and swarthy in his dark complexion, was the first to speak, "Dad, it's bad....*real bad*. Channel 10 has been streaming from the IDF satellites. There are hundreds, thousands of armored troop carriers, tanks and artillery racing out of Damascus....you know....on the southwest side of the Syrian capital, coming down Highway 7."

Moshe rubbed his forehead and said, "I know, Yitzhak, I know. I just heard on the car radio an IDF report on Reshet Aleph, you know, 104.8. It's pretty clear that there are as many as a hundred thousand soldiers, armed troops, maybe twice that, *storming towards Israel*. If that's true, that not only means that our precious peace treaty is *worthless*, it also means that Israel will soon be at war....*again*."

Sophia, who was a bit more conservative in her political views than her husband, replied, "I *told* you, Moshe, when the US put a headlock on Israel and made us sign that treaty that it was *a mistake*. The U.S. President has never liked Israel. Look at his background. He set us up to make a fake 'peace'. Why? To give Russia and Iran, and knows what other Muslim countries, time to get ready to *take us out*....to shove us into the sea....as Iran promised."

"OK, Sophie, OK. You were *right*, I was wrong. But, that's history. So, Israel got snookered again. *What's new?* Look at the holy scriptures. Israel was always a sucker for a peace agreement. God told Israel *not* to rely on Egypt for its security. He warned them that Egypt would be like a reed, when it counted on Egypt the reed would splinter and pierce Israel's hand."

"Why do we Jewish folks," Golda asked, "like to depend on everybody else, *except* the Creator?" Golda, an attractive raven-haired beauty, was the more spiritual of the four Guttmans, telling her parents when she was twelve that someday she wanted to teach the Torah. "As we were leaving soccer to come home we heard that the Chief Rabbi has called for a national fasting, prayer and mourning. He'll lead it at the Wailing Wall. Why don't we pray, Dad, OK?"

Moshe led the family in prayer, asking for protection for Israel and for his family. After each Guttman prayed, Moshe suggested that it was still too early to enter the family safe room. The Guttmans gathered around their large screen television, with Yitzhak managing the remote control. Sophie put frozen pizza in the oven, as she didn't want to take the time away from breaking news to make dinner.

The normally coiffed and made-up newscasters on Channel 10 didn't look so coiffed or made up, looking instead like they were under the pressure of breaking news, having to report to their Israeli viewers news that could eventually mean their death and destruction. The male talking head looked down at a paper just handed to him, scanned the document and looked at the wrong camera, reading at least two octaves higher than his normal broadcast voice.

"An undisclosed source in the IDF is being widely quoted in Israeli media as saying that the IDF picked up a private conversation between the Presidents of Russia and Iran. This report suggests that the two leaders actively discussed an invasion of Israel, using men and armaments stored in large warehouses southwest of Damascus....Unh....What makes this report most believable is that the day to launch the attack, the day which was supposedly discussed between the Kremlin and Tehran, *is today*....Let me repeat....An undisclosed source in the IDF intercepted a conversation recently about an invasion to be launched *today* against Israel, launched from Damascus."

The female newscaster was pale, her hands visibly trembling. She asked, "Ben, do you have a degree of confidence in this report? With the troop movement that the satellites are picking up, doesn't that make it almost a certainty that Israel will shortly be....*invaded*? If so, then how do we explain the White House's earlier claim that these are just *joint military exercises*?"

Sophia asked Yitzhak to switch channels, to channel 2, which she preferred to 10 as she believed that the station was generally more candid with viewers on Israeli security matters. Channel 2's news desk was centered on the screen, with a famous face having a discussion with the station's lead newscaster. Moshe said, "Hunh. This *must* be serious....he was the *top guy* at IDF for almost ten years. Turn it up, son."

The retired IDF general was saying, "....and that would be *an accurate assessment*. This is no joint training exercise."

"General, can you tell us *why not*? The administration in Washington initially claimed that Russia and Iran are just engaged in some *war games*, nothing more sinister than that. What say you?"

"Oh, I agree that they're playing *a war game*, but the end result will be *a real war*, not some game, not some exercise. Look, you don't put that many tanks, and armored personnel carriers and artillery, let alone over a hundred thousand troops, into an exercise. Look at that satellite feed on your wall. In an exercise you pretend you are at war by maneuvering your various forces to simulate battle strategies and such. You do not load them onto a highway, at full force and speed hurtling towards a target of invasion. Highway 7 is a well-known and used entry point to the nation of Israel. These troops are heading southwest straight into Israel. Anyone who claims otherwise is *deluded*."

"General, that's strong talk. Are you going on record to claim that the White House, that this President, was *fooled....*to use your word....*deluded,* into thinking that this was just a military training exercise, and not an invasion?"

"I'm just saying that it has now become *quite clear* to the entire world that Israel has been invaded and that a major war has erupted in the Middle East. Even if the...."

An off-screen hand pushed a document across the news desk. The newscaster apologized to his guest, saying, "General, so sorry. I've just been handed a released statement from the Israeli Defense Force press office. The Commander of IDF has just confirmed that Russian and Iranian forces have not only *crossed the Syrian border* with Israel, they are heading across *the Golan Heights.* There is also an unconfirmed report that Russian saboteurs may have disabled several air base facilities in the Negev. I repeat....*unconfirmed.* General, it looks like we won't have to wait any longer to find out if this is an *actual invasion* of Israel. Your reaction, General?"

"Let's face the facts. The Golani Brigade and the mechanized elements of the IDF Northern Command were withdrawn and merged into other IDF forces as an integral part of the U.S. brokered 'peace agreement'. This President made us pull back the forces that could have been used to help stop this invasion in its tracks. The same President who originally claimed this invasion was a training exercise had better change his mind against getting involved here and issue the order to send in American troops, quickly. What's needed now....what's *urgent* now....is for the President to pick up his red phone and tell the Russian and Iranian Presidents that the US military is *on its way* to the Golan Heights....that only an *immediate* withdrawal of their invading forces will avoid their total *destruction.*"

"Agreed, General, but what do you see if the U.S. sticks with the President's earlier refusal? What happens if the U.S. *won't* get involved in defending Israel?"

The General at first appeared to be speechless, pondering the question. He leaned forward and slowly said, "*If*....that is, *if*....the US refuses to abide by the terms of the Camp David Accord Memo of Understanding....if America *stabs Israel in the back* and turns tail....then....well, I guess we'll see if Israel ends up covered in blood and shoved into the sea, or if the IDF, weakened under US pressures, can save our country. Apart from America and the IDF *there's no other power in the universe that can save us.*"

10

America's Kitchens and Family Rooms

America's network and cable systems were simultaneously interrupted by a National Emergency Message. Most viewers assumed that it was about the invasion of Israel. The President must have changed his mind and would announce that the U.S. would now come to Israel's defense. But, instead of the President making a prime time public service announcement, Americans saw a different President on their TV screens. Seated in front of four American flags was former President Wilbur Jackson Calhoun, staring straight into the lens of the digital television camera. He wore a red and white striped regimental tie, bright white shirt and a finely tailored suit. The expression on his carefully powdered face was one of stern concern.

"My fellow Americans. Your local station or cable network has made this time available for me to come to you with an urgent plea. As your former President, I am urging all Americans to support our President during this time of national crisis and war in the Middle East. Many are violating the law by criticizing our President's decisions regarding the defense of Israel. These harsh and illegal attacks on our Chief Executive come on the heels of several months of widespread civil unrest in America. Much blood has been shed. Our President has taken steps to quell this unnecessary violence, including the imposition of martial law. In response to the President's much-needed actions, though, some have violated our nation's hate speech laws. Hate speech is against the law. I am urging you to report

anyone whom you hear criticizing our nation's President, which also violates the McAlister Act. Also, be sure to turn in anyone you know of who has not yet turned in their hate weapons, their weapons of violence, their firearms. To report hate speech and hate weapons, just call the FBI at the number on the bottom of the screen. It's your duty as a loyal American citizen to help stop words and weapons that violate the law. Thank you for your attention to your civic duty. Together, we can stop hate speech in America against our brave and beloved President.....May God bless America."

Ten days after the PSA message was carried across the nation, the Director of the FBI, an appointee and fellow college classmate of the President, released a news statement to America's media. The release read, *"As a result of former President Calhoun's widely-viewed PSA message, the Bureau has received many thousands of calls, in all fifty states, identifying hate speakers in the callers' communities. America's dedicated FBI Agents are following up on each and every tip and will insure that appropriate criminal charges are filed where warranted. Hate speech is illegal in America. There is no right to criticize our nation's leaders, especially the President of our country. Hate speech criticizing, attacking or ridiculing our nation's elected Chief Executive is illegal and can result in significant time in jail. The FBI is serious about enforcing these laws. You are so advised."*

11

Ambergris Caye, Belize

"Yes, Mister Madison, we *are* Mirandizing you. You think just because you avoided going to prison once, that you can get away with the crime of harboring a fugitive? If you do, just think again, *sir*."

John Madison was seriously concerned that he might suffer a cardiac problem. He knew that his blood pressure was nearing a dangerous level. He was close to physically grabbing the FBI agents on the porch of his Belizean condo and heaving them over the side. John had at least 50 pounds on each of the agents and at least four inches. He briefly considered what the prison sentence would be for assaulting a federal officer and whether the fact that it happened offshore would affect the number of years he would have to serve. Eventually, though, his better senses kicked in. He half-listened to the younger agent read him his rights. He had, after all, been read his rights back in Texas when the government tried to convict him for exercising his Constitutional rights of free speech.

"....if you can't afford an attorney one will be provided to you. Did you understand these rights that I have read to you, sir?"

"*Of course*, I understood them," John replied in anger. "Now would you be *so kind* as to tell me why you're here? Can you tell me why my government is so fearful of *its own citizens* that it has to spend tax money to give you guys a trip to the tropics? Don't you know there is a war about to set the Middle East on fire? Don't you have *better* things to do?"

"*Look*, Madison, you obviously think we're not aware of how much trouble you're in. Your son is a fugitive from justice. The Texas jury may have exonerated him on the hate speech charges, but whether you know it or not, though we suspect you are well aware of it, he was then indicted in a sealed indictment, and...."

"*What?* He's found *not* guilty and the government still comes after him? *For what?* Sealed? What the...."

"Calm down, sir....I'm not at liberty to reveal the new charges, but we think your son must have gotten word from somebody right before he jumped the border into Canada. Though his wife and children haven't been charged with any crimes....*yet*....they appear to have fled with him. We have good reason to believe that they have come here to Belize and that you and Mrs. Madison are *harboring your son*. Thus, you, sir, are about to be charged with *a class D felony*."

John Madison said nothing in response. He stared at the two agents, gritting his teeth, gripping and then releasing both hands.

Recognizing that John Madison didn't intend to reply, the lead agent barked, "*Mister* Madison, do you intend to *cooperate* with our investigation Are you going to tell us where your son is located? *Where* have you hidden him?"

John Madison continued to be silent, just glaring at the agents.

"*Sir?* Are you going to answer my questions? Failure to cooperate with an ongoing federal investigation can have serious consequ...."

"Now *you look*....I'm *not* 'harboring a fugitive'. I have *no* idea where my son is located....I wish I did. I just can't believe that he's been charged *again* with federal crimes right after being found not guilty in the first witch hunt. Gentlemen, if there's nothing else, I have an important appointment with some Tarpon."

"*Very* funny, sir. If you won't cooperate that's up to you. The district attorney will be duly advised of your failure to assist in the investigation."

"The district attorney? *Which* district attorney would that be, exactly? Thanks heavens, there are no U.S. government district attorneys here in Belize. I no longer live in the U.S., so I don't know *what in the world* you are talking about."

"We don't provide legal advice, sir, but I would highly recommend that you consult with your Texas attorney, Mister Webster, as I recall? He can advise you as to the federal grand jury sitting in Dallas and the evidence that has been presented to them concerning your son....and yourself. The federal government doesn't take lightly to persons charged with crimes leaving the jurisdiction of the United States."

"*Really?* Even when they don't know anything about the charges? You did say a *sealed* indictment didn't you? To quote Jack Nicolson, why don't you fellows try selling *crazy* someplace else? We're done here. Enjoy your trip back to the asylum."

12

St. Patrick's Cathedral

Manhattan, New York City

Cardinal Thomas Micah Bolton was wearing his most casual clothes, which for a Cardinal of the Catholic Church was never very casual. He wore the mandated black wool cassock, the rabat Roman collar and red silk skull cap. He preferred this most acceptable non-formal clothing when he was in his working office at St. Patrick's, the 150 some year old edifice which occupied a full city block, from 50th to 51st streets and from Madison Avenue to Fifth Avenue. Today was a working day, as he needed to finish his remarks to be delivered as part of the upcoming Sunday service, though normally, he didn't participate in the weekly mass, which was handled by one of the priests honored with the task. Cardinal Bolton had wrestled with the title for his homily, which he recognized would ruffle feathers at the White House. No stranger to doing so, the Cardinal had frequently stood up for the church when it was under attack by the administration. When the White House ordered that religious organizations must provide abortion coverage to employees, he spoke out, leading the legal challenge in the courts. Consequently, Cardinal Bolton was widely perceived as a leading vocal opponent of the President by many Americans, most of the mainstream media and certainly by the President and his advisors.

Cardinal Bolton had been watching the news with rising horror as he realized that his country was apparently not going to come to the defense of its most valued Middle East partner, the State of Israel. With each

41

hour the news from northern Israel got worse, as Russia and Iran rolled south. The video showed hundreds of tanks and troop carriers manned by troops numbering in what appeared to be many tens of thousands, prepared to kill Israelites. Cardinal Bolton knew that he could be quiet no longer. His church had remained largely silent during the holocaust. This Cardinal, for one, was about to assail his own government for not defending Israel. He was well aware that some within his denomination did not see Israel as God's chosen people, but his reading of scripture and history convinced him. He knew that it was time to call on the President to do the right thing.

Earlier that morning he had shared breakfast with his best friend in the media, the international affairs reporter for Fox news. During their sharing of everything bagels and cinnamon cream cheese, the Cardinal let it be known to his friend that he would strongly assail the President this Sunday. His reporter friend asked if Fox could run a trailer at the bottom of its news screen revealing that Cardinal Bolton during Sunday services at St. Patrick's would call on the President to come to Israel's defense? The Cardinal thought about it for a moment, decided it couldn't do any harm. In fact, as he shared with his media friend, advance notice of his upcoming words might even push the President to help Israel, now, rather than later after more Israelis were dead. The Cardinal's hope that the White House would take action once it read the trailer on Fox reporting on his upcoming verbal assault was correct. What was incorrect was what kind of action the President would order.

13

Hannah and Gary's Family Room

Birmingham, Alabama

Scott was angry at what the three couples in their small group Bible study were seeing on TV. "You just heard the same thing I heard. The Russians and Iranians invade Israel, the President announces that the US *won't* come to Israel's defense and then no other country is willing to do so. I was hoping that maybe Canada or France, who have been friendly to Israel recently, would step in and help little Israel survive. Blood is about to start flowing in Israel. How could this be anything *except* what the Bible said would happen?"

Beau, who had demonstrated through the years his widespread recall of scripture, responded, "Yup. Jeremiah said it in chapter 51. Let's see....here it is....verse 35....and 36. *May the violence done to our flesh be upon Babylon, say the inhabitants of Zion. May our blood be on those who live in Babylonia, says Jerusalem. Therefore, this is what the Lord says: 'See I will defend your cause and avenge you'*....and I think there's a similar verse a little later....yes, here it is. Verse 49. *Babylon must fall because of Israel's slain.*"

Hannah asked, "Beau, didn't we study a verse in Psalms along the same line?"

"Good memory, Hannah. It's in 137 as I recall....un-hunh....verse 8. *O Daughter of Babylon doomed to destruction, happy is he who repays you for what you have done to us.*"

43

"We all concluded from the thirty prophecy clues revealing the identity of Mystery Babylon, that *it has to be* America, our country. It's also named in scripture as the Daughter of Babylon and Babylon the Great. Beau, didn't one of the prophets label Babylon as a betrayer?"

"Again, good memory guys. It was Isaiah. Let's turn to Isaiah, very powerful language. Go to 21:2....You all there?....OK, here's what Isaiah said. *A dire vision has been shown to me: The traitor betrays, the looter takes loot. Elam, attack! Media, lay siege! I will bring an end to all the groaning she caused.*

Audrey looked up from her well-worn Bible and asked, "*Who* are Elam and Media again? I know we discussed this before."

Gary said, "Didn't we learn that both Elam and Media are in present day *Iran*? And just as Ezekiel said, some of those troops that we're seeing on TV invading Israel are from Iran. Look....right there....see those tanks, look at the emblem on the turrets. Looks something like a bird. That's the emblem of Iran, it's in the middle of their flag. Iran and Russia, and the other Muslim nations that Ezekiel listed, are definitely invading Israel. *To kill Israelites.* What's *wrong* with our country....that we can't keep our word....that we *betray* our *only* friend in the Middle East?"

Scott had been paging through his notes as the others talked. "Do you all recall The Message translation of Lamentations 4:17 that we looked at last year? Let me read it, *We watched and watched, wore our eyes out looking for help. And nothing. We mounted our lookouts and*

44

looked for the help that never showed up." What a sad description of what the people of Israel have been going through since the invasion started. America promised to bring the full might of our military into Israel to protect what? The trees? The buildings? No, *the people* of Israel. The millions of men, women and children who may either *already* be dead or facing *imminent* death. We are truly betrayers. I love my country, and I don't want to see it destroyed, but I completely understand why God is about to do what He said He would do. *Completely* understand."

There was silence in Gary and Hannah's family room as the three remaining couples of the small group realized the enormity of what would soon happen in America.

Audrey, tears obvious on her cheeks, broke the silence, "Men, we women have talked and we're scared. *Really scared*. Once America's major cities are nuked, it looks like that's what's prophesied, then it won't take long before every grocery shelf in town will be cleaned out. We've all laid up a fair amount of canned goods, rice, beans and such, but we all know that our minimal prepping efforts won't last very long. People....we are going to be out of food *soon*. Maybe, by scrimping, being very careful, we might make it two months, not much longer."

"Audrey," Hannah, also crying, sniffled, "We gave a lot of our food to Uncle Paul's family. Since he was killed, they've had some financial problems, so we wanted to help them out. So....I doubt that we could feed ourselves for *even a month*....what....*are*....we....going....to....do?"

14

The Moshe and Sophia Guttman Home

Petah Tikva, Israel

The General's words sent Moshe, Sophia, Golda and Yitzhak into stunned silence. Israel had been invaded and it might not survive, especially since the U.S. reneged on its written promise to defend Israel were it to be invaded. Not wanting his family to see his reddened eyes, Moshe went to the restroom. Drying his face, he returned to find three tearful watchers of the televised pictures from an IDF drone flying above the Golan Heights. The televised pictures were in almost HD clarity compared to the previous satellite shots, taken at a significantly greater height. Seeing the Russian and Iranian tanks, helicopters, multiple rocket launchers, self-propelled artillery, assault breachers and troop carriers, including their nation's bright markings emblazoned on them was a jarring sight. These were massive machines of war being driven rapidly into Israel for a single purpose – to kill Israelis. As potential death targets the Guttmans could do nothing but shed tears and cry out to God for help. Moshe suddenly realized that maybe there was something he could do.

Moshe excused himself and went to the back hall. He punched in his brother's long distance number in Fairfax, Virginia. He looked at his watch. He would be up by now.

"Moshe, great to hear from you, what's up?"

"Ben. Have you been up long enough to see the news? Do you know *what's happening* here?"

"*News?* No. I've been out of cell range. Our synagogue had a camping retreat, with our sons. What's happ...."

"Ben, *listen.* We're being *invaded.*"

"What? *Invaded?* What do you mean *invaded?* Who would be that crazy? This is the 21st century."

"Russia. Iran. Maybe Libya. Muslim radicals. You get the idea. They're already across the border with Syria and into the Golan."

"Oh, no....What's the IDF doing?"

"So far, Ben, even though the IDF is on heightened alert, it looks like the nation's armed forces are waiting to see what the U.S. does. Saudi Arabia just issued a challenge to Russia and their old enemy Iran asking them what the heck they're doing, are they coming into Israel to take a great spoil? Don't they have enough oil and gas that they need more from a conquered Israel? The European Union a few minutes later raised similar questions."

"So, why is the IDF *waiting?*" If you're being invaded, why not massively respond? Throw *everything* at them, including nukes. That is, if you have any. I know that's been a not very well-kept secret?"

"Think about it, Ben. As soon as Israel launches its full forces it invites a full scale counter by the invaders. Full scale, as in nukes. Russia and Iran both have nuclear weapons. Iran has made it clear that they want to nuke Tel Aviv, for starters. So we start to fight back and then the nukes rain down *on us.* Israel's destroyed and the invaders pick up the pieces, including the new oil and gas fields."

"Humh. I get it. So....there's only *one way* to halt the invaders. America *has* to intervene. Right?"

"Correct. I'm bothering you because you once told me that one of your dental patients there in northern Virginia worked at the Pentagon. Am I remembering right? A general or an admiral or some ranked officer?"

"Yeah. He's a great guy. But, he was promoted and he's not stationed in the DC area. Not sure where exactly. We became fairly close, so I can locate him from our records. Why?"

"It was a long shot, Ben, but I couldn't think of anyone else I could call. Here's the deal. You know where we live. Anybody east of Tel Aviv is on the entry point to the city. If America decides to help us, we'll probably be alright. Your nephew and niece will live to become adults. But, if America continues to turn its back on us and walks away, we could be....well, *we wouldn't likely survive.* I'd just like to know from someone on the inside, if that's possible, which is it going to be? Will the U.S. keep its word, does America *have our back,* as the President once said, or instead, will the President not change his mind? Can you make an inquiry? America *has* to help us, Ben. You promised."

"I'll find the General and see what he can tell me, if anything. He'll be limited, as you can imagine, in what he can divulge, if he even knows anything. Maybe America can be convinced to get in, Moshe. Israel's our *best friend* in that part of the world."

"Ben, you know as well as I do that the U.S. has *not* been Israel's true friend. Things have gone downhill ever since the President came into office. Why did Israel give up *so much* land? Why is there a Palestinian capital located in East Jerusalem? Why is our remaining land now so narrow, not really defensible?"

"Well, Israel was sold on the idea that its security was guaranteed by its Muslim neighbors. That sounded good when you all were sitting under your fig trees in peace and security, to use a Biblical phrase. But, now....Israel is being invaded. America *has* to come to Israel's defense. *We must.* I'll get back to you as soon as I can reach the General."

15

Western/Wailing Wall (Kotel)

Jerusalem, Israel

Chief Rabbi Isaac David Herzog loved Israeli food, lots of it, but not today, maybe never again. He knew when he called for Israel to fast and pray that he would not be eating again until the invading army was destroyed. He knew, though, that the invading army could conquer Israel. He concluded that now was the time to earnestly seek God, to fast and pray for mercy and God's protection from the invaders flowing from the north into Israel. He made his calls on other Jewish religious leaders, quickly organizing them, and their followers, to meet and implore God to save Israel.

Rabbi Herzog, the Sephardi rabbi for Jerusalem for the last five years, walked slowly from his office in the Jewish Quarter to the Kotel at the western side of the Temple Mount in the Old City. As he walked, with nearly a thousand rabbis and Jewish religious leaders in his wake, he recalled that for 19 years after the establishment of the State of Israel, no Jewish persons were allowed to worship and pray at the Wall. In 1967, however, when Israel was attacked, it captured the Old City, opening the Wall to use by Jewish worshippers. Most in Israel considered the Western Wall and the adjoining Temple Mount as the most sacred sites in the nation.

Rabbi Herzog said nothing on the way to the Wall, his head downcast, his hands clasped. His somber demeanor was observed by Israeli media walking with him and the crowds gathering along the way. Tears began to flow from those watching and waiting for the Chief Rabbi. As Rabbi Herzog walked slowly onto the stone plaza adjoining the wall, he also began to quietly weep as the enormity of his task came upon him. The very continued existence of Israel, and its 7,700,000 residents, three-fourths of whom are Jewish, was at hand.

Rabbi Herzog turned in front of the Wall, facing the growing crowd and numerous media, with cameras relaying his words to Israel and the world. He nodded to the sounder of the Shofar, the long Ram's horn used since ancient days. The first sound, the Tekiah, was a long, loud wailing sound used to announce God's intent to establish the area He will occupy. Next came a series of several short, sharp 'breaking sounds', the Shevarim, announcing God's intent to break through barriers and shatter resistance to his will. Thirdly, the Shofar was sounded in nine staccato notes, the Teruah, the sound used to announce God's arrival on the scene. The last sound from the Shofar, traditionally known as the sound to declare God's complete domain, was an unbreaking, commanding sounding of the Shofar trumpet.

As he prepared to speak, the Rabbi felt a strange stirring in his body, unlike anything he had ever experienced before in his fifty-seven years. He felt as if God Himself had placed his hand on his shoulder. Rabbi Herzog was so overwhelmed by the sensation that for at least a full minute he was unable to speak. During his silence the Rabbi felt he was being given dictation for his message.

Finally able to speak, the Chief Rabbi said, "The Prophet Joel foresaw this day. *This very day.* We read Joel's prophetic words in the Holy Scriptures. He was shown a day in which a great and powerful nation would come down from the north against the Holy Land, like has never been seen before. The assembled armies that have entered Israel have come with *fire and sweeping destruction,* just as Joel was shown. These armies of invaders were shown to Joel to have teeth like lions and fangs of a lioness, and to resemble great war horses and chariots, leaping on the tops of mountains. We look at our television news reports and we see the great and powerful armies that Joel was shown by Jehovah over 2,700 years ago, even including Russian assault helicopters which we see on TV leaping across the mountains of the Golan Heights.

"What is Israel told to do when *this day of darkness and gloom* comes upon us? Joel was given the answer by the Almighty. We are told to consecrate a fast, call a solemn assembly and gather the elders and the inhabitants of the land....*to cry out to the Lord.* Joel tells us to blow a trumpet in Zion and *sound an alarm* on his holy mountain. Today we are crying out to the Lord, as a people whose faces are pale and who are trembling as we face imminent death and destruction. The priests and ministers of the altar are called on by God through Joel to put on sackcloth, to fast and to lament. *Will it be enough?* Can Israel, and its people, be spared in the face of this great and powerful army invading *God's Holy Land?*

"Our media in Israel are filled with only two questions: They ask first, *will* America intervene to save us? Secondly, if America doesn't save us, are Israel's armed forces *strong enough to save Israel?* My reading of the Holy Scriptures shows me that *no nation,* not the United States, not any nation will come to Israel's assistance. If our strongest ally lets our blood flow at the hands of this great invading army, will our military be strong enough to win the war which has already started? Again, the Prophet Joel was shown that the invaders will charge, scale walls, leap upon cities and....burst through our weapons....and....and....*not be halted."*

The Chief Rabbi stopped, recognizing fully the enormity of what he had just said, that Israel had no hope, no defenders and insufficient military strength to survive the invasion from the north. Millions of tears flowed from millions of eyes across Israel as Israelites glued to their televisions watched as the Chief Rabbi of Jerusalem delivered his fatal message. News commentators all day reported America's refusal to keep its treaty commitment to Israel, but to hear it from the lips of such a respected religious leader was more than many could take. Just as difficult was the thought that Israel's military might not be able to throw off those who were coming into Israel to kill, maim and destroy. Many viewers in Israel decried their nation's decision to give up part of the land, contrary to God's directive not to do so. Now in an untenable, indefensible position, Israel faced annihilation, invaded by foes committed to wiping Israel and its 7.7 million people off the map.

As grim as his message sounded, the Chief Rabbi wasn't quite finished.

16

St. Patrick's Cathedral

Manhattan, New York City

Cardinal Thomas Micah Bolton made it a point to arrive at sunrise on Sundays at St. Patrick's. His weekly custom was to change into his Vatican mandated formal attire, his red wool cassock and red silk skull cap, well before the morning services were to commence. After being dressed appropriately, he would proceed to the altar at the front of the historic cathedral and pray for what would occur in the historic building later in the morning.

As the Cardinal prayed, the altar boys, designated priests and other staff busied themselves in the sanctuary, doing their best not to disturb the Cardinal's prayers. Concluding his prayers, Cardinal Boland genuflected, stood, turned from the altar and looked out at the 2,200 seat Cathedral. It was what he expected to see. What he did not expect to hear, though, was what sounded like loud voices, raised in anger, coming from the Cathedral's entry doors. The Cardinal walked down the altar steps from the front to the main central aisle, heading towards the source of the increasingly raucous noise, puzzled by what was disturbing the sanctity of this sacred space. He soon learned the source.

As he was half-way down the central aisle Cardinal Bolton saw several green-uniformed DHS Conservators shoving persons whom the Cardinal recognized as employees of the Cathedral, including two armed plains clothes security officers who worked for the church.

"You *can't* come in here with *weapons.*"

"*Stand back* or we will be forced to *arrest* you."

"Arrested *for what,* for defending our church from uninvited, armed men?"

"We have a warrant. *Stand back.* This is your *last* warning."

"I told you, that you *can't* come into the...."

Two shots exploded into the echo chamber of a sanctuary, reverberating like two thunder claps across the long sanctuary.

The Cardinal stopped, thirty feet or so from the two church security guards who were now bleeding out on the marble floor of St. Patrick's. For a brief moment the Cardinal wondered if this was another one of those weird dreams he had been having, of strangers invading the sanctuary. But, his doubt only lasted a moment as he smelled the gunpowder. This was no dream. It soon became a nightmare, as the Cardinal looked up from his fallen employees to see that the men who had just fired their revolvers were now aiming them at him.

"*Whoa there,* whoever you are, what do you think you are *doing?* This is a house of God."

"Shut up, whoever you are. Oh, so you are *Cardinal Whatever?* We are *the government.* We have a warrant. We are here to protect the City of New York. *Stand back....Now.*"

"A warrant?....By whom?....For *what?* Do you understand *where you are*? Do you have any idea how much *trouble* you are in? I don't care what government you say you work for, you can't just shoot peo...."

"*Shut up*, old man."

"Have you *no respect* for...."

"*Respect?* You are harboring terrorists, you *silly old man* in a red dress. We're here to *shut you down*. We protect the City of New York. *No more 9/11s*, do you understand, old man?"

"Terrorists?....*Terrorists?*....How can you *seriously* say....?"

"*Enough* of this....*Cuff* the old man....*Nail this* to the entry door....*Padlock* the doors."

The armed, uniformed DHS Conservators cuffed Cardinal Bolton, man-handling him out of the cathedral to a black armored DHS detention vehicle parked in front. The large red sign nailed to the ornate front door of St. Patrick's Cathedral read:

CLOSED
UNTIL FURTHER NOTICE
BY ORDER OF US DISTRICT COURT
THIS STRUCTURE HAS BEEN DESIGNATED
AS A POTENTIAL TERRORIST SITE
IT IS A FELONY TO
ENTER THESE PREMISES
By Order of US District Judge Lawrence Barrasso

17

Trinity Episcopalian Church

Bellevue, Washington

Pastor Mick Kirkland was looking forward to todays' sermon. He had been working on the text for several weeks. One of his pet peeves was Christian writers and commentators who tried to convince the church that the end times were near. The Pastor's theology was simple. The Bible was a helpful guide book, though not inerrant by any means. Jesus was a great teacher, but don't look for Him to somehow come back to earth. People who believed that the Bible accurately prophesied the future undoubtedly also wore tin foil hats to ward off microwaves from the NSA.

The Pastor kept his sermons short, never more than twelve minutes, as he had learned that his messages tended to encourage his parishioners to nod off if they went much longer. Today's sermon was to be no exception, including a catchy title, which the Pastor devised each week to attract attention.

"Today, my dear congregants, I will be addressing the subject of prophecy. The title of my message is PROPHECY – ARE YOU KIDDING ME?" As was their norm, the congregation chuckled upon hearing the title of his sermon. Leaning over his carved stone pulpit, Pastor Mick stared at the people in the pews, then asked, "Does anyone here *really* believe that God, he or she, can actually know the future?" He waited for his words to sink in. "I mean, certainly a God who is as powerful and all-knowing as our E---vangelical friends would have us believe, might have such a parlor trick ability. But, I'm talking about *reality*, my friends." He paused for a second round of light laughter. "Come on, folks, don't forget that our God is a god of *love*. Since he loves us why would he want to *scare us* by telling us that all manner of catastrophic events will happen....some....day....in the future? Do you know how many E----vangelicals have been wrong about what they call the end times, or the latter days, the final days, the day of the Lord?

"Oh, I know that there are some Bible literalists who point to Israel coming back as a nation in 1948 as *proof of prophecy*. My view is simply that the re-creation of Israel was the world's way of making up for the bad treatment of Jews in the Second World War. Certainly not some kind of miracle. Don't get me wrong – *I believe* in miracles. How else could you explain the *Seahawks* winning the Super Bowl?" More laughter, stronger this time. As his listeners showed their appreciation for his words, Pastor Kirkland looked out the side window of the sanctuary across Lake Washington. His thoughts briefly went to his comfortable home which was east in Sammamish, an upscale suburb of Seattle. The last thing he would ever do, he pondered, would be to flee what he called his 'heaven on earth'.

Pastor Mick continued for the next few minutes bashing Christians who believed that the Bible contained prophetic verses which accurately foretold the future. He was now nearing his wind-up, what he had decided was the favorite part of this sermon. "My dear congregants, there are, I am told, tens of thousands of people, not just here in Washington State, but all over this country, who seriously believe that *America is doomed.* I'm not just talking about a high level of federal debt, we can all agree that it needs to be trimmed a bit, but they go even further. Much further. You may know some of them. They come in at least two different categories. Some are called 'preppers'. And others are fleeing our beloved country. Preppers are, may I say this? They are unusual, strange, maybe even wacky folks who store food and ammunition for when *the end times* arrive. Let me see if I get this....they want Jesus to come back....so they're storing up hundreds of bullets? I'm sorry, *I just don't get that.*

"The other certifiable folks are those who say that America will be destroyed, claiming that the Bible names our country as Babylon. They throw out verses saying that Christians....and American Jewish residents....must flee the country and move offshore. One verse they use says to flee to avoid participating in her sins. Sins? *Sins?* What a *quaint* word. Don't they know that this is *the 21st century?*" Snickers and laughter could be heard across the sanctuary. "America isn't perfect, what nation is? But *'flee from her sins'*? But that's not the worst of what these extremists preach. For example, I don't think America will be destroyed, which is what these folks argue, because it won't come to Israel's defense in that dust-up that we've all been watching in the media. What *difference* would it make? It's just one of a couple hundred nations on the globe, certainly *not* a 'chosen nation' and definitely *not* God's *'chosen people'.*

"I met with a family from our church recently who were in tears, asking me for advice. Why were they upset? The parents of one of the parishioners in my office had decided to move to Central America. Why are they moving, I asked? Because the parents think America is Babylon and will be destroyed once it turns its back on Israel. They think, believe it or not, that the Bible tells them to *'flee the wicked nation of Babylon/America'*. Well, congregants, I told them that before their parents left the country they should consider seeking a court order and have them *committed.*" Applause. "God will *never* destroy this nation, even if he or she could. We are *too important* in the grand scheme of things. A little insignificant country like Israel may not survive....who really *likes* them anyway....but the United States of America will *never* fall. The media is full of stories about Israel's neighbors invading them. So what? Israel should have *gotten along better* with its neighbors, that's what I say. It's certainly not worth the lives of *any* American young men or women to *defend* them. They can fend for themselves.

"So the next time a friend or a family member criticizes our great country, and breathes heavy about hoarding food and ammo, or worst yet, leaving the country, just tell them what you just heard from an expert on the Bible. America's not in the Bible. The Bible doesn't predict anything about the time in which we live. That's voodoo Christianity. *You have nothing to fear. No* destruction. *No* downfall of America. *No* reason to hoard nor to flee. Things will *continue* in our great country just as they have *in the past.* You heard it from a man of the cloth, so you can count on it. Now, go and be warm and blessed."

The congregation jumped to its feet, cheering their Pastor's comforting assurances.

62

18

The Moshe and Sophia Guttman Home

Petah Tikva, Israel

At midnight in Israel the Guttman phone rang with a call from Moshe's brother in northern Virginia. Ben told Moshe that he was able to reach his military client, but that the General didn't have any knowledge that he could share as to the intentions of the U.S. The General did advise Ben, though, that a morning press briefing was scheduled at the White House, at which it was expected there would be a new announcement concerning the U.S. response to the invasion of Israel.

Neither Moshe nor Sophia could sleep well for the balance of the night, though their two teens had no problem. Sophia frequently said that youth was wasted on the young. At 4 AM Moshe was tired of tossing in his bed, so he got up, started the coffee and turned on the kitchen TV. He was soon joined by Sophia. They sipped coffee and watched the news of the invasion of their country, while they waited for the morning news conference from the White House. The hours crawled slowly by before it finally came time for video coverage from the Press Room of the White House.

At just after 3 PM a news bulletin flashed across Israel's TV screens. It was being reported by the Israeli government that "after several attempts" the Prime Minister had finally gotten through to the US President and that the two leaders were currently in an "extended planning conversation". Upon hearing the news flash

Yitzhak and Golda jumped up and shouted in joy. Moshe and Sophia hugged each other. *"Such good news"*, the four said, *"such good news"*. Sophia didn't share her concerns with her celebrating family, but she was puzzled as to why it took so long for the PM to speak to the President. The invaders crossed into the Golan yesterday at mid-day, she recalled. Why so long?

Moshe was so cheered by the news, though, that he went to the kitchen and starting cooking an afternoon treat, his famous blintzes, with strawberries, blueberries and red raspberries, which he usually reserved for special occasions. The Guttmans' conversation was animated, as they enjoyed the sweet afternoon treat and rejoiced over what they believed would be the imminent insertion of U.S. troops and missiles into northern Israel. In the background, television reporters disclosed that the invading force was mostly now past Israeli Highway 91, with the lead units rapidly heading south on Highway 6, the Yitzhak Rabin Highway, one of four major north-south roads in Israel. A reporter on Channel 10 came on the screen, with clouds of black smoke behind him as he spoke into his microphone. Golda saw it from her seat in the kitchen and asked Yitzhak to go turn up the sound.

Almost out of breath, the Channel 10 reporter, dressed in a desert camo flak jacket with red letters saying MEDIA, said, "....and one IDF source described this invading force as like *a cloud covering the land*....Based on what we have just seen and been told by IDF sources, we've learned that the village of Kfar Tavor, at the foot of Mount Tabor, has been decimated....*totally gone*....every building either flattened by the force of the artillery or now in flames....It looks like the invading forces went out of

64

their way to run over and destroy the vineyards for which the village is famous....This area is on the route the forces from Russia and Iran have apparently chosen from Damascus into Israel's heartland....There is no estimate at this time as to the casualty count of the twenty seven hundred residents here, though several apparently dead bodies were spotted lying near the highway out of the village....Hold on....I'm getting a report on my earpiece that....Yes, it appears that the town of Afula, southwest of our location, has *also been destroyed* by the invading forces on their way to Highway 6....When we can get closer to Afula, we'll update viewers with what we learn. That's all we have right now from the war zone."

The mood in the Guttman kitchen ratcheted down, as they realized that brother and sister Israelis just north of them were being attacked and killed. They left the kitchen to huddle around the television awaiting the news conference from the United States of America, Israel's military defense treaty partner. Within minutes the station announced that they were switching to their U.S. affiliate for coverage from the White House Press Room.

The President's Press Secretary, a diminutive, bespectacled former reporter for the New York Times, strode briskly into the Press Room. He stepped up behind the podium. Sophia noticed that he had no document binder with him, which was his normal approach, as he would consult written talking points in order to answer media questions. The President's Press Secretary only briefly glanced at the assembled reporters, his eyes looking up at the ceiling.

He only uttered one sentence, saying in a steady voice, *"In spite of enormous pressure on this Administration, there will be no change in the position of the United States regarding the inter-regional disagreement in the Middle East."* The President's Press Secretary turned and walked out of the Press Room without taking any of the several questions shouted at him by reporters.

Moshe looked over at his family. He could see that Sophia and Golda were both crying. Looking away but wiping his face, Yitzhak was the first to speak, saying in anger, "I can't believe it. We're *dying* here."

Golda just held her head in her hands. Sophia murmured, *"Disagreement?"*...."Is the President that *dense?*....This is a *full-scale war* with at least three countries, *no friends* of the US I should add, who are invading your *only* friend in the Middle East. What does it *take* to get you to help us before we're all *dead? What?"*

Moshe started to speak, cleared his choked-up throat, then suggested, "It's time we get ready to go into the safe room. Everybody take a good long hot shower, it'll be the last one we get for a while. Let's do a big meal, not a diary meal like we usually have at night. We'll use up the last of the fresh meat, lettuce, you know, food that's refrigerated, since we don't have refrigeration in the safe room. Let's get busy guys, those troops coming south on Rabin Highway are headed our way....and *we're* on *their way* into Tel Aviv."

19

War Room – Israeli Defense Force

IDF HaKirya Compound, Tel Aviv

Israel's Prime Minister slowly placed the red handset back on the crisis phone on the massive table in the Israeli War Room. All twenty of the people in the room, three levels below street level under the HaKirya Compound in Tel Aviv, were carefully watching Israel's leader. They were all ear witnesses to one side of the Prime Minister's heated conversation with the President of the United States. Though none heard the words spoken by the leader of the free world, it was painfully obvious that he was offering Israel nothing. No change of mind. No defense. No military assistance. Nothing.

Israel's Defense Minister was standing against the wall of the war room. He moved forward, placing his hand on the Prime Minister's shoulder. "*It's OK*, Bebe, you did what you could. We knew when he wouldn't take your many previous calls that he was going to choke, to refuse to help us. I take it that he's still *sticking with* his 'we won't interfere in your little local conflict' line."

"*No*, Ben, the U.S. won't be helping. *God help us.*"

"I appreciated your conversion of his promise that America 'had Israel's back' into 'you're stabbing us in the back'. I take it he didn't exactly *appreciate* that, right?"

"Actually, that's when he terminated the call. By that point in the conversation I knew it was over, so what harm was it to call it like it is? As he hung up he said he would let me know if there's any change, but we all know how *likely* that is."

"So, gentlemen, since we can't count on any military assistance from our former closest ally we need to structure our response to the invaders accordingly. Alert our remaining undamaged air wings to be ready for *launch.* What's the current most forward location of the armored columns? How many kilometers from Tel Aviv? "

The General tasked with coordinating the defense of Israel replied, "We're about an hour, maybe fifty minutes, from *massive bloodshed.* Our recon shows that the initial strike will be east of Tel Aviv at Petah Tikva. We've of course alerted everyone. As you know, there are about 200,000 residents in Petah Tikva. It looks like they will be the largest metropolitan area hit first."

The Prime Minister rubbing his temples, clearly in distress, suggested, "Well, it's appropriate that the battle line will first be in the Valley of Achor, at the city named from Hosea's prophecy, *'the opening of hope'.*"

The Defense Minister nodded in agreement, saying, "As you may recall, the first attack on our Jewish ancestors took place in Petah Tikva, back in the late 1800's. So, yes, it's very appropriate that the first major assault will be at Petah Tikva. My grandchildren live in Petah Tikva. Let's pray that our IDF boys and girls can hold off the invaders long enough for Petah Tikva's residents to either flee or get securely behind their safe room doors. If not, let it be always known that the blood of our brothers and sisters....and grandchildren....will be on *the hands* of America's President. *On America itself.*"

20

Western/Wailing Wall (Kotel)

Jerusalem, Israel

The Western Wall had been called the Wailing Wall for centuries, as mourners would kiss the stones and bemoan the destruction of the Temple. Jewish tradition held that Solomon had placed the foundation stones underlying the Wall, with others holding that Herod the Great had authorized the edifice upon that foundation. The Western Wall is revered as a holy site, as close to the Temple as one could come. Mourners frequently write prayers on small pieces of paper, roll them up and place them in the cracks of the wall. Today's tearful, mourning reaction to Rabbi Herzog's words by the now overflow crowd was in keeping with the name of the Wailing Wall.

Rabbi Isaac David Herzog was weeping also, having just emphasized the difficult news from scripture that no nation would come to Israel's aid and its weapons would be insufficient. The Chief Rabbi was only able to continue speaking because he knew the rest of the story, the prophetic revelation given to the Prophet Joel. Wiping his face, he continued, "Joel said, '*Alas*, for the day!'....'*Alas, for the day!*'....But....*then* Joel wrote....for the day of destruction....*from the Almighty*....will come. Yes, *this is a day of destruction*. Yes, many of our brothers and sisters have died and more will die as *this evil* army from the north sweeps south....but...the Almighty confirms this in His word. The invasion will happen, which it has, just as He said. There will be blood shed in Israel, but Joel tells us that *the Almighty will become jealous for His land and* *will have pity on His people....*As Joel urged, *'Fear not, O land, be glad and rejoice, for the Lord has done great things'* and *'Be glad, O children of Zion and rejoice in the Lord your God'.....Why?*

"Joel conveys to us a special message written just for *this day.* God revealed to Joel that He will remove the northerner far from us and will drive him into a parched and desolate land, destroying the army, some in the eastern and western seas, with the stench and foul smell arising from *their slain bodies.* The Prophet Ezekiel foresaw the same invasion of Israel. He prophesied God's anger would arise against those *defiling His land* and coming to *kill His people. He promised* that the invading fighting men would *fall* on the mountains and on the open fields. *Will you join me as we pray?*

"Almighty Jehovah God, just as you instructed, we have sounded the Shofar, we have gathered *a Solemn Assembly,* we are *fasting, praying and seeking Your face and Your will.* We thank You that You knew from the beginning of time that this great and powerful army would come against *Your land and Your people.* We pray for our people in Your land who are suffering and dying. *We weep, we mourn, we implore You* to fulfill Your Word given in the Holy Scriptures to Joel and Ezekiel. We pray that *You turn in your righteous anger and act.* We pray that the great earthquake, and torrential rains, and hailstones and fire and sulfur, about which the Prophets wrote, will soon fall on these evil invaders of *Your sacred land.* As the Prophet Joel wrote, *'*The Lord utters His voice before His army, for His camp is *exceedingly great;* He who executes His Word is *powerful'. Please, Almighty Jehovah....save us,* we pray, for there is *no force on this earth* that can do so, *except for You.* Amen and Amen."

In response to Rabbi Herzog's pleas, millions in Israel, denying their bodies food by fasting, also earnestly and fervently prayed for a miracle of God.

The Shofar sounded a long wailing, rising sound.

21

Hannah and Gary's Family Room

Birmingham, Alabama

The six remaining members of their small group Bible study were huddled around the television. What they were seeing was not only history in the making, but spiritually disturbing. Israel's Prime Minister had just finished making what he called a 'final plea' for the United States to send its military resources into Israel to stop what he said would be the 'wholesale massacre of Israelites' in Tel Aviv and soon throughout Israel. Fox's network talking head summarized the PM's passionate call for help from America, but was interrupted by breaking news from the White House.

"Whew!" Scott exclaimed, "This could be it. The President may have seen the light and reversed course. It may be that we're about to hear that America is coming to the rescue. It's really late....the invaders are close to entering Tel Aviv....lots of dead people in towns on the way to Tel Aviv. But....if we send in American jets and our troops now, we could still spare millions of people....there, watch. It's the Secretary of Defense....never liked that guy much....but....okay....here he goes...."

The Secretary of Defense had apparently been delayed by media on his way into the Executive Avenue entrance to the West Wing of the White House. The wind had tosseled his silvery hair, giving him a frazzled, even wild look. The look in his eyes as he stared at the reporters who had stopped him further enhanced the look of an important person who didn't like being disturbed. Glaring at the assembled media, he snarled, "We have, *again*, just heard from Israeli officials in Jerusalem. They have, *again*, requested that the US *interfere*, uh, that is, intervene, in the *regional disagreement* in the Middle East."

Scott dropped his head into his hands, groaning, "*Oh, no*, this is *not* going where it should."

After looking at his watch and looking for any nearby aide who could rescue him, the Defense Secretary continued, "The official position of the United States government has *not* changed. We will *not* exacerbate what is already an obviously tense situation by throwing our military might into *some other nation's* controversy. We would urge Israel to settle its *own problems* and to desist from continually *badgering us* to do something that we have made clear we will *never* do.....That's all....I have a meeting with the President."

Audrey and Hannah were hugging each other. Sally, who had said for the last two years that there was nothing that would cause her to move from the US, was crestfallen. Wringing her hands, she burst out, "Can you guys *ever* forgive me? I know we talked about this earlier, I apologized, but I just can't get over the fact that we had a chance to flee, and we willfully....*I willfully*....decided *not* to listen to what God was telling me in His Word. If I hadn't been so stupid, you all might have followed Marty and Tom and Liz and Max out of what is about to happen to us."

Scott put his arms around his wife, comforting her, "Sally, my dear, I knew the same things you knew. I studied the same verses. I knew in my heart that America is the Daughter of Babylon prophesied in the Bible. It *can't* be any other country. It *can't* be ancient Babylon. I just read in my Bible reading this morning that God told Jeremiah that after Israel was captive in ancient Babylon that He would impose on Babylon an *everlasting* destruction. He kept His word. Ancient Babylon is *still* a pile of rubble. *America*....is....the descendant of *Babylon*. It was *both* of us, honey, who decided not to obey all those verses to flee the Daughter of Babylon."

Everyone was quiet, then Beau said, "I suggest that we go straight to prayer. It's quite obvious that the President of our country has not only stabbed Israel in the back, now we're *twisting* the blade, telling Israel to stop bothering us with its repeated cries for help. God forgive us for *what we are doing to Israel*. But, we *know* what He promises for those who mis-treat Israel. So....we *know* we're toast. The only remaining question is *when* do we head to our bolt hole, our safe house?"

Gary, who had been quietly contemplative up to now, said, "Here's the deal. God's response to our country's betrayal of His chosen people *is imminent*. If I had to guess, I'd say with this final announcement from the White House that we're not far from doom. If you ladies are right about how long our food supplies will last, then getting us and what food we have over to our safe house in a timely manner is *critical*. Scott, you've been our point guy on the safe house. What's your plan once we see America under attack?"

75

Still hugging Sally, Scott replied, "As you know, there are guys from twenty small groups who've been planning what we would do if....*when*....disaster hits. We've been meeting monthly. Though we've kept it very quiet, I can share with you that we've selected an older, abandoned grade school building between here and Pelham. It was closed due to school consolidation, mothballed for years. It's not on any major road. It was built back in a wooded area probably forty years ago. Just one floor. All brick. Windows, of course, but not so many that the building can't be defended. Central courtyard, so we can use the outdoors, without going out of the building. Kitchen facilities so we can prepare food for the hundred or so men, women and children who will live there."

Audrey, dabbing her eyes, whispered, "I just can't believe that we're talking about hiding out in some *bunker*....Is it really going to come to that? *Really?*"

Beau not only looked like he was military, he had just retired from the Army Reserves only a year ago. He replied, "Audrey, dear Audrey. We're not the *first* Christians, nor the first humans to face truly tough times....war, destruction, death. In fact, we've been blessed for years, for decades when we've lived quiet, plentiful lives. But, nothing lasts forever, that is, except for God's word and people. What we do now, in face of what we know is about to come down on this country, is we do what the Bible says, we see the danger and *we flee from it*.....I get that it's too late to flee the country. Foreign air travel has been restricted since August, but that doesn't mean that we should stay here, stay in our homes and get picked off by every marauder, thief and murderer

76

who knocks on our door and asks for food. We have to *protect* ourselves, *protect our kids.*"

Scott joined in, standing as he spoke, "Brothers and sisters. The way we left it with the other small group leaders who've been meeting to plan our safe house is that we are *not* going to wait around, mouths agape, scared silly once we see the US has been attacked. Most folks will be so shocked in the first day or two that they won't know what to do. But for many all they will need is the mere hint of widespread problems and they'll be off to the grocery stores *like a shot. Wham.* Let's grab all the food we can, they'll say, before somebody else does. *The result?* Empty store shelves everywhere. The gun stores that still have weapons or any remaining ammo will likewise be picked clean. Gas stations won't last long."

Gary asked, "What's your estimate on *how long* it will take?"

"Picture this scene....because we're about to actually see it. The nukes go off. The media that survives report that American cities, all across the country, have been hit....hit with nukes. The average Joe watching it on his big screen at first won't believe what he's seeing. *How can this be*, he'll ask? His wife will say *what* are we going to *do*? That will make Joe start thinking, yeah, what *are* we going to do? He'll remember that his truck is below a quarter tank on fuel – most guys can tell you the gas level on their cars, believe it or not, ladies. So he jumps up, grabs his keys and starts for the door. His wife asks, where are you going? He says, to get some gas before everyone runs the tanks dry at the gas stations. She says, but what about food? All we've got is what we've got in the pantry and the frig. We were gonna stock up at Costco this weekend, she says. He replies, okay, I'll hit the grocery as soon as I get some gas."

Beau added, "Multiply that scenario by the population of south Birmingham. Everyone *panicking* at once. Remember what it was like in 2003 when the blizzard warnings came out?"

"Yeah. Within a few hours you couldn't find a gallon of milk or a loaf of bread. The lines at the gas stations were up to a mile long, before they started waving people away because they were out of gas."

"So, what do we learn from all that?", Sally asked.

Beau spoke slowly, "We....learn....that....we can't wait around once the first news comes that we've been attacked.....We would have literally....*no time*....to get organized. We have to be organized *now*, which is what Scott has been doing. Scott, what did you guys decide we should be doing once we got to this stage?"

"What we decided was that we really don't wait until the bombs go off. That will trigger panic. Clogged roads. The whole bit. We're suggesting that everyone load up the trunks of the cars with food that's not refrigerated, guns and ammo, our warmest clothes for when it gets cold and we don't have power and, for the sentimental, a few family pictures. Forget the laptops, and ipads, iphones, ijunk, none of that's going to be working a few days after the attacks. Forget electric razors, too. And once the razor blades wear out, every man will be bearded. The school is about ten minutes away for most of us, so we'll possibly be able to make a second, maybe a third trip back home,

78

but *that's it*. Then, once everyone's in the school, we lock it down and get ready for all hel....heck....to break loose."

Hannah, the practical member of the small group, asked, "But, Scott, we can pack our trunks full now, but we're not going to drive over and move into the school *before* the nukes go off, are we? How does the timing work?"

"Good question, Hannah. We wrestled with that for some time. What we decided was that everyone needs to keep their cell phones with them. Not in the car. Not in the bedroom. But, *with us*. Once anyone in our group hears of the attack, even if it's a sketchy early report, call my cell. I'll send a group text and alert the other small group leaders. The plan is to get our family members gathered up, wherever they may be, *quickly*. Loaded up. Then get over to the school. We can park behind the school and wait while we listen to the radio reports. Once we know for sure that the U.S. has been attacked, we start unloading our stuff in the school. One of the other leaders who was an administrator at the school has keys to the school. Then we'll try for a second load and pray the roads aren't clogged yet. We should be okay at that stage because most folks will be in initial shock before *full panic* sets in."

"But Scott," Beau asked, "What about our cars and trucks, we can't leave them *there*, they would be a huge sign saying *'there are people in here'*."

"Correct. Our plan is to drive to and scatter park the cars in a small sub-division, about a mile away. Then walk back to the school. They'll be close if we need to get to them, but they won't tip off our location."

"It sounds like you fellows have thought of everything," Audrey said *"Have you?* Are we forgetting anything?"

Beau responded, "In war and in similar situations like we are about to face, the one rule is that planning is *always* faulty. You can't know what you don't know, but I agree with you, Audrey, Scott's group has put a lot of thought into how we survive the train wreck headed our way."

"I don't want to be too negative," Scott said, "but what we have planned is for short term survival *only.* Medium and long term? Well, that's *another* story that we can talk and pray about when we have a lot of time at the school. On that somber note, I think it's time that we pray."

22

The Moshe and Sophia Guttman Home

Petah Tikva, Israel

Several hours had passed since the President's White House Press Room news conference in which he had announced that America would not get involved in the invasion of Israel by Russia, Iran and Libya. During ten of those hours the Guttman family inhabited their flat's safe room. Though they didn't have cable in the safe room, a small radio kept them apprised of the latest news. They were temporarily cheered when the radio newscaster announced that Israel's PM was making what he called "one last attempt" to change the President's mind and obtain American military help against the forces invading their country. That good news allowed the four family members to finally get some sleep on their cots, which were none too comfortable.

Just after 6 AM Moshe awoke and turned the radio on at a low volume so as not to awake the others. He listened carefully to reports of the location of the invading forces. He heard a reporter who was located at Israeli Defense Forces headquarters in downtown Tel Aviv confirm that the lead units of the invading force were still traveling south on Highway 6, Yitzhak Rabin Highway, and were just now south of Highway 5. With a sinking feeling Moshe realized that the invaders of Israel were now only about four miles from Petah Tikva and their apartment building. Moshe knew that if the armored column pushing south left Rabin Highway and headed west towards Tel Aviv on 483, then moved to 481, one direct route to Tel Aviv, that his building and his neighbors in east Petah Tikva might escape harm. On the other hand, if the forces turned south on 40, the Yerushalayim Highway, they would soon be on their doorstep. Maybe, just maybe, they'll take 483 and 481 straight into Tel Aviv. If they do in Tel Aviv what they've done already in Israel, he realized, his dental office would be no longer, but at least they would still be alive.

Sophia was also awake. She could hear the radio reports of the location of the invading forces. Being the practical member of the family, she immediately realized when she heard that the invaders were south of Highway 5 on Rabin Highway, that their community offered too attractive of a bombardment target to ignore. She said her prayers quietly, not wishing to wake the children, whom she knew would be awake soon enough once artillery shells began to rain down on their neighborhood.

Moshe heard Sophia's fervent prayers. As reports were broadcast that the invading forces were turning south on Highway 40, Yerushalayim Highway, next to their home, Moshe reluctantly realized that the Guttman family might not survive the next hour. When they purchased their flat the salesman had been quite specific that the safe room would afford only limited protection if larger rounds of ammunition were to be used. His expression at the time, Moshe recalled, was, "This is *not* a bomb proof room, and just *barely* a bullet proof room, depending on the size of the munition being used". Moshe decided he needed to pray also.

As he finished his prayers, Moshe heard two things simultaneously, the radio newscaster announcing the latest location of the armored column on Yerushalayim Highway, just a block from their building, and the sound of exploding ordinance. The armored column made its way south on Yerushalayim Highway, blasting each residential tower on its way, moving west to downtown Tel Aviv. As numerous shells tore the buildings apart, screams of the residents could be heard in the loud explosions. A Russian artillery unit pulled up next to the six story apartment tower in which the Guttmans lived and fired four devastating rounds into the building. The blasts had the effect of collapsing the first floor, which led to the pancaking of the upper floors. The apartment tower was no longer a tower, but was now a pile of rubble, surrounded by dust, in the midst of which flames erupted from opened gas lines, consuming what was left in the building that could burn.

Moshe, Sophia, Golda and Yitzhak Guttman were no more. The Guttman safe room and flat on the third floor of the apartment tower collapsed into the rubble. Their bodies were torn and crushed by the explosion which destroyed their home. Moshe, Sophia, Golda and Yitzhak's blood flowed from their smashed bodies, mixing with the concrete dust, disintegrated timber and what was left of their family home. Thus, the four Guttmans' lives flowed out of their bodies as their blood ran onto the Promised Land. Though what had just happened in Petah Tikva was of no great concern in America, it was noticed where it counted.

23

The Old Cemetery

Rosh Pina, Israel

For the site of the curse the Rabbi chose the Old Cemetery at the back of the 135 year old town known as Rosh Pina. The town was settled in 1878 by orthodox Jewish farmers, financially supported by Baron Edmund de Rothschild. The town boasted the nation's second oldest modern Hebrew school and Baron's Gardens modeled after Versailles. Buried in the Old Cemetery is Shlomo Ben-Yosef who died at the age of 25 in 1938. He was the first Jewish resident of the British mandate area executed by the British. Ben-Yosef led an attack on an Arab bus in retaliation for the killing of six Jews by Arab militants. When his death verdict was announced, two months after the attack, Shlomo Ben-Yosef stood and shouted, *"Long live the Kingdom of Israel on both banks of the Jordan"*.

The Rabbi selected the Old Cemetery not only for its notable history, but also because it was the same cemetery where he had some years before performed a Pulsa Dinura curse. He called then for a curse on the Prime Minister of Israel who gave away Gaza, leading to the forced eviction of ten thousand Jewish settlers from 21 communities, many of whom had lived in Gaza for decades. The Pulsa Dinura curse was performed by twenty bearded, married Jewish residents over the age of 40 and under a rabbinical order for the curse. Four months after the Rabbi called in the curse for angels of destruction to come against the Prime Minister, Israel's leader lapsed into a vegetative coma, dying several years later. In the years following the Rabbi's call for the curse and the PM's stroke, the Rabbi frequently referred to the Pulsa Diura curse as the underlying cause of the Prime Minister's stroke and eventual death. He also noted that the hurricane which became America's costliest natural disaster slammed into the southern U.S. during the last two days of the forced evacuation of Jewish residents of Gaza, which started on August 16th and ended on the 30th. The Rabbi suggested to anyone who would listen that when America pushed Israel to force the Jewish residents out of their Gaza homes that God then allowed a hurricane to push Americans out of their homes.

On this day of great danger and turmoil in Israel, the Rabbi gathered the same group of bearded, married Jewish residents who had earlier assembled near the grave of Shlomo Ben-Yosef for the first Pulsa Diura curse. Each was dressed in black, with the exception of the Rabbi who was dressed in white. Prior to their meeting, a question had been raised by one who participated in the first curse as to whether the second curse which the Rabbi was proposing was in keeping with rules for the kabbalistic ceremony. The Rabbi had let it be known that the new curse would be upon America for failing to keep its word to come to Israel's defense if Israel were to ever come under attack. Under halacha, traditional Jewish law, the ceremony was to be against people who are Jewish. The Rabbi, after studying halacha and consulting with other scholars, concluded that such a curse would be appropriate, given the fact that America had many Jewish residents, several of prominence being in the U. S. government at high levels.

The invokers of the curse walked solemnly into the Old Cemetery just before dusk, the sun just finishing its job for the day as it lit the dust and pollen motes circulating in the air. They said nothing as they made their way to the sacred burial site of Ben-Yosef, revered by many in Israel as a young man willing to give his life for the formation of the State of Israel. They stood around the burial site, their hands clasped and their eyes either closed or filled with tears. The Rabbi prayed, then briefly reviewed the unforgiveable crime of America, that the world's most powerful nation had given its solemn, written commitment to Menachem Begin, Prime Minister of Israel on March 26, 1979. To induce the signing of the Camp David Peace Accord, America, through its President, gave its promise to come to Israel's defense were it to be militarily attacked.

The Rabbi recited the facts of the current invasion of Israel from the north. He reminded everyone present, though they were all quite well aware of the facts, that America's promise was being breached by its refusal to help little Israel, it's only ally in the Middle East. Thus, he cried out, America has become a betrayer of Israel, as scripture prophesied. The Rabbi mentioned the several verses in scripture pointing to America as the rich, influential and powerful end times country described as the Daughter of Babylon. He finished the charges against Israel's former friend and protector and lowered his head. The assembled men prayed fervently for God's justice. After their prayers, waiting for a few moments, the Rabbi gave for all to hear the basis for the Pulsa Diura curse, as he then read aloud from Jeremiah 51:33, 35, 49 and 56:

"For thus says the LORD of hosts, the God of Israel: The daughter of Babylon is like a threshing floor at the time when it is trodden; yet a little while and the time of her harvest will come."

"May the violence done to our flesh be upon Babylon," say the inhabitants of Zion. "May our blood be on those who live in Babylonia," says Jerusalem.

"Babylon must fall because of Israel's slain, just as the slain in all the earth have fallen because of Babylon."

"A destroyer will come against Babylon; her warriors will be captured, and their bows will be broken. For the LORD is a God of retribution; he will repay in full."

The Rabbi then prayed and called upon God to send angels of destruction on the nation which betrayed Israel, as Isaiah warned in 21:2 - *"the traitor betrays"*.

"Oh, God, we only ask for *justice for Israel* and to avenge the blood of our people, your people, which will be shed in this evil invasion. We ask you to *keep your promise* given by the Prophet Jeremiah that the violence done to our flesh and our blood shed *will be upon the betrayer*, upon the Daughter of Babylon, upon the United States of America, just as you promised. *A Pulsa Diura curse we call for on the Daughter of Babylon, on America.* May you have *mercy* on their souls. Amen and Amen.

24

Highway 40

East of Tel Aviv, Israel

It started with a single large raindrop hitting the windshield of the Russian Commander's armored mobility vehicle, which was mine-resistant and designated as INV-1, the command vehicle for the invasion. The Russian Commander, who had been studying ground invasion terrain maps, heard the rain drop hit, looked up and saw that it had splattered right in front of him. His first thought was that it had be from a bird, as they had carefully chosen this day based on perfect weather to move massive machines and large numbers of troops quickly across Israel. Couldn't be rain, he thought, as he looked back at his maps.

Shortly thereafter, though, another large drop splattered his windshield, followed by another and then many drops began to pummel his column of armored vehicles and armed soldiers. Within ten minutes the rain had turned into a torrential downpour. Some of the force's armored fighting vehicles had windshield wipers, but many of the larger vehicles had not been so designed or built. As the rain increased in intensity it was soon obvious that the column would have to stop, as the drivers of the larger vehicles with no wipers couldn't see to stay on the road. Even in vehicles with wipers, set at the highest speed, drivers were not able to see clearly through what looked like buckets of water being thrown on them from above.

Commander Nikolaevich issued the order to halt their advance to Tel Aviv, temporarily, until the rain slackened. He radioed his column control officers who were further back, some still in the mountains of the Golan Heights, to warn them that they might encounter exceptionally heavy rain when they arrived further into Israel. Each officer with whom the Commander spoke responded that they were already experiencing a great deal of rainfall, which had forced them to halt their advance. Strange, thought the Commander of the invasion force, that there should be so much rain over such a large area, yet with no prior weather warning. He concluded that it was nothing like he had ever before encountered, he'd just have to wait it out.

As the rain continued to pour down in increasing intensity, the Commander received a flash message from Moscow asking why they were stopped, as the satellite feeds in the Kremlin confirmed. After being strongly reprimanded by the Kremlin for 'letting a little rain slow you down', the Commander hung up, adjusted his uniform, pulled on his General's high-peaked hat and opened his side door, noticing as he did so that there were now some sizeable hailstones mixed in the falling rain. He stood up on the side platform, tried to look at the road ahead, which he could just barely make out, then turned his head to see how much of his column he could see in the downpour.

As he turned he was thrown off of the side platform onto the ground. At first he thought he had just slipped on the wet platform, but then as the ground was violently shaking below his fallen prone body he realized that an earthquake, an exceptionally large quake, had shaken his

90

vehicle so violently that he was thrown off. He looked up at a small building near the edge of Yerushalayim Highway. It was being shaken like a pit bull ripping apart a small dog. Cracks appeared in the walls, followed by the building shaking apart and collapsing to the ground. He looked the other direction at the mountains that he could just barely make out in the rain. The mountains were undulating up and down, with walls of what looked like large rock sections shearing off and falling off the mountains. One large cliff appeared to bolt straight up, then fall sideways and pitch down the side of the mountain.

The Commander's last conscious thought was to ask himself how there could be such an enormous, damaging earthquake in an area of the world not known for seismic disturbances. As the thought came to his mind, something else came to his head. A falling seven pound hailstone split the rain and the Commander's skull, killing him instantly. The driver of the command vehicle saw his Commander's body on the rain-soaked ground, blood spewing from his smashed head. He jumped out of the vehicle to assist the fallen officer, only to himself be struck dead by multiple softball and larger sized hailstones.

Most of the invading troop carrier vehicles were of the same design used in prior wars, with canvas tops and sides. The plummeting hailstones quickly split open the canvas of the trucks, hurtling onto the soldiers lined up inside. Within minutes, no matter how the troops tried to avoid the armament from heaven, most couldn't and died from traumatic injuries, head concussions and smashed rib cages and limbs. Those who tried to escape by jumping from the personnel carriers were quickly struck down, as the hailstones were pervasive across the invading column and beyond. Armored vehicles with metal tops were pounded by round after round of increasingly heavy hailstones, collapsing the roofs, crushing the troops within. The world had rarely witnessed such an exhibition of cosmic power, but it wasn't yet over.

The earthquake aftershocks grew in intensity with the rain and hailstones also not slacking. In the IDF War Room Israel's military leaders were monitoring the rain and hail on weather radar. The earthquake seemed to be centered on the invading armored column in the Golan and south into the plains of north central Israel. Its effects swayed the IDF tower and other buildings in Tel Aviv. At the same time, a wire service news bulletin reported that record-sized earthquakes were happening in Moscow, Tehran and other cities of nations whose troops were part of the Israel invasion force, with reported widespread destruction caused by unusual fire falling from the sky.

Just as IDF's commanding general turned from the wire bulletin to make a comment to Israel's PM, a blinding flash appeared on several of the television monitors in the war room. The PM shouted, "*What was that?* What was *that?* I haven't released our nukes, yet. That looked like a nuke detonation. *What* was...."

A review of the electronic monitoring resources in the room disclosed that three explosions had just detonated, in the Golan Heights, near Mount Tabor and northeast of Tel Aviv, near the intersection of Highways 5 and 6. The PM reviewed the monitoring results, sipped more coffee to moisten his throat which was made dry by the tension and stress of watching what certainly appeared to be the world's first nuclear war-time detonations since 1945, and again asked, "*What?* These weren't *our* nukes. We *know* that. But, none of the three were detonated on our population centers. I don't get it. Are you telling me that these are maybe *less* than a megaton? That's close to normal ordinance as far as blast effect, but of course, the radiation will kill thousands. Uhm, I don't....Do you think? Uhm. Maybe. Get me Rabbi Herzog. *Now.* He prayed for this....it sure looks like the Prophet Ezekiel's prophecy that the Rabbi called down on the invaders at the Wailing Wall, praying for Israel's invaders to suffer. What did he call it? *'Fire and sulfur'?* That sounds a lot like the effects of a nuke. You don't suppose?"

Rabbi Herzog's office thanked the PM's staffer for the call, but explained that the Chief Rabbi was in prayer at Yad Vashem and couldn't be disturbed. The staffer conveyed the response to the PM, who replied, "The *last thing* I would do is to interrupt Rabbi Herzog as he prays at Israel's national memorial to the victims of the Holocaust. His prayers at the Wailing Wall may well have saved us from *a second holocaust,* here in our own land. When he calls back, connect me *right away.*"

25

War Room – Israeli Defense Force

IDF HaKirya Compound, Tel Aviv

Upon his return from praying at Yad Vashem, Jerusalem's Chief Rabbi tried to return the PM's call. He was immediately refused access by the PM's office, but he suspected that given the invasion, he would most likely be at the IDF HaKirya Compound, in the IDF War Room three floors below ground level. The process of getting his call through took some time, but during his wait he was fully apprised as to what had been happening in the last hour. He heard a click on the phone line, after which he was greeted by the surprisingly upbeat voice of Israel's elected leader. "Rabbi Herzog. What *an honor* to hear from you."

"Umh....That is....Mister Prime Minister. The honor of course is mine."

"Before we discuss why you called, let me unofficially....later it'll be more formal....thank you, Rabbi Herzog, for calling Israel to a solemn assembly, to fast and to pray for divine intervention. Along with watching by drone as Russia and her friends stormed into our sacred land, I also watched you at the Wailing Wall. I will be the first to admit, Rabbi, that *I didn't have much faith* in what you were calling down on the invaders, but it appears to *certainly be working.*"

"Sir, it wasn't *me.* I just did what Joel said to do and....well....*Almighty God is doing the rest.*"

"No one can argue with that, Rabbi. As men we can do a lot of things, but we *can't* cause earthquakes, or send torrential rains, or hailstones that weigh over twenty kilo. And *fire and sulfur* – it looked like large sheets of flames falling from the skies, consuming everything it landed on. I've asked our science office to figure out what that was....and how we could possibly replicate it."

Rabbi Herzog quietly but assuredly said to the leader of his country, "Bebe, this is nothing but the hand of *Jehovah Himself*. Ezekiel 38 tells us that when Gog and Persia and Cush and Put, that is today's Russia, Iran, Libya and others, would someday invade Israel that God would rain on them, send hail on them, shake the earth and send, yes, *'fire and sulfur'* on them. Ezekiel says that Israel will be burying dead invaders *for months*. The Prophet says that the nations that sent these invaders will suffer greatly. What we have seen today is God honoring His word and glorifying himself. The nations of the world will see this and know that *He is the Lord*."

"As you might say, Rabbi, *Amen and Amen*."

"Sir, have we lost *many* Israeli lives? We want to organize to help the families of those who died."

"Rabbi, it's too early to know. We have lost *several thousand*. They shed their blood while the U.S. dithered and swithered and then betrayed us, as you know. I wouldn't want to be *anywhere near* the White House, or DC, or even in America for that matter, after what this President did to us. Don't the scriptures say that God repays for the shedding of innocent blood?"

"Yes, Bebe, He demands *an accounting*. Joel, by the way, tells us that one of the results of the miraculous divine intervention we are witnessing will be that Israel will know that *God is in the midst of us*, that He is the Lord our God and there is none else. Ezekiel says that through this *God will make himself known* in the eyes of many nations."

"Rabbi, you can help insure that Israel *never, never, never forgets* what the Almighty has done on this day.

"Well, sir, I agree with the sentiment, but *God* will ensure that we *don't forget*. Joel says that afterward, that is after these acts of God in Israel, that He will pour out His spirit on all flesh, that our sons and our daughters shall prophesy, and our old men will dream dreams, and our young men will see visions. We should be ready to see *great and mighty wonders* in the days ahead."

"Rabbi Herzog, I truly do appreciate all that you did for Israel in this perilous time. You heeded the call of the Lord given through Joel, and Israel has *survived*, praise His name. Sorry, but I need to get back to managing the mop up. Anything else?"

"Just one thing, sir, if you have another few seconds Can we pray?"

"*Certainly*. Please."

"Almighty and gracious God, we thank you for loving this land and its people. We praise you for telling us *in advance* how you would save us when wicked and evil men would seek to destroy Israel. Help the families of those here who lost their lives and shed their blood today....Almighty God we know that many, if not most, of those who sought to do us great harm have themselves instead lost *their own lives* today. We pray for their families....And, finally, we pray for the nation which *betrayed us.* We know from the Torah that those who curse Israel will be cursed. *You have blessed America* in the past when it *blessed Israel,* now we pray for your mercy on America....in the midst of your *severe judgment.* Amen and amen."

26

Beau and Audrey's Bed Room

Birmingham, Alabama

"Beau, its Scott. I'm *really sorry* to call you at this hour of the morning."

"*Whoa*....what time is it....uh....3:40? Sure hope this is import...."

"Listen, Beau, my brother just called. You remember Carl, he's the one who works at that secret Air Force installation under Cheyenne Mountain."

"OK. So....I'm still wakin' up, sorry. So....*what* did Carl say?"

"He just read a flash message out of Israel. Something's happening in Tel Aviv. Something *big*....Carl knows what we believe about what the Bible says, so he went out in the hall and called me on his cell."

"I'm awake now, Scott. *What's happening*? What did he tell you?"

"You're *not* gonna' believe what....oh, yeah of course you will. The Air Force is getting reports....and video from Israel showing what look like *fireballs and sheets of flame*, lots of them, falling from the sky and taking out the invaders. One report, he said, described them as 'burning sulfur. He said that the guys in the Pentagon are perplexed. They stay in touch with Israeli defense agencies and they've heard nothing about such a weapon. Carl says....get this....coming from my brother the unbeliever....I'm sorry to say. He says that the guys in the Pentagon are referring to this as *'the fire and brimstone weapon'*."

"*Whoa!* What do these things do when they hit?"

"Beau, this is where it gets *weird*. Carl said the first reports show that these fireballs and sheets of flame are *only* landing on the invading troops and their equipment. They don't appear to be hitting areas of Tel Aviv, or outside Tel Aviv in the areas still under the control of the Israeli Defense Forces. When they hit, they splatter and splash burning substances on the soldiers and their trucks and tanks. What's even weirder, if that's possible, is that they have video showing the Russkies spraying fire foam on the fires started by these celestial fires and it doesn't do any good. But, *get this,* besides these fireballs and sheets of flame, they are getting heavy rain and hailstones, all at *the same time.* You'd think the rain would put out the fires when they hit, but instead he said it's like the rain and hailstones are *spreading the fires.* Nobody's ever seen *anything* like this. When you were with the Army do you recall hearing anything about these burning sulfur fireballs and sheets of flame?"

"Nope. Never. Without jumping to a conclusion, this sure sounds like God at work. Fireballs from heaven? That sounds like *fire and brimstone.* Rain and hailstone? Scott, we looked at the prophecies, I think it was in Ezekiel, in either chapter 38 or 39, that *God Himself* would intervene when Israel would be attacked in the future. But, you know, Scott what this *undoubtedly* means? You know....what's going to ....to....happen *next?*"

"I know, that's all I've been thinking about since I hung up from Carl's call. Now that God has stepped into the battle to save Israel from total destruction, how long can it be before the U.S. is toast? Ezekiel, as I recall, said that when God comes to Israel's rescue it will be....what was his phrase? Oh, yeah, *hot anger.* Ezekiel said God's hot anger would be aroused. Since He has had to come to Israel's defense, given that the President as late as yesterday continued to say no to Israel's cries for help, then we can only come to *one* conclusion. Right?"

"It's over....*it's over.* America is about to be *nuked.* My heart rate is about *double* what it was when you called, Scott.....You know we need to *get ready.* We need to...."

"Check. It's almost four AM, so given what we suspect about God's patience with America about to run out, we'd better gather everyone *early* tomorrow morning. We've discussed this before. The attacks on the country will come on a work day for maximum deaths. Tomorrow's a work day. The prophecies we studied imply that when God acts to punish the Daughter of Babylon/Babylon the Great He *won't wait around.* When the destruction that He allows happens it will take place in *one day, one hour and one moment.* We need to gather at Hannah and Gary's *very first thing* in the morning. We can watch the news and then, if we're right about the timing, we can leave immediately for the Irwin grade school before the roads fill up with panicked people."

"Agreed. Let's not wake up our wives and kids or Gary's family now. Right before six I'll roust our family up, feed them and head over to Hannah and Gary's house."

"OK, Beau, I'll call Gary at six. See you at their house in three hours give or take. Say your prayers, brother. Our lives are about to not only *change*, but in a few weeks we won't even recognize them, for how different things will become. *May God help us.*"

27

Air Force One

Above West Virginia

The President was livid. The White House Communications Center had just attempted, again, to get him to take a call from the Prime Minister of Israel. He wasn't about to talk to him. He was tired of the constant pleas, multiple times a day, for the U.S. to intervene in the invasion of Israel by Russia, Iran and other Muslim allies. What part of *no* does he not understand the President wondered? Have I not been clear?

The Air Force Colonel assigned to convey messages to the President while he was on Air Force One opened the cabin door to the air borne Presidential office. He was met by a visibly unhappy President. "Colonel, didn't I *just say* I *won't* take the PM's call? Is he calling me *again*?"

"Mister President, sir, yes, but he says...."

"No buts. Just tell him *no....got it*?"

"But....Mister President....he said he *understands* you won't take his call, but he wants you to know something *before* it's all over the media."

"Hunh....what? *Exactly* what did he say?"

"I'm reading, sir, just as he said it. 'Tell the President that something *major* has just happened in Israel.'"

"*What?....*What's he talking about? *I swear*, Colonel, if this is *another* attempt to get us involved in his messy little problem...."

"The rest of his message, sir, is, 'Israel is experiencing what he called *fireballs and sheets of flame*, falling selectively on the areas where the invading troops are concentrated'."

"Say it one more time. I don't understa...."

"Fire falling from the sky and enormous amounts of rain. Oh, and he said they've had a major earthquake. Maybe an 8.9. Maybe higher he said."

"Is that *it?* Didn't he ask, *again*, for military help from the US?"

"No, sir."

"Humph. *That's a first.* Wonder why he didn't ask for...."

"Right before he terminated the call, Mister President, the Prime Minister said....I didn't write this down, sorry, sir. He said something like, 'It looks like we won't need America, our defense is coming from a *higher* source, *mightier* than the US.' Or something like that, sir, I got the idea."

"Humh....Send Jeff back here. I need him to pull up some intell on the monitors and find out *what the heck* the PM's talking about. Like *now*."

II

THE

DAY

 .

"Flee from Babylon! Run for your lives! Do not be destroyed because of her sins. It is time for the Lord's vengeance; he will pay her what she deserves." (Jeremiah 51:6)

"I am God, and there is none other; I am God, and there is none like me, declaring the end from the beginning, and from ancient times the things that are not yet done, saying, 'My counsel shall stand, and I will accomplish all my purpose....' " (Isaiah 46:9-11).

28

Ten American Cities

The signals from Moscow and Tehran were flashed simultaneously and received immediately by operatives on their encrypted cell phones. The words were in Russian and Pashto, but interpreted they meant the same thing: CLIMB MOUNT NIITAKA. It was the same signal sent in 1941 from Tokyo to Japanese forces poised to attack Pearl Harbor. Vladimir, a student of history, had chosen the words to be used in the signal as a Russian form of dark humor, as the nuclear weapons about to exploded in response to the signal would be detonated inside the only nation ever to have used nuclear weapons on humans.

Designated secure cell phones in ten American cities vibrated, alerting their owners that a message had arrived. The Russian and Iranian operatives carefully followed the news from the Middle East and were quite well aware that the time for action was near. The hour on which they were to fulfill their highly-trained tasks was fast approaching.

Upon receipt of the early morning coded message each agent knew that the clock was now ticking. At 12 noon central standard time the nuclear weapons under their control were to be detonated. Six of the operatives knew that their lives were almost at an end, as they were committed to manually trigger their assigned weapons, with no possible way to escape the detonation zone. The others had been furnished with timing devices attached to the nuclear weapons for which they were responsible.

Washington, D.C., New York City, Chicago, Los Angeles, Atlanta, Boston, Miami, Las Vegas, Houston and Seattle. Ten cities. Ten future cemeteries.

The clock ticked. 12:00 Noon central standard time approached. The hour had been chosen to maximize the deaths in the chosen cities. Not too early in the morning before employees arrived, not too late in the day. Maximum deaths.

11:58 – The world turned. The economy of the world and of America had been experiencing significant, even catastrophic problems. But the dollar was still the globe's most accepted currency. Millions of former employees in the United States were out of work, but millions more were working. Many were working in the office buildings in the ten chosen American cities.

11:59 – The digital counters in four cities counted down. In six cities the agents sat or stood next to the nuclear devices previously smuggled into the country, with their fingers on the detonation button. They recited their prayers, saying *"Allahu Akbar, Subhana Rabbiyal A'ala, Subhana Rabbiyal A'ala Subhana Rabbiyal A'ala."*

29

The Mall - Washington, DC

Abdul Azim Mahaz drove the cargo van which appeared to be owned by a carpet store in Falls Church, Virginia. His brother, Yaqubi, drove the van bearing the identification of an automobile glass repair service. At the last minute, Abdul decided to substitute his wife, Naveen, as the driver of the third van, labeled as owned by a house remodeling business. His cousin was to have driven the van, but Abdul had last minute doubts of the young man's ability to accomplish the mission.

The doors on the large garage on the rented home in Landover Hills, Maryland were opened and the vans exited into the home's cul-de-sac. Abdul, Yaqubi and Naveen checked that their cell phones were working properly. Abdul didn't need to give a pre-determined signal, as each van's nuclear weapon was on a timer now set for 1 PM. The three vans left the Maryland upscale sub-division and headed towards U.S. 50. Once on the heavily traveled highway, the vans separated by several car lengths. Abdul knew from his previous practice run that he could easily make it down New York Avenue and onto the federal Mall area before 1 PM, which was 12 noon central standard time – the moment set for detonation.

Naveen was in the lead van. As she neared the outskirts of DC she had to hit the van's brakes as traffic in front of her came to a standstill. She nervously picked up her cell. After punching her husband's contact number, she said, "Abdul. This could be *a problem*. Traffic is stopped. Up ahead I can see red flashing lights and at least three police cars. Should we *turn around?*"

"Naveen. Don't worry. It's probably *nothing*. I have an app that carries traffic alerts. I'll check it and call you right back. Allah is in control, blessed be his name. Oh, here's Yaquib calling in. *I'll call you back.*"

Abdul quickly checked his WAZ app and learned that there was a traffic accident less than a mile ahead, that it involved a semi-truck and a cattle truck. Estimates for the length of delay were up to forty-five minutes to clear the highway of cattle carcasses spread across the DC bound lanes as a result of the collision.

Abdul was concerned, edging on panic. Sweat began to cover his neck and forehead. This day was the day for America to die. He had been entrusted with the destruction of the capital city of the Great Satan. He could not fail. He could not even be delayed, for he knew that all of the nuclear devices were to be detonated at the same time today. If he failed to get the three vans into governmental DC by the ignition time, by even a few minutes, the city would escape destruction, merely blowing up adjoining suburbs. He had been warned that, upon hearing of detonations in other cities DC would be put into a full lock down, barring any future incoming traffic into governmental Washington. The three cargo vans must not miss the time, miss getting to the Mall and miss the most critical part of today's planned destruction of America, cutting off the head of the snake. Washington, DC could not be allowed to survive. He had to get his vans out of this traffic, but how?

Abdul pounded his steering wheel. He wiped his brow. Just as he was about to lose control he remembered that his app included an alternate route option for traffic stoppages. Grabbing the cell, he opened the app again and saw that not a quarter mile behind him was a crossroads that would lead to a local road which ran straight south to New York Avenue. Abdul alerted Naveen and Yaquib to the new plan. Then he slowly drove out of his stopped lane, across the grass median and headed north. He saw in his rear view mirror that there were several vehicles also crossing the median, including the other two vans. Encountering no additional significant delays, at 12:32 PM Abdul, Naveen and Yaquib arrived at the Mall in Washington, DC. By prior arrangement, they made sure that their weaponized vans were several blocks apart as they drove continuously around the four sides of the long grassy park area known as the Mall. Not wanting to alert any potential cell scanners, Abdul's only message to his fellow van drivers was a texted *"We will be with the Blessed One in just a few minutes"*.

30

Unit 4501, 700 Lake Shore Drive

Chicago, Illinois

It was windy in Chicago. Not that a windy Chicago was unusual, but the wind today off of the lake was so blustery that it made the condo tower slightly sway, just as it was designed to do. When Muhammad ben Sarkori went to the bathroom he noticed the small ripples on the surface of the water in the toilet, which he had only witnessed on rare occasion. Well, he thought, high winds will be the least of this city's worries in a few more minutes. Finishing the visit to his marble lined bathroom, he glanced up at the clock in the long hallway of his condo. Ten more minutes. Ten minutes....and then the world will change. Forever.

As soon as Muhammad ben Sarkori, whose cover name in America was Alfred H. Carlsberg, received the *"Climb Mount Niitaka"* message on his encrypted cell phone early in the morning he began to make his preparations. The actual detonation of the nuclear weapon, which was contained behind two inches of lead in his massive coffee table, was by remote control. His only, and singular, assigned duty was to live in the sumptuous Chicago high rise condo until the time of the detonation, insuring that no one, especially no government snoop, came into the condo and somehow discovered the weapon. When he received the coded signal for detonation from his Iranian contact in the US he knew his job was nearly over. As *dhuhr* prayer time arrived, he unrolled his prayer mat and began, *"Allahu Akbar. Subhana rabbiyal adheem. Sam'i Allahu liman hamidah, Rabbana wa lakal hamd."*

.   Down below the high rise, traffic on Michigan Avenue was flowing slowly, as it did normally, accommodating the tens of thousands of vehicles conveying the workers of Chicago to their offices. Muhammad ben Sarkori finished his prayers and walked over to the full length windows which looked south to the loop and downtown Chicago. He mused that this would be his last time to look out on one of the world's great cities, but he delighted himself in remembering that America, and Israel, must be destroyed in order for Islam to conquer the world. 'Allah be praised', he breathed, *'Allah be praised'.*

31

Northwestern Memorial Hospital

Prentice Women's Pavilion

Chicago, Illinois

This is the part of being a doctor that I hate the most Doctor Harold Campbell thought. In his twenty one years as an OBGYN he had frequently been required to disclose to patients that they had cancer, in many cases that they were short-termers. In his outer office were seated a delightful forty-three year mother of four and her husband. Doctor Campbell again reviewed the test results. There was no question. Sharon Larson had pancreatic cancer. The worst variety.

The doctor turned in his chair, staring out his office window on Chicago Avenue in downtown Chicago. In the distance he could see the city's impressive lake front skyline, including its imposing condominium towers. He had several times considered buying a condo in the 700 Lake Shore Drive building, with its sweeping 360 degrees view of Navy Pier and downtown Chicago. Had he made the purchase he could have dramatically shortened his commute time to Northwestern Memorial Hospital from his home in Evanston, where he almost finished raising his children. Maybe someday, he mused. But, he realized he was just trying to delay the inevitable. It was almost noon, and he didn't like to delay his patients beyond their appointment time, unlike most of his colleagues. It was time. He buzzed his assistant to bring in his doomed patient.

Not one to avoid bad news, when necessary, as soon as Sharon Larson and her husband were seated, Doctor Campbell launched into his report, saying, "Mrs. Larson, I *don't* have good news for you. The tests show that y...."

"It's cancer....*it's cancer*, isn't it?"

Sharon Larson was already wiping tears from her cheeks.

Once the doctor had confirmed her worst suspicions, reading to her the lab results, he then described how fast acting was her type of pancreatic cancer and that modern medicine had no known cure.

Don Larson asked, "How *long* does she have, Doc?"

The timing question was inevitable, but Doctor Campbell nevertheless was loath to tell a fellow human being how many days they would have on the earth. He glanced up at the clock on his wall above their heads, noticing that it almost noon, the second hand sweeping up the left side of the clock, about to confirm twelve noon as the time.

"Mr. and Mrs. Larson, I am so sorry to have to tell you that, with this virulent form of pancreatic cancer, you will only have two....at the most....three....months."

Both Larsons were now in tears. Don Larson tried to wipe away his tears, not able to look at the doctor, instead fixing his eyes out the window at the looming silver-windowed condominium towers on Lake Shore Drive. Doctor Campbell looked away from his grieving patient and her spouse, noticing as he did so that the second hand had just marked that it was now twelve noon.

As Don Larson stared away at the condo towers, suddenly from high up on one of the silver towers a brilliant flash of light enveloped Chicago. The nuclear device in the tower instantly vaporized not only Doctor Campbell and his grieving patients, but the entire women's pavilion, all of the buildings in the medical complex and every structure within five miles, along with their human occupants. Frame houses as far away as Oak Park were instantly flattened, or if built of brick or stone, ignited in flames.

Sharon Larson didn't live to see her estimated final two to three months.

32

THE MALL

WASHINGTON, DC

Abdul Azim Mahaz drove his carpet store labeled cargo van east on Independence Avenue near its intersection with 1st Street. Abdul had been driving a circuitous route north on 1st Street, which runs between the U.S. Capitol and the Supreme Court, west on Constitution Avenue, then south on 14th Street, back to Independence Avenue. Abdul earlier mapped out the route so that his van would be as close as possible to the Capitol and to the Court at 1 PM.

Abdul's brother, Yaqubi, drove his automobile glass repair labeled van on a route just south of the White House. His route along 14th Street, Constitution Avenue, 17th Street and Independence Avenue circled the Washington Monument.

Abdul was concerned that his wife, Naveen, who was driving the third van, bearing the name and logo of a non-existent house remodeling company, might not do well trying to follow a prescribed route. Instead, she was to drive the length of the mall from the U.S. Capitol to the Lincoln Monument. Abdul told Naveen not to be concerned where her van was located as the hour came.

12:53 PM (EST) – Abdul stopped at the red light at 27th Street and Independence Avenue. He was sweating profusely, though the temperature both inside and outside of his van was moderate. He knew he would soon be vaporized, along with hundreds of thousands of others. He wasn't concerned about the people he saw walking along Independence Avenue, they were after all, all heretics, part of the Great Satan. He wiped his brow, drumming his fingers on the steering wheel of the van. Reciting his prayers. *'Allah Hoo Akbar. Subhaana Rabbiyal Azeem.* Looking at his watch. Looking again. He was still about a mile from 1st Street and Capitol Hill. 'When would this light change', he asked no one.

12:54 PM – Yaqubi turned north on 15th Street. He could see the Washington Monument to his left and the Ellipse across Constitution Avenue. Having driven his route now several times he knew that he would most likely be just south of the White House very close to 1 PM. He smiled, thinking of the waiting virgins who would greet him soon as a hero of Islam.

12:55 PM – Naveen was not smiling. Women in Islam are not promised sexual adventures in paradise. She knew that she would soon be no more. Her children, she had repeatedly been told, would call her blessed for her efforts to strike America. Naveen was committed to her assigned role of killing Americans, but in her deepest core she had a level of doubt. If Islam is the only true faith, she asked herself, then why do we have to kill the infidels? Why not just let them discover how marvelous are the five pillars of Islam, Shahadah, Salat, Sawn, Zakat and Hajj? Without killing them? But, she shook it off, turned left on 17th Street, then looked down the length of the reflecting pool at the Lincoln Memorial. She pulled over to the curb and parked, keeping her gaze on the large Presidential marble statue surrounded by Greek columns.

12:58 PM – Abdul looked at his watch as he pulled up to the curb on 1st Street on Capitol Hill. He put his van in park, exited the van and rolled out his prayer rug on the grass next to sidewalk. He knew that it was too late for a law enforcement officer who might see this unusual scene to stop and do anything. *Allah Hoo Akbar, Allah Hoo Akbar.*

12:59 PM – Yaqubi looked to his right as he came to the South Lawn of the White House. He noticed that a section of the metal fence appeared to be newly installed. Rumors of a coup de' etat attempt the prior year had been rampant in the world outside of the U.S. As he pulled his right two tires up on the narrow grass strip in front of the fence, his last thought was whether or not the new fence was where the trucks had breached White House security.

1:00 PM – Captain Roger Rice's US Airways Flight 127 had just been cleared by his FAA controller to land on main runway 61 at Reagan International Airport. He banked slightly left, flattened out and began his descent. Captain Rice first saw an enormous flash of white hot light straight ahead of his plane, behind the U.S. Capitol's white dome. As he was processing what he had just seen, the pilot immediately saw two other immensely bright fireballs flash further down the Mall near the Washington Monument and the Lincoln Memorial. Within five seconds the shock waves coming from the nearly simultaneous blasts tore the Captain's US Airways Airlines 737 into multiple pieces, bursting it into flames from the immediate heat and fire that followed the shock waves. Flight 127 was no more.

Had the Captain been alive to see it, he would have witnessed the instant vaporization of Reagan Airport's terminals, parking garages and support buildings. The three nuclear devices totally destroyed and leveled to the ground every structure from the airport and the Pentagon on the south, up past DuPont Circle more than a mile north of the White House, from the Marine Corps Memorial in Virginia to the west and twenty blocks east of Capitol Hill. Gone were the limestone temples of the U.S. Congress, the U.S. Supreme Court and the White House. The Jihadists' nuclear weapons were equal opportunity destroyers, taking out the executive, legislative and judicial branches of the American federal government. The head of the executive branch, though, at the time of the detonations was safely in Air Force One on his way to a fund raiser in California.

33

Air Force One –

Over the Arizona – California State Line

The world's most famous airplane was at 43,000 feet preparatory to making its final vector approach to Los Angeles, now less than forty-five minutes away. The President had showered, shaved and dressed on the plane for the noon luncheon fund raiser in downtown Los Angeles. The time in Washington DC, which the President always maintained on his Rolex, was 12:56 PM.

In spite of the President's insistence, the Pentagon had not been able to explain to the President what had been happening in Israel. They had video. They had on the ground reports. What they didn't have was any clue as to what weapon system was being used to fire on the foreign troops invading Israel, nor who used the weapons. The Chairman of the Joint Chiefs of Staff had just informed the President on an encrypted call to Air Force One that the military was still working on solving the weapons mystery. He was able to report that the weapon systems, whatever they were, combined with the deluge of rain and a devastating earthquake, had decimated the invading troops. Preliminary body counts of dead invading troops, he said, could be in the hundreds of thousands. The remaining troops, the Chairman told the President, were being tracked by satellite imaging heading back north and east, out of Israel.

The President was slouched in his executive leather chair, gazing out the window at the barren areas below in

Southern California. What in the world happened? He couldn't call Vladimir. Not right now. Not after he may have lost most of his front line troops. He knew, of course, that his friend Vladimir was going to invade Israel. Vladimir didn't ask him for permission. The President had simply let Vladimir know that the U.S. wouldn't get involved in what the two decided in advance to call a regional controversy. But, what the President was worried about now was simple. Would Vladimir think that the US had somehow developed and kept secret this fireball weapon? Would he think the U.S. attacked his troops? Would he lash back at the U.S.? It wouldn't be seemly, he concluded, to call Vladimir and deny knowledge of the fiery weapons. That could just fuel his suspicions and move him to conclude that the U.S. had attacked Russia and her allies.

The President again looked at his watch. It was 12:59 in DC. What to do? Call Vladimir? Don't call Vlad...... *"WHAT WAS THAT?"* he shouted as a flash of white hot light filled the office cabin of Air Force One. He grabbed the phone next to his leather chair connected with the pilot. *"What was that?* That *huge* flash....the light....what...."

"Mister President," the pilot replied, "this is *not good*. We 're a hundred miles out, but....it sure looks like a nuke just lit up....flash and cloud over LA....*oh, oh....oh....*Here comes the shock wave....*belt in....belt in....*We're going to take a hit and....". The pilot didn't finish as he fought to control his pitching and yawing aircraft. The shock wave pushed the nose of the plane sharply up, then the plane pitched to the right, followed by a slow dive towards the ground.

124

The President wrestled with his seat belt, finally getting it secured and grabbed the wide arms on his chair. His eyes wide, adrenalin pumping, he struggled to look out his window to see if he could make out what the pilot had just described. As the massive modified 747 began to level out, now down to under 20,000 feet, the President could see a distinctive shape on the horizon, a growing mushroom cloud. He again called the pilot, "Where....*where*....are we heading *now*?"

"Mister President, thank your lucky stars that we were twelve minutes delayed due to head winds. Otherwise we would have been close enough that the shock wave that just threw us around would have knocked us out of the sky....That cloud and the shock wave could *only* come from a *nuke*....sorry to say, sir.....To answer your question, sir, we' have few options. San Diego's out, too much chance of radiation blowing south out of LA. Same problem with San Bernardino. Looks like Phoenix, maybe an Air Force base. We're pulling choices, now. It will take us about. W*hoa*....wait a minute. Mister President....You'll want to have Jeff get your monitors up. I just heard an FAA controller say that there appears to have been another nuke....so not limited to just LA....repeat....repeat sir....*another* nuke. Appears to be *Las Vegas*, sir."

The President couldn't speak. He couldn't move, as he felt locked into place. All he could do was stare out his window at the mushroom cloud over Los Angeles. What had caused this disaster? Why didn't we have a warning? Why? Why? A sliver of thought crossed his mind. Did I blow it by refusing to come to the assistance of Israel? Surely not, he thought, as he immediately discarded the thought. What he hated most was the thin possibility that

125

the religious pests, whom he referred to as 'Bible thumpers', who had warned him that these things would happen, may have been correct.

34

Hannah and Gary's Family Room

Birmingham, Alabama

The sun over Birmingham had been up for three hours. Six adults who were nervously sipping coffee, visibly on edge, looked over at the television frequently to see if anything had yet happened. The children appeared to be happy, playing in the back yard or on their i-pads, as their parents had kept them out of school for the day.

Gary toggled back and forth between CBS and Fox on the theory that anything that would happen of a catastrophic nature would either be reported on one of the networks, or alternatively, that one or both would go off the air.

Beau, Gary and Scott were talking quietly around the television while Audrey, Hannah and Sally were busying themselves in the kitchen, preparing sandwiches for lunch later in the day.

Gary glanced up at the clock on the family room wall. It was just now 1 PM. Gary suggested, "If we don't hear anything by four or so this afternoon, then maybe we should....*oops*....look....CBS just went to black screen....let's see what Fox is doing." Gary pushed the button on his remote control. "*Oh oh*....nothing but snow....*no* signal. How could *both* go off at the *same* time, unless...."

Beau choked and said, "*Unless*....New York City just got hit. Both CBS and Fox are in New York. Go to channel

13....WVTM....it's an affiliate with NBC, but it's all local for Birmingham news. Let's see what, if anything, they're reporting on New York."

Gary changed the channel to the local channel. A soap opera was playing. Scott exclaimed, "Look at that. They are *barely* dressed. Good grief. I haven't watched daytime TV for years. Many years. I didn't know you could show on over the airwaves television what that couple is doing."

"Beau replied, "Scott, the FCC took away the final barriers a couple years ago. The networks argued that cable could air indecent shows, so why not allow the networks to do so. It's just further evidence of the status of America of the Mother of Abominations....Now, *come on*....he's removing her...."

The television screen switched to a screen saying CHANNEL 13 EMERGENCY NEWS ALERT. The screen stayed up, with no sound. Gary yelled into the kitchen, "*Hannah*, you guys better come over here and *watch* this."

Audrey, upon seeing the news alert on the screen said, "Oh....*no*....*no*....oh, *please* Lord *help us*."

Eventually the silence on the television screen was broken as the news alert screen was removed. The screen showed the station's well-watched news broadcaster looking down to adjust his lapel mike, then glancing up to see that the red light on camera one was on, confirming that he was being broadcast live.

"UH....We've....uh....interrupted   our   regular programming in order to...." WVTM's leading newscaster stopped speaking as he pushed his hand up to his right ear, leaning into his ear bud, concentrating on what he was hearing from the station's control room, and not addressing his TV audience. The newscaster appeared to be speaking to his control room, saying, "Are you *sure*?....I can *go* with that?....OK....Umh....Sorry....As I said, we've interrupted our regular programming to bring you *breaking news*....Umh....We are being informed by *foreign* news sources, because our normal wire services are not currently functioning, that there have been....*multiple detonations* of what appear to be *nuclear weapons....in....America.* Reuters is just now carrying an emergency news feed reporting that Washington DC and New York City have experienced nuclear weapon detonations. Let me *repeat* that....*international news services are reporting that at least two American cities, Washington DC and New York City, appear to have been hit by nuclear explosions."*

All six people in Hannah and Gary's family room were in tears. Two were down on their knees praying. Scott was on his cell phone alerting the other small group letters who may not have yet heard the news.

The WVTM newscaster was again silent, pressing his ear bud, then he continued, *"Oh my....*I regret to announce that the BBC is reporting that satellites over the US appear to have detected as many as *eight,* one source says as many as possibly *twelve,* separate *nuclear explosions* at almost exactly *the same time,* across America. The nearest nuclear weapon detonation to the Birmingham area appears to be in *Atlanta,* I am *very sorry* to report. Viewers in our most *eastern* Birmingham viewing area are calling to tell us that they are seeing what

129

appears to be a mushroom cloud on the far horizon, in the approximate location of Atlanta....As we learn more from either US sources or from foreign news services....we will....we will certainly inform you. Unfortunately, we can't switch you to our normal network coverage out of New York, or....or....apparently any other major city from which we would normally get news coverage. Until we can get *more* news, our program director tells me we will return to our regular pre-recorded programming." The screen changed to two actors in the act of an intimate relationship.

Gary snapped off the television, saying, "Folks, that may be *the last* television any of us may ever see....*It's time to go*....Get the kids. I heard your calls, Scott, to some of the small group guys. Are they heading to the school?....Let's load up our cars and get over to the school....*before we can't.*"

35

Air Force One –Over Oklahoma

"The king of Babylon has heard reports about them, and his hands hang limp. Anguish has gripped him, pain like that of a woman in labor." (Jeremiah 50:43)

The President's Chief of Staff had reluctantly agreed to fly to California for the fund raiser. He generally preferred to stay in DC, usually spending fifteen to sixteen hours per day at his desk in the White House. The President, though, had insisted that he accompany him, as his Chief of Staff was formerly the Mayor of Los Angeles and thus could be expected to help raise significant funds at the event.

The President generally excluded staff members from his airborne office while flying, unless they had a reason that the President concluded justified their sharing his expansive office space. Nevertheless, the President's Chief of Staff knocked on the cabin door and entered the office. His face was drained of color. His hands were visibly shaking as he held a print out from the plane's communication system.

"Yeah, Carlisle, what have we learned about Los Angeles? It *was* a nuke, wasn't it? You look *terrible*, Carlisle, what have we learned? You better sit down before you fall down. We'll make it through this. We'll find out who nuked LA and Vegas, then we'll *nuke 'em back*. But before you tell me what you know, I want to know....where *are* we going? I need to be on the ground. Who knows what they may plan to do to Air Force One?"

"Mister President, Nellis Air Force Base isn't available due to the nuking of Las Vegas. We're headed to Vance Air Force Base, in Oklahoma....But you need to know what the Penta...."

"Where is that? Where in Oklahoma? I don't want to land in some hayseed...."

"STOP, sir....uhh, Vance AFB is in Enid, Oklahoma, sir. It's the furthest installation from the cities that are gone. What I haven't been able to tell you yet is that it now appears that *ten cities* have been nuked. *Gone. Destroyed.* DC, New York, Atlanta, Houston, With radiation fallout we have to be careful not to fly into radiation nor land you in an area that will be overblown by fallout."

"Did you just say DC? *The Capitol?* Nuked?"

"We're *toast!*....It's over....*Over.* The total count now appears to be fifteen nuclear devices detonated in those ten cities. Mister President, this could be *the end of America.*"

"DC?.... You did say DC? Is that *confirmed?*....What's our level of confidence in....?"

"It looks like they used *three nukes* on DC, so there's no way that anyone could...."

"*Oh, no....*I can't....I....At least the wife and kids were *gone* from the White House. Have the guys in front patch me through to Air Force Two. She should be half-way to Paris by now. I want to tell her *I'm alright* and make plans for...."

132

If possible, the Chief of Staff looked even worse than when he walked into the airborne office. "Mister President.... *I truly regret*....being the one to have to inform you....but....but...."

"But *what*? What is it? My family's plane wasn't...."

"The First Lady and the kids didn't take off when they were supposed to....She delayed the departure....It had something to do with adding some more staff to the flight to France....and they couldn't get ready in time....and...."

"WHAT?....*What are you saying*? My family is....are you saying *they're dead*? They didn't get out of DC? *They're dead*?" The President's head fell into his hands. He pitched forward in his chair, his knees hitting the floor. Tears streamed down his face, his hands now hanging limply at his sides.

"I'm so sorry, sir. The Secret Service last showed the First Lady and the kids in transit to Andrews AFB at the time of the detonations. Their limo was on South Capitol Street bridge when the nukes went off....The communications center confirmed with NORAD. There could not possibly be *any* survivors in metropolitan DC. It's a smoldering cauldron of fire and radiation, sir. No buildings left. Just ashes, and burning, and some limestone blocks, not many. DC is gone."

NO....NO....It can't be happening....*NOOOOO!!*" The President arms were wrapped around his body. He was rocking back and forth. Excruciating pain spread across his face. *"WHAT HAVE I DONE?....WHAT HAVE I DONE?"*

36

Lake Sammamish State Park, Washington

On the morning of The Day, Pastor Kirkland was enjoying reading a book on a bench alongside Lake Sammamish, the state park of the same name. He had just finished a dramatic chapter in the novel he was enjoying. He closed the book and looked west across the wooded lake front. Without warning, the sky west of the lake flashed from an azure blue to a brilliant white. The flash only lasted a brief time, but it was so intense that the Pastor was temporarily blinded. He rubbed his eyes, hoping to clear his failed vision. Blinking. Blinking. Finally, he could make out his surroundings, though his forehead hurt as if he had banged it on a wall. What was that, he wondered? Some kind of explosion? Just as the thought passed his mind, he heard a roaring, rumbling sound, not unlike the loudest thunderclap he had ever heard. Just as the sound began to subside, the trees across the lake bent sharply down, towards him and away from the source of the light and sound. The wind pushing the trees down was so strong that several small and medium sized trees snapped off, landing in the lake.

As the hot wind grew in intensity it blew the book out of the Pastor's hands and knocked him back over his bench, hitting his back and head hard on the cement pathway. Pastor Kirkland briefly lost consciousness. When he came to he had no idea how long he had been in darkness. All he knew was that his head was throbbing. He tried to sit up, grabbing the back of the bench, the legs of which were anchored in the park's concrete path. He again rubbed his eyes and his head. He looked around in the park. The lake was littered with broken trees and limbs. The sky over Seattle, west of the broken tree line, was glowing a peculiar orange-rose color. Again, he asked himself, what in the world has happened? He didn't have a clue, as he'd never seen or experienced anything like this before.

Grabbing the bench, he moved around it and sat down. It hit him that all five of his senses had been assaulted in a matter of just seconds. Sight and sound were first. Overwhelmingly. Now he could smell what seemed to be dirt, or sand, and looked like flakes. As he parted his lips, whatever was in the air, now almost visible to him, touched his tongue, tasting just like it smelled. As he sat trying to collect his thoughts, he felt something and looked down at his bare forearms. They were coated by the dusty flakes floating through the air. The longer he looked down at his arms it seemed that they were accumulating layers of the particulate matter. He brushed his hand across the top of his head and saw that he had knocked loose some of the same dusty material. He watched the particles float from his hair down onto his pant legs and shoes. What is this, he wondered? If the Pastor had possessed a Geiger counter he would have learned that his body was being massively irradiated by the fallout from downtown Seattle.

III

AFTER

THE

DAY

"For the Lord's purposes against Babylon stand – to lay waste the land of Babylon." (Jeremiah 51:29)

"I will kindle a fire in her towns that will consume all who are around her." (Jeremiah 50:32)

"Daughter of the Babylonians; no more will you be called queen of kingdoms." (Isaiah 47:5)

"Fallen! Fallen is Babylon the Great!" (Revelation 18:2)

"The Commission believes that unless the world community acts decisively and with great urgency, it is more likely than not that a weapon of mass destruction will be used in a terrorist attack somewhere in the world...In our judgment America's margin of safety is shrinking, not growing." (*World at Risk*–The Report of the Commission on the Prevention of Weapons of Mass Destruction Proliferation and Terrorism, appointed by the United States Congress, December, 2008).

37

London, England

LONDON (IRN News Network) --- Al Qaeda today confirmed in a videotaped statement aired on al Jazeera television that, along with Russia and Iran and others, it was responsible for the detonation of multiple nuclear weapons in America the day before yesterday. Though the exact number of nuclear devices was not disclosed in the statement, most British military experts now believe that the number was between 10 and 15, apparently of varying kilotonage. It is believed at least two major cities, Washington, D. C. and New York City, were hit by more than one detonation. The death count of the surprise attack is as yet unknown, but expected to be in the several tens of millions. If confirmed, the attack on the world's leading military power would easily be the largest loss of life in one day in history. The al Qaeda spokesman claimed in the broadcast statement that "America, as we first warned in 2006, is destroyed, and will never again persecute Muslims".

British military sources said that it was still too early to determine the full extent of the deaths in the cities hit by the nuclear weapons detonated in what appears to have been a coordinated attack, with the weapons exploding within seconds of each other. There has been no immediate armed response from what remained of the American military, possibly complicated by the inability to target the location of al Qaeda operatives. The electromagnetic effect of some of the nuclear explosions knocked out most communication with America, the effect of which is continuing. For those areas of the States in which communication is still possible, a disturbing picture has quickly emerged of highways clogged with Americans seeking to flee from areas detonated under obviously apparent mushroom clouds. It was reported that medical facilities near blast sites were quickly overrun by blast and radiation burn victims.

No official statement has yet been released by the U.S. government, most of the officials of which appeared not to have survived the three known nuclear devices which destroyed Washington, D.C., the seat of the American government. It is anticipated that a statement will soon be made from a ranking U.S. official who did survive the attacks. Some isolated media reports received here have said that most surviving petrol outlets have been drained of their supplies and that food markets' shelves were quickly emptied. With winter approaching, some unnamed sources in Her Majesty's government suggested that significant numbers of Americans may die in the next few months from the radiation effects from nuclear weapons, and also as a result of lack of food resulting from a paucity of petrol and any meaningful way of paying food suppliers. The sources also cited early reports of what may be widespread violence by those seeking to obtain remaining food supplies and petrol.

Her Majesty, who had earlier expressed her shock and dismay at the news from America, is expected to make a televised statement by week's end. Her spokesman, on background, indicated that Her Majesty will respond to published statements by Jihadists that Britain, and other European nations, would suffer a similar fate as America if the star and crescent aren't flying over government offices by year's end. Her Majesty's troops, as was earlier reported, are on full alert. A full shut down of British ports has been ordered, on a temporary basis. The House of Commons convened in executive session late today. No reports have thus far emerged as to actions taken, nor statements made, in the closed door meeting. Some M.P.s called publically today for Her Majesty's government to immediately vacate London and its environs. No decision has been made on their suggestions, according to government spokespersons, who asked not to be identified.

Reginald Sloane, press spokesperson for the Archbishop of Canterbury, suggested to reporters in a hastily called news *conference that the Archbishop would have no problem with a Muslim "presence" at No.10 Downing Street, even if that eventually meant a PM of Islamic beliefs. Sloane dismissed as "rubbish" claims by columnists and others that the attacks on America had been prophesied in certain Biblical verses. Reports had circulated for some time before the attacks that many hundreds of thousands, possibly millions, of American Christians, and American Jews, had emigrated from the U.S., apparently relying on what they claimed were scriptural warnings about the future destruction in the "end times" of a rich and powerful nation. Leaders of the emigration had earlier expressed concern about America's refusal to support Israel should it be attacked by a coalition of nations led by Russia and Iran. Readers may consult news archives for more historical details on the outcome of the invasion of Israel.*

Leaders of leading British charitable organizations who were contacted today expressed their sorrow at the attacks, and indicated that they are beginning to collect medical supplies and food for transport to America, if suitable transportation can be arranged. Numerous international corporations, who have now lost most if not all of their ability to sell goods to the world's leading consumer nation, expressed outrage and shock at the attacks on America. Some privately questioned their future economic viability, given the economic loss of their largest trading partner. One CEO, who refused to be identified for this article, suggested that the nations of the world reform and move the United Nations, whose headquarters and most of its staff were destroyed with the nuclear destruction of New York City, to Geneva, Switzerland, in order to deal with what he privately called 'this incredible Islamic violence problem, before we're all blown up'. No United Nations official was available for a comment on his suggestion.

38

The Harlan Robbins Farm

Crown Point, Indiana

Once Harlan and Dorothy Robbins realized that America had been hit with multiple nuclear detonations, their next thought was how the nuclear destruction of Chicago would affect them on their farm near State Road 2, just south of Crown Point, Indiana. The Robbins received most of their news from cable, with channels broadcast from South Bend and Lafayette. For several days after The Day they were able to receive television signals, that is, until their electric power finally went off. The diesel powered generators at the television stations didn't help the Robbins any once they lost electricity at the farm. Dorothy had nagged Harlan for some time to buy a generator, but he never quite got around to it.

During the time that the Robbins were still able to watch the news they learned that Chicago's nuke had been particularly devastating, one commentator guessing it as large as 50 kilotons. They saw helicopter footage of a totally destroyed downtown Chicago extending out past the Dan Ryan Expressway. Casualty estimates for Chicago alone were in the millions. The Robbins could hardly say a word most of the afternoon once they saw the horrific video on the noon news. Within 48 hours of the detonation, the Robbins knew from the newscasts which they could still receive that the winds which normally blew from the northwest, had not changed their course. The fallout from what used to be Chicago was nearing their part of northwest Indiana. The next morning Harlan decided that they needed to make plans.

"Dot, we're only about forty-five miles from Chicago. Interstate 65 is just *four miles* east of us. Even though downtown Chicago is gone, there are still several million people around Chicago who must have lived, who knows how many? Those folks will eventually run out food. No food grower will want to try and ship their harvested crops into a nuclear zone. There'd be no assurance they could be paid, plus they'll want to save their crops for themselves and their neighbors."

"Honey, doesn't that mean that once they run out of food that they'll start moving towards where the food is grown? Towards the farms in Wisconsin, and Illinois, and of course south, *right here* into Indiana?"

"Yup, Dot, that's what I've been thinking. I've been doing a fair amount of praying and asking for wisdom."

"Me too, dear, but I had to confess my anger when I realized when I started praying that our shepherds, all those preachers we watch on TV, let us down. We don't have seminary degrees, that's for sure, but we agreed years ago that those verses about Babylon, the reborn Babylon, or whatever the exact name is, *has to be* the United States. Couldn't be anyone else. But, we never heard any of our favorite TV preachers say anything about America facing the destruction that the Bible said would hit the new Babylon. *Never.* Why not?"

Harlan responded, "I don't even recall anyone preaching about how God has been sending natural disasters to get our attention. Earthquakes, hurricanes, forest fires, floods, tornadoes, drought, worse than we've *ever* experienced before. What were they thinking? *Why didn't they warn us?"*

"Once I got my anger confessed, I remembered what that fellow said that they interviewed from the South Bend Hospital on the news. He said that if we are in the fallout area, where the radiation from Chicago lands, that we will *only have a few weeks or maybe months* to live. The black rain he said would fall on us could start tonight, based on what the sky looks like. Honey, it's quite likely that we won't be alive very long, we may be with the Lord in just a few weeks."

Harlan scratched his head, looked at his wife and then said, "Dot, sweetie, we *will* be in heaven soon. Think about it. We're in the fallout pattern, so give or take a few weeks, we're dead from radiation poisoning. But, I've been thinking and praying about it. I think we will be gone *well before* the radiation takes us."

"You mean the *mobs* that will come out of the Chicago suburbs? The starving people? I've thought about them, of course. My heart goes out to them. They'll be scared, and they'll all be hungry and....very desperate. But, Harlan, *what are we going to do* when they come up on our front porch asking....maybe *demanding*....that we give them food?"

"The root cellar."

"Hunh? The old root cellar behind the milk house? We haven't used that *in years."*

145

"I know, Dot, but it's the *only* place that we can hide the food we have left. More important than that, though, is that there's enough room in the root cellar for both of us to lie down, closing and locking the doors. We can scatter straw, and a cow flop or two on the doors, to hide the cellar from the marauders, once they rampage through the house and see that there's *nothing* to eat."

"I see where you're going. We could leave a few cans and bottles in the kitchen, to make it look like we just up and left. But, Harlan dear, how long can we hide in the root cellar? Once the mobs start coming across the farms in this area, they won't be content with just a couple of cans of peas, they'll pour through the barn, and the machine shed, and maybe even *burn* the house. What are we going to...."

"Dot honey, let's just take a day at a time. I'll start moving our canned and dried food into the root cellar. I'll nail plastic sheeting on the back side of the doors, since those doors aren't waterproof by any means."

"Okay. I'll start packing the canned and dried foods into boxes. But, you haven't said anything about the two shotguns you packed in grease and buried in the barn after *the geniuses* in DC passed that horrible law making our ownership of firearms illegal?"

"I haven't forgotten our guns, Dot, but like I said, *let's take each day at a time.*"

146

39

Indiana State Road 231 (East Joliet Street) and South Indiana Street Crown Point, Indiana

Interstate 65 had become a parking lot within hours of the nuking of Chicago. Those living south of Chicago who saw the mushroom cloud and who recognized what would happen jumped in their cars, with some food thrown in the trunk along with their firearms, if they still had them after Congress outlawed gun ownership under the McAlister Hate Speech and Hate Weapon Act. Some remembered to grab the family pet, while others didn't bother, figuring the pet was just another mouth to feed.

The entry ramps to interstate 80/90 east from Chicago soon filled, as thousands tried to get on the six lane wide freeway, hoping to make it to the interstate 65 exit, heading south to Merrillville, Crown Point and points south. Motor vehicle breakdowns and crashes caused by fleeing motorists blocked two of the I-80/90 east bound lanes, narrowing escape out of the cauldron that Chicago had become. Within the first 48 hours of The Day over a million persons, men, women and children, had managed to flee the suburbs of Chicago, fleeing north to Wisconsin, west into Illinois and southeast to Indiana. Empty gas tanks, coupled with service stations that quickly exhausted their supplies before the power went out, resulted in traffic eventually coming to a halt on I-65. The two lanes south towards Indianapolis were soon blocked by stranded and abandoned vehicles, denying motorists any chance to drive any further south.

147

Stranded motorists, their families and pets on the I-65 exit at Crown Point left their cars, vans and trucks and hiked west along Indiana 231 two miles to Crown Point. As they trudged along 231, which became East Joliet Street, they were stopped at its intersection with South Indiana Avenue. Crown Point Police cars were parked across Joliet Avenue, blocking any further access to the city of Crown Point, which was just under ten blocks further west. In front of the police cars was an armored SWAT vehicle, provided to the city by DHS, complete with gun ports along both sides of the dark green vehicle. The twelve police officers manning the roadblock were dressed in SWAT uniforms, each holding a firearm.

The roadblock went into place within hours after the Mayor of Crown Point received a report from the Indiana State Police describing the devastation of the nation's third largest city just miles north west of his small city. He checked his almanac confirming that Chicago had about 2,700,000 residents. If one third died in the nuking, he calculated that would result in well over a million and a half people fleeing into the three adjoining states, meaning at least half a million souls would be heading into northwest Indiana, with many of those coming into his city. He ordered the Chief of Police into action, who quickly called up the entire 15 man police force of Crown Point and the reserves. The majority were assigned to the main entry point from Chicago, Indiana 231 from I-65.

Not everyone who walked up to the police roadblock at Huron and Indiana Streets took kindly to being told they couldn't come into the city. One of the earliest stranded motorists to approach the roadblock was Chuck, who was tired, hungry and scared, which was a dangerous combination. He had his wife and two grumbling teen agers with him. He refused to be waved off by the officer standing point, who motioned for the approaching refugees to head south down Indiana Avenue, away from the city. "Sir, you can't come into the city. The Mayor's put a quarantine on for the next several days or weeks or...."

"Look, pal, I used to work for CPD. I know what a police officer can do....and *what you can't do*. We have *a right* to walk on public roads. We have *a right* to come into your cruddy little town, so *get....out....of....our....way*. We're *real* hungry and we're *real* tired, *if you get my meaning*."

The lead officer stepped forward two feet from Chuck's face, slightly raising his M4A1 assault rifle. "Now, *sir*, we don't want any trouble. So just take your nice family and *head south*, that's to your left, down Indiana Avenue. You'll surely find someone who can help you. The City doesn't have any food supplies available for you. *None*. Now, sir, Indiana Avenue becomes Grant Street a few blocks south, then it turns into County Road 55. The county road runs down to State Road 2, two, maybe three miles. There's a county park not far from there, to the west, where you could bed down for the night."

Chuck's face reddened during the point officer's street directions. He clinched his fists, trying to decide what to do. He wanted to get into the city because he knew that he would eventually find food there. He wasn't nearly as confident if they were turned away from where people lived close by in neighboring homes. The point officer carefully watched Chuck's body language, prepared to handle him if it came to it. After what seemed like a long time to both the officer and to Chuck, finally Chuck controlled his anger, instead pleading, "Sir, if we don't get some food *soon*, we won't....like I said, we're *real* hungry, we haven't eaten *anything* since we left our home in Pullman, Illinois eight ten hours ago. *Please*....sir....you must have a family. What would *you* do?"

The point officer studied Chuck, saw that his fists were no longer clenched, and his normal facial color had returned. He felt for the man, and his family, but he had his orders. He lowered his gun, stepped a little closer and quietly said, "Sir, just do I what told you. Go left down Indiana Avenue. Keep going. Don't try and turn back west at Center or South Streets. A block away you'll run into more roadblocks. The Mayor's serious. He's got folks, with guns, posted to keep people like you out. Keep going until you get to the cemetery, then head west across the cemetery until you get to the Wells Street Park. You can bed down there. When you look for food in town, just take one of your kids. It'll be less intimidating when you knock on a door. Ask *real nice* and you may get fed. *No* threats. *No* clenched fists. If people say no, just move on. *Got it?*"

A tear ran down Chuck's cheek. "Thank you, I won't forget you. God bless you."

"It's OK. Now, move on. *Now*....I see a bunch of folks walking up 231. I can't send them *all* your direction - lose my job. They're gonna' have to head out into the country and take their chances. Now, scoot. Get. God be with you."

Chuck and his family headed south on Indiana Avenue as fast as they were able.

40

Sam and Laura's Kitchen
Minneapolis, Minnesota

Sam and Laura's power went out the day after America was nuked. Sam and Laura shared some of their food with needy neighbors on both sides of their house in their aging sub-division. They stopped answering the door soon after the power went out, though, because they knew what was coming. Hungry people would come knocking at their door demanding food. Though several had come up on their porch and pounded on their door, so far no one had attempted to kick in the door. But, now Sam and Laura were down to two cans of pork and beans, small quantities of un-cooked spaghetti and rice and three withered potatoes. It was time for Sam and Laura to talk.

Sam reached across their small kitchen table, grabbed Laura's hands in his and said, "Laura my dear, we *both* know where this is going. *Right?*"

"Umh. You mean, because we're almost out of *food?*"

"Yeah....That's the *obvious* problem, since the stores have all been stripped clean. I'll never forget what Coborns and Fareway looked like inside. I couldn't find anything worth picking up in either store. *Picked clean.*...All within just hours after The Day. No one in this neighborhood has any extra food that they can share with us. Heck, we could have lasted another two or three days if we *hadn't shared* with the Smiths and the Svensons."

"But, Sam, it was the *right* thing to do. You know that."

"I'm okay with what we did, but what we need to look at is....well....you know....the *future*. We're going to be out of anything worth eating *very soon*. Then, what will we do? Laura, we're *too old* to go out and search for food, either in homes or by hunting in the state parks. And Laura you know that...."

BANG....BANG....BANG...."OPEN UP. WE KNOW YOU'RE IN THERE"....BANGBANGBANG. "We saw your lights on last night." BANGBANGBANG.

"*Sam*, get the *gun*."

Sam jumped up from the table and grabbed his antique Colt revolver from the counter between the kitchen and the living room where he had placed it for convenience sake. Waving for Laura to hide in the hall closet, Sam walked over and stood to the side of the front door.

"What do you want? You don't need to bang on our door *so hard*. We can hear."

"*We* can hear, hunh? So there's at least two of you. Probably also *a woman*, right? We're here for *food*. We're out of food. *We're hungry.* We want some of what you've got stored away....*Open up....or we're comin' in.*"

Sam grimaced as he realized his mistake in letting his uninvited visitors know that there were two of them, most likely including a wife. He raised his Colt revolver, pointing it at the door, saying, "That would be *a really bad* idea....whoever you are. We don't have any food. *Go away.* Leave us alone."

"*No* food, hunh? Who do you think you're lying to? If you've got candles or flashlights...whatever we saw lit up last night....that means you've also got *food*...probably plenty of it....We're hungry....*Real hungry.*...This is your last warning before we come through this flimsy little door."

"Listen *pal*," Sam said with his voice quivering, "I have a gun pointed right at *your gut.* Bullets go through flimsy doors, as you called it. If you're not gone in ten seconds we'll both find out how flimsy this door really is. Now go. *Get outta here.* Leave us alone. *Don't* come back....I've got plenty of ammo. *Got it?*"

"Yeah, smart mouth, we *will* get it. Thanks for telling us about all your ammo....food *and* ammo....and *a woman.*...what a *deal.* You can put away your gun, mister macho man. We're going. But you better be able to stay awake at night, *all night,* because *we'll be back.* Sweet dreams, macho man. Tell your woman we're lookin' forward to *meeting* her, if you know what we mean."

.

41

Columbia Food Distribution, Inc.

Columbia, Missouri

Thad Stevens was an admitted workaholic. He loved his job, and had done so ever since he took over Columbia Food Distribution, Inc., when his only uncle suffered a fatal heart attack, leaving him sole owner of the company. Like everyone else in central Missouri he watched what little news he could get on the television channels still broadcasting after The Day. Neither St. Louis or Kansas City appeared to be on the nuclear target list, so Thad was able to get updates from channels in both cities on his cable system in Columbia, located in Missouri about midway between both cities. He often reflected on the wise planning that led his uncle to locate the warehouse midway between the two metropolises.

Two days after The Day, Thad, as was his custom, unlocked the secure door at 6:30 AM to the offices of Columbia Food Distribution, Inc. He was usually the first employee to appear at the warehouse, so he wasn't surprised that his car was the first in the large parking lot. He noted that semi-trucks were backed into 18 of the warehouse's twenty loading bays. What did surprise him though, was that by 8:15 AM only two employees had driven their cars into the parking lot and were in the company's kitchen drinking coffee. Usually, all forty-seven personnel were on hand by 8 AM to grab a cup of Joe and start to work.

Thad walked back to the kitchen, filled his cup and sat down, saying to neither employee in particular, "Where the heck is everybody? Hunh?"

The two employees present, Jim and Nick, looked at each other, with Nick saying, "Boss, we were just wondering the same thing. KC and St. Louis weren't hit, so why did everybody stay home?"

"Got me, boys, I don't get it either. We've got work to do. Those trucks out there still gotta' be loaded, and then driven to our customers' stores. We can't do that without people. I know they're scared after what happened to the country. *Whew!* Who coulda' seen that coming? It sounds like lots of folks....*millions*, maybe....are dead. What a *disaster*, but we still got work to do. People are still gonna' have to eat....you know....the ones who survived....the people in our part of the country....you know....the areas that didn't get nuked. Life has to go on....and....you know...."

"Boss, Jim and I were just talking about that. Do you see any problem with our getting any diesel fuel for the trucks...like....*after* we draw down the tanks out back and *run out* of our reserve supply? Whatchathink?"

Thad stopped mid-sip, looking over the edge of his coffee cup at Nick, his inquiring employee. Late last night and early this morning Thad had been thinking about a lot of potential problems, like continuing their food supply lines and insuring that their food market stores maintained their banking relationships so Columbia would get paid, but he had totally spaced any concerns about diesel fuel. Diesel fuel. Columbia's fuel tanks held

156

just over five thousand gallons, and were re-filled twice a week by his petroleum supplier, the Stone River Refinery, located in Roxana, Illinois 15 minutes from St. Louis. Missouri had no refineries. It was time to call Stone River.

Back in his office, Thad looked out at the parking lot which still held only three vehicles. He picked up the handset on his desk phone, pleased to hear a dial tone. He punched in the number for Stone River Refinery. The number rang....and rang....and rang....but no one answered. Maybe I dialed wrong in my haste Thad decided. He hung up and dialed again. Same result. Ringing, but no answer. He looked at his wall clock, they're an hour ahead, so it's well after 9 AM in western Illinois. Stone River has people there 24/7/365, since they refine crude oil around the clock. Thad put the ringing call on his speakerphone and laid the handset on the desk, hoping that someone would answer, eventually.

42

The Harlan Robbins Farm

Crown Point, Indiana

The first people to walk onto the Robbins farm front porch looking for food were a sorry bunch. The husband/father looked like he would not be able to take another step without collapsing. The wife/mother didn't look any better. She was holding an infant on her left hip and a toddler on her right hip. Three children, with dirty faces, aged from nine to twelve hung onto their parents, staring up at Harlan and Dorothy Robbins who were standing just outside their front door. They arrived late in the afternoon, as dusk was falling over northwest Indiana. Harlan was explaining that they couldn't help them with food as they didn't have any to spare. But Dorothy laid her hand on Harlan's arm and whispered in his ear, "Honey, we can share *a little* of what we have. Look at these pitiful folks. They could die, literally, if we don't help them. I'll get some grub, you take them out to the barn and get them a place to lie down and rest some. Okay?"

Harlan wasn't happy about what his wife of over fifty years had just whispered. He knew that their actual supply of food would soon be gone if they gave it away to everyone who knocked on their door. But in those years of marriage Harlan had learned that when Dorothy made up her mind....well, he knew what they would have to do. His underlying concern was not giving some food to these sad-looking folks, but what would they do when the next hardship case came to their house asking for food, and the next, and the next. He pondered the problem as he nodded his affirmative response to Dorothy. She turned and went into the farm house to get food. Harlan led the family out back to the barn, showing the family where they could lie down in a clean stall.

That night, after Harlan and Dorothy shared a small meal, Harlan brought up his concern, "Dot. We have to *talk*. We can't keep doing what we just did."

"But, Harlan, honey, they were *starving*. We *had* to help them or else they...."

"I know. I know. But, Dot, my dear, we will be *out of food* soon, even if we don't give any more away. What we've stored in the root cellar may keep us alive for two to three months, maybe more if we skimp. These folks we just fed are only the first of *many* who will come. Dot, we can't feed *everybody*. *We just can't.*"

Dorothy wept. Harlan was silent, looking down at his farm-roughened hands.

Finally, Harlan said, "I'm alright with sharing....like....I don't know, maybe a third of what we've got. But no more. Otherwise, we'll...."

"Harlan, I understand. But, you said yourself that the fallout might kill us before we ran out of food. So, what difference does it make if we...."

"*Die* from starvation before we *rot* from the radiation? Is *that* what we're saying, Dot?"

"Pretty much, Harlan. Let's take your idea and bring some of the root cellar food back into the house, not much. And we'll share it with folks who show up looking for food. When it's gone, it's gone."

"OK, I can live with that Dot, my dear, but *then what?* We'll then still have only about half of what we started with. We'll leave, as we discussed before, a few cans in the kitchen for those who decide to break in the house, when no one answers the door. Then, I suggest that once we decide that we are done giving away food, that we hide out in the root cellar during the night when visitors willing to shoot us for food are more likely to show up at the farm."

"*Seriously?* Through the *whole night*, Harlan? In the *root cellar?* I don't think we can...."

"*I* don't like the idea much either, but what are the alternatives? If we stay in the house, with no food, and the hungry visitors come, what do we do then? If they're armed, they won't believe that we live on a farm, but we don't have any food. They'll either *shoot us* or *threaten to shoot us* if we don't tell them where the food is hidden. Our options are *very* limited."

Harlan and Dorothy Robbins didn't have to endure lying in their root cellar. Their fourth food visitors the next day were five dirty and bedraggled men, all packing weapons stuck in their belts. Dorothy tried to convince them that all that they had to give them was a can of pork and beans and a mason jar of canned dill pickles. They grabbed the food, demanding more, assuring the Robbins that they knew that they had to have more food. They were farmers, after all, they said. Harlan insisted to the increasingly angry men that they had already given away everything else they had. The hungry men standing in their kitchen would have none of it. The dirtiest, angriest hungry man pulled his gun, laying the barrel next to Dorothy's head. Harlan started to reason with the wielder of the gun. He fired directly into Dorothy's right ear, instantly killing her and splattering Harlan and the Robbins kitchen with her blood. Harlan lunged towards the shooter, only to be hit mid-chest by the second bullet fired. Harlan and Dorothy Robbins went to be with their Lord, never again to worry about sharing their food with hungry, angry people.

43

Stone River Refinery

Roxana, Illinois

Frank Talbot was talking to himself, not for the first time in the days since The Day. *"Don't they know that this country was NUKED? Why do they keep calling? I'm the only guy who was stupid enough to stay here after the bombs went off, but somebody had to shut this humongous puppy down. What if I hadn't had six years of engineering and graduate school? What if I'd only worked here for a year or two, instead of twelve. It takes skill to gradually turn off an oil refinery, that is without blowing it up along with half of Roxana. Can't whoever keeps calling just get the message and hang up? I need some sleep."*

The phone in the Dispatcher's office at Stone River Refinery continued to ring. It was directly across the hall from the refinery's Primary Control Room, making it difficult to ignore. Now that the final steps and procedures for shutting down the refinery were completed, Frank Talbot thought again about sleep, which he desperately needed after 36 straight hours without any. But, he knew that he couldn't just curl up on the floor and power nap, not as long as that pesky phone continued to ring. Oh, alright, jerkwater, I'll answer your call. It better not be a sales call or I will give you such a tongue lashing that you...."

"Yeah. Stone River Refinery. What can *I do* for you?....Is anyone even there? Well, I'll be...."

Surprised that his call had actually been answered Thad took a moment to snatch up the handset and answer, "*Hey....hey*....this is Thad Stevens over at Columbia Food Distribution....you know....in Columbia, Missouri. We're one of your fair sixed customers. Usually north of thirty to thirty five thousand gallons of diesel per month."

"Hunh....well, you're talking to Frank Talbot. I'm the Chief Engineer and I don't have a clue who buys what. Sounds like you buy our diesel product....but you won't be....buying it, that is....not for a *really* long time."

"What? That's why I called....and by the way, thanks for finally taking my call. I needed to know if we're still scheduled for a Thursday afternoon delivery of our normal four thousand gallons...like I said....of diesel?"

"Simple answer is *no*. No one will be getting any products from Stone River for some time....I don't know how long....*if ever*, frankly."

"What's *that* supposed to mean? What's *happened* there?"

"Well, here's the deal. This refinery gets its crude from two pipelines. Pipeline number one runs just west of the Chicago area, southwest across Illinois. Pipeline two comes up from the Gulf of Mexico, starts in Houston. Number one is still functioning, but it's close enough to Chicago that anything flowing through the line is radiated, you know, with gamma rays and such. Our Geiger Counters started going crazy within just a few hours of the nuking of Chicago. As an immediate consequence, pipeline one was shut down."

"When will it come back up, Frank?"

"That's the thing. We can't allow radiated crude oil into the refinery. As soon as it started flowing into our system it would *radiate everything* here. Then even if we did start refining again, we would be cracking petrol products that were radioactive. Think of that. You stop by your local gas station and your choices are regular, super or *radioactive.* I don't think so. The half-life of a normal nuclear explosion is between 1,000 and 10,000 days, depending on several factors, like the concentration of Cessium-137 and the...."

"*Whoa,* mister engineer man, you're already over my head here. I get why you can't use radioactive crude oil, but what happened to the *second* pipeline, the one from the Gulf?"

"Not good. The static pressure on the crude flow....uh...let's see....in layman's terms the amount of the flow through the pipe started slowly declining this morning. For the first few hours after the nukes went off I didn't see any difference that could be measured, but...."

"But, was that because of what was already headed your way, in the pipeline, so to speak?"

"Yeah, so to speak. But, about six this morning the alarms monitoring the flow started going off. Then, within an hour it was lower than 40%. Now it's *a trickle.* I shut down the line, because it causes damage to the cracking system if the flow's not over 40% capacity. That's all by way of saying that Stone River Refinery is *offline.* No petro products. Not now. Not for a long time. If *ever.*"

"Why do you say maybe *never*? Couldn't the Houston flow come back?"

"Houston was nuked."

"*Ouch*. I hadn't heard that. So the oil fields, and oil docks and just about everything dealing with oil in that part of the U.S., coming in off the Gulf, I take it, are *toast*? If they *could* pump to you, which doesn't sound very likely, it also would be radioactive crude oil, right?"

"Thad, you sound like you had some oil background. Want a job? I'm the only one still at the refinery, but I could use some help holding this place together, until somebody a lot smarter, and a lot richer, than me decides what to do with it."

"Thanks for the offer. My dad was a wildcatter for a while, but he lost it all. My love is shipping food to grocery stores to feed people. But, Frank, what I'm hearing is that my job, apparently much like yours, *is over*. You're telling me you're not going to be refining any petroleum products. If I can't find a refinery in Kansas that is still in business, *I'll* be out of business, too. *Whoa!* You know what that's going to mean for several hundred thousand grocery store shoppers in another few days?....How do you spell *hunger*?"

"Sorry to be the bearer of bad news, but we're only just two small cogs in the giant financial system which is shortly going to be totally shut down. We supply four electric generating plants with petroleum products to run their generators. We're still able to talk on the phone and have electricity in our offices today because those electric plants are still cranking out wattage. They have back up

166

storage capacity allowing them to make it through a natural disaster, but not for more than a week, some for just four days. Pretty soon, though, *lights out.* The electric plants that burn coal to make electricity will soon find that the trains in this country that haul the coal don't run on water. Without diesel fuel they'll be *done.*....I don't know how you get deliveries of food to your warehouse in Columbia that you then ship to grocery stores, but I suspect it's by semi-truck, maybe by train. Right?

"Spot on. I was just thinking as we were speaking that I'm out of business *two ways.* I not only can't get the food shipments to the groceries, but I won't be receiving much, *if any*, food since it all arrives here by truck, a small amount by train, but, as you said, the trains run on diesel. Actually, a third big problem, come to think about it, is that the food distribution business operates on almost immediate payment to food suppliers. If the banks are closed and the internet is down, *we're done.* Plus, the just on time system of food shipments and deliveries in this country has been fine-tuned so that the average food market is virtually empty, cleaned out, of food products within four to seven days, depending on size and location, not including cleaning products, paper goods, that kind of thing. And....that's with normal shopping, not the looting that's hit the stores that the radio's been warning everybody not to do. They might as well advertise it. *'Get to the store quick, while there's still a can of soup left.'* Most of today's younger generation think that food comes from the super market. What a shock they'll have. Whew! *We're done,* Frank. Heck, the *country's done.*"

"On that *cheery* thought, Thad of Columbia, Missouri, I wish you well. Sorry we won't be selling you

167

guys any more diesel. You'd better load your car's trunk with some canned corn, though. Know what I mean, Thad? Good luck."

"Thanks, Frank, but I don't think *lucks* got much to do with it."

44

Sam and Laura's Kitchen
Minneapolis, Minnesota

Sam's hands were still shaking, even though their unwanted visitors had left their porch several minutes before. Laura, still red-faced, was dabbing tears from her eyes. Both recognized that they had just escaped the event that they both feared the most. Since The Day they had frequently discussed what they would do if someone forced their way into the sanctity of their home. Now it was decision time.

"Sam....oh, Sam....those men are *serious*. They'll be back tonight....or tomorrow night."

Sam finally laid his revolver back on the counter. Trying to calm his nerves and control his still wavering voice, he said, "Laura....We've *talked* about this. We both know that I *won't* kill anybody, not just to protect what little food we have left. If they break down the door, we should just let them take what's still in the kitchen. I won't take somebody's life, especially when they're probably starving. We talked about that poll that came out last year that said that 58% of Americans would kill someone who threatens their home or family. Less than 20% said they couldn't do it, which is where I am. *I can't do it.*"

Laura was just able to talk, sobbing as she said, "I know, Sam....*I know*....You made that decision right after the nukes went off and you knew *then* what was going to happen. But....Sam....you heard what they said about

169

me....your wife....*a woman,* as they said. If they come back....that is....*when* they come back, they'll surely take our food and our gun and that box of bullets, but then....Sam, they're going to....*to take me.*"

Sam looked over at his wife, who had been barely able to speak. He carefully chose his words, saying, "My dear....you *know*....I would *never, ever* let anyone hurt you. Not if I could do anything about it....*but....*"

"But?"

"But....since I can't pull the trigger and actually take somebody's life....it seems to me that we only have *one* good option. We don't have any place to escape. No relatives or close friends in the wilderness. We don't know anyone who has any food. Everybody we know is in the same fix."

"Well, Sam, if we have no place to go and you won't use your gun *to protect me*....to protect *us*....then what are we going to do? *What's our plan?*"

"This is difficult for me to say, but, Honey, we need to seriously think about an early exit."

"An early exit? What does that mean....oh....oh....You mean *taking our own lives? Suicide? Seriously, Sam?*"

"I don't like the idea *either*, Laura, but *what else* can we do? Without food, we're going to be dead within a few days, no more than two or three weeks, anyway. We're not willing to kill people who break in our house.

170

So....so....since we're not going to live long term, I'm just suggesting that we *speed up* the inevitable."

"*Speed up?* Like what? *When*, Sam?"

"Before I answer that, I think we should talk about what my sister said to us last Thanksgiving."

"Thanksgiving? I don't remember what she said. What did she say?"

"Remember, we were all talking about the news report the day before that a couple over in St. Paul had committed suicide. My sister brought up the Bible. You know she's a so-called evangelical Christian, whatever that really means."

"Laura, I know where she's coming from, religiously speaking, but I don't recall what she claimed the Bible said about suicide."

"What she said, quite simply, was that taking one's own life is *a sin*....and the Bible preaches against it. She quoted a verse about our bodies being temples of God, or something like that.

"Well, your sister certainly *preaches* against it, I do recall that now. She went on and on about the Bible being against murder and she argued that suicide is self-murder. But, since I don't buy most of what the Bible says, I don't see that your sister's weirdo religious beliefs from a year ago, before The Day, should affect us, *now*."

"No, I guess not. *I just hope we're right.*"

Sam and Laura looked into each other's eyes, neither saying anything. After thirty-two years of marriage they could almost read each other's thoughts. Once Sam and Laura rejected the Biblical view of what they were about to do, they realized that they had arrived at a life-ending decision.

45

St. Antonio Hospital

Crown Point, Indiana

Harlan Robbins promised his wife Dorothy, after she ran out of her pills, that he would make his way to the hospital in Crown Point, south of town, to try and get her medications. As he walked out to his pick-up truck, he was concerned that it might not start, based on some articles he remembered reading about EMP effects. He said a prayer and turned the key, starting the six cylinder engine. Whew, that's a relief, he thought. He couldn't image trying to tell his wife that he couldn't get to town to get the pills she had to have.

What Harlan didn't know as he pulled out from his farm was what he would encounter on the ten minute drive to Crown Point. As he drove north on County Road 55 he was surprised to see that not much seemed to have changed. He expected to encounter several stranded vehicles, but the further north he drove he realized that whatever the nuclear blast did in Chicago, it didn't send out electromagnetic pulses to fry the electronic circuits of newer motor vehicles, at least in their area of the country. Seeing no abandoned vehicles along his route he started looking at the farm houses and then the homes close to each other, south of town, to see what people were doing. He saw very few people outside their homes, which didn't really surprise Harlan, as he anticipated that most folks were still just hunkered down in their homes, waiting to see how the attacks on America would affect them.

He further relaxed as he saw the five story hospital building up ahead. Pulling off the road into the hospital's mostly deserted parking lot, he changed his mind. He watched as two men ran out the main entry doors of the hospital, their arms full of blankets and what appeared to be bed sheets. What is this, he asked himself? He pulled up by the entry doors, switched off his truck and headed into the hospital. He noticed trash, smashed bottles and empty medicine boxes lying on the sidewalk. Before he got to the doors, a petite woman, obviously distraught, rushed out of the hospital.

Harlan reached out, grabbed her shoulders, stopping her and asked, "*Whoa*, what's wrong little lady? What's going on here?"

The sobbing woman, whom Harlan could now see was a nurse, based on her uniform and Crown Point hospital name badge, at first tried to twist away from his grasp, but then looked at his face and age and realized he wasn't a danger. She leaned her head forward on Harlan's chest, crying and saying, "*They shot Doctor Scott....*and Doctor Belcher, and I don't know who else. The hall is full of dead....There's *blood* everywhere. They've cleaned us all out....they took everything....they *just came in* and...."

"*Calm down*, now....*Who* shot the Doctors? Who took what, little lady?"

Collecting herself, the fleeing nurse sobbed out her reply, "About two hours ago several men....with guns....came into the hospital. They shot the receptionist, my friend, Molly, up front....*oh, Molly, Molly*....then they went down the hall, shooting *anyone* they saw. I was at

174

the end of the hall when the shooting started. I hid in the supply storage closet, near the pharmacy....I could hear them talking as they cleaned the pharmacy out. They took pillow cases and dumped all of our meds in them. They broke open the narcotic cabinet...took it all....*everything.* I stayed in the closet....but I finally came out after they were gone. By then, the rest of the staff had either been shot dead....or scared away....apparently all of them, nurses...the business staff. *Everybody's gone.* When I left the closet I glimpsed two men who grabbed blankets and bed sheets running down the hall and out the door."

"I saw them. I can't believe that they would shoot doctors....And nurses....What kind of animals would....*Lord, have mercy....*I can't believe....Now, little lady, are you saying that you're *totally* out of pills? No more meds?....My wife has to have three different medications....or else....she....may. Oh man, this is *not good....*But, what about the patients?"

"We have twenty eight patients who need care. The two docs who were on duty are dead. I didn't see any nurse who's alive. The ones who didn't *get shot* must have left. I expect some may be back, but sir, without any meds, how are we going to provide medical care? I don't know what we're *going to do.*"

Harlan relied sadly, "I don't either, little lady, *I don't either.*"

46

Abilene State Savings Bank

Abilene, Kansas

Harry Weaver considered himself to be a relatively savvy businessman. He had, after all, sold appliances at Weaver's Home Appliance Store on downtown Cedar Street for almost twenty years. As soon as a customer in Harry's store brought his attention to the breaking news flash on one of the television sets on the wall of Harry's store, though, Harry knew that the world had just changed. Big time. Harry excused himself and went to his office at the rear of the store. He first tried to call his brother in Las Vegas. Uncharacteristically, his brother, who was retired and almost always at home, didn't answer. Next Harry tried to call his sister at her beauty shop in Los Angeles. Again, no answer. Harry then began to seriously worry. He hesitated to call his only child, who was an intern at Baylor Medical Center in Dallas. His first thought was what he would do if his son didn't answer the cell phone which had been a gift from Harry. The news report he had just seen on the display model television in his store didn't give a full list of American cities which had been hit. What if Dallas was on the list? He didn't think he could handle the loss of his son. As a widower, his son and his two distant siblings were his only close family.

Saying a silent prayer, Harry punched in the numbers for his son's cell. "Hello, Dad. Are you alright?"

"Yes, son, but more important....*how are you*? Did Dallas have any....you know....bombs....*nukes*? I'm sure you've heard about New York and DC and...."

"Look, Dad, I can't talk long, we're on emergency status. No bombs in Dallas, thank God, but Houston, we understand, was hit. We're packing up medical supplies to take to Houston, or whatever's left of it. As a precaution, you should put about 100 drops of iodine in some water and drink it. Do that every day for a few days, until the fallout has dissipated. Even where you are in Abilene, you're likely to get wind-blown fallout from the west."

"Thanks, son, I'll do it, but you need to get back to work. Be *real* careful if you get very close to ground zero in Houston.....Just be careful.... *I love you, son.*"

Harry closed his store and walked home to follow his son's iodine regimen. After slowly sipping the fluid, Harry began to think. What should I be doing, he pondered. What *should* I be doing?

In the shower the next morning Harry knew what he had to do, and do quickly. If the U.S. has been hit as hard as it sounded from the isolated news he was able to get, what with all of the major news and cable networks no longer broadcasting, he knew his business would be hit almost as hard. Who would want to buy an appliance when the nation was partially destroyed? As a businessman for two decades Harry suspected that the multiple nukes would have a devastating effect on the country, even out in the plains of Kansas. His business was effectively done for – finished – kaput. In the months before The Day Harry had laughed at some of the news coverage of so-called preppers, whom he viewed as extreme. When he heard that a pastor of a small church in Abilene had moved his family to Panama to avoid participating in America's so-called sins, he just shook his head, wondering why anyone would voluntarily give up living in the greatest country on the globe?

After thinking it all through, Harry headed to his bank, the Abilene State Savings Bank, where Harry maintained his personal and business accounts. Harry wasn't wealthy by any means, but he mentally calculated on his brisk walk to the bank that his personal account held over thirty thousand dollars and the store's account was north of a hundred thousand, most of it in low interest paying certificates of deposit. It was a few minutes before nine, the time that the bank opened for business, when Harry turned the corner and soon realized that he wasn't the only bank customer with the same idea in mind – to get their money out of their bank. As he walked up to the bank's still-locked doors Harry counted eleven people standing in line.

Harry knew the two people standing at the end of the line, a couple who had done business with his store, almost since he opened in 1994. Turning, the couple saw Harry as he approached. "Harry, how are you today?....Did you hear about Russia and Iran. Both Moscow and Tehran were hit hard, but *not* by Israel. I heard it on my short wave right before we came over here. Looks like the same kind of fire and brimstone that was rained on their troops which invaded Israel. Those *cowards*. Those *murderers*. They're getting *exactly* what they deserve. A guy in our church says that the Bible prophesied that when they invaded Israel they would pay for it. Can you *believe* it? God help us."

"Murderers," Harry replied, disgust in his voice, "*Why in the world* would they do it?....Russia? And Iran? We should have *stopped Iran* from getting nukes when we had a chance. How many died?"

"They didn't say. We haven't heard anything about death tolls. Are you here for the same reason that we are?"

"Yeah. To get my *money*." As they were talking, several more walked up, joining the line, which was now around the corner of the bank building.

At 9 AM promptly the front door was unlocked, but instead of allowing the waiting customers entry to the bank lobby, a bank uniformed guard came out and announced, "Folks, I've been asked by management to tell you that the bank is *closed* today." His words were met by shouts of anger,

"*What?* This is a business day."

"*You can't do that!*"

"We want our *money*."

"*Where's* management? Bring the *cowards* out here. We'll show them what they can...."

The guard ducked back into the bank. The line was no longer a line, but was instead a mob, gathered at the front door, banging on the glass of the doors and the front windows. Frightened bank employees peered out at the angry mob. Harry caught the eye of the branch manager whom Harry had known from his first day of business. Harry nodded his head slightly, indicating that he would meet him at the bank's service door, located in the alley behind the bank. Harry mumbled that the bank obviously wasn't going to open today and slowly pulled away from the Bank's customers who were taking out their anger on the bank's doors and windows

Checking behind him to insure that he was alone in the alley, Harry knocked softly on the bank's rear service door. It was immediately opened by his manager friend. "*Get in here*, Harry, what's that all about out there? Who organized *that mob*?"

"What? Are you deaf and dumb, ol' buddy? *We just want our money.* My business now will be toast, at least for a few months....or maybe years....*who knows* at this point in time how bad it's going to get, even out here in the plains, away from the nuked cities? My son in Dallas tells me they hit Houston. That means that a *huge* percentage of our refining capacity is gone. *No* refined gasoline or diesel fuel will translate pretty soon, I'm sure, into *no* food being hauled to stores, which means violence, massive thievery, *you name it.*"

"Aren't you just *a bundle* of morning joy? But, Harry, why were you at the bank this early? You generally make late afternoon deposits."

"Well, duh, why do you *think*? I need my *money*....and I need it today. Look at that crowd, it'll be a hundred times larger once people figure out what's happened. So, fork it over, I wanna get outta here before things turn ugly."

"Well....uh....Harry....uh....we *can't* do that."

"Can't do *what?* I want my *money.* I only have a little over a hundred and thirty thousand dollars between my two accounts....give or take. So, give me the form I need to sign and I'll get out of your hair."

"Harry....I just told you....we *can't* do that."

"I heard you the first time, but I need my *money....now.*"

"Look, Harry, let me explain this. We don't carry that kind of cash in the vault. Your money, most of which as I recall is in CDs, is invested in loans to other customers, Harry, it's not *here.*"

"Who do you think you are....George Bailey? I know how fractional banking works, but I know you either have or can soon get a measly hundred grand or so. That's *chump change* for you guys. So *come on,* I'm not leaving until I get my money. *Got it?*"

The Abilene State Savings Bank branch manager looked over at the two bank guards who were standing in the bank lobby at the bank's front doors, their hands resting nervously on their holstered revolvers. One of the guards looked back and saw the manager motion for him. He strode back to the manager, who was standing next to an obviously irate Harry.

Harry recognized what had just happened, hissed, "So, that's how it is, *hunh?* You threaten to shoot a good customer who only just wants his money. I get it....*I get it.*"

"Harry, nobody's going to *shoot you*, or anyone of those people pounding on the front of the bank. That being said, we *don't* have the money you want, so you're going to have to leave. Tom, will you take Harry to the back door, please?"

"Wait....*wait*....I understand that you've got a lot of people that are going to want their money, I'm willing to compromise....just for now, you understand. Later, I'll want all of it. But for now, how about just *thirty thousand?*"

"Harry....Harry....I really wish we could, but we only keep *a few thousand bucks* in cash to handle the very few people in this day and age who need actual greenbacks. With banking online and credit cards, we just don't have a call for that much cash."

Harry wiped the sweat off his forehead. He had worked himself into arrhythmia, stressing out over money, which he had told himself he wouldn't do. He tried one more approach, "As a favor, to one of your best, long-time customers, how about *five thousand*, the rest next week, after you get more cash? What do you say?"

"Harry, we *can't* do that....But....well....here....come over to the teller cage."

Once there, the bank's manager unlocked the cash drawer. He counted out five one hundred dollar bills, six fifties and enough twenties and tens to total an even thousand dollars. He counted it out in front of Harry, handing it to him, and in a lowered voice said, "You *didn't* get this here. If it becomes known that we're giving out money to some, even to a few customers , they'll *break through* the doors they're only pounding on now. Stick this in your pocket and get out of here. But, Harry, you better be prepared for what is quite likely about to happen."

Harry looked at the small stack of bills in his hand, looked at the manager and said, "Only a grand? *That's it? A measly* thousand bucks?" Seeing that he had just been given all he was going to get, he asked, "*What* should I be prepared for....a grand *sure* won't help all that much."

"Harry, those bills may buy you some food or gas or whatever...*today*....but see if *anyone* will take paper money for food in another day or two. My point is that even if you had all one hundred plus grand, very soon it won't do you *a bit of good.* Think barter, Harry, *think barter.* The dollar was sinking fast *before* the attacks on America, but now the dollar's *all but dead.*"

47

Lee's Gas Station and Food Mart

Abilene, Kansas

Harry Weaver left the Abilene State Savings Bank through its alley door, still munching on what the bank's manager had just said about the worthless dollar. Whatever happened, Harry thought, to the 'almighty dollar'? Didn't seem very almighty now. But, Harry had just over a thousand dollars in his pocket, so he decided to test what the bank manager had just said. He didn't want to get rid of too many dollars, as he expected they would come in real handy in the days following The Day, but the only way to find out was to find out. He walked the seven blocks to his modest home, entered the garage and grabbed his red metal five gallon gasoline can, which he used when he needed to fuel his 4000W generator, when the power was out. He shook the can, realized he had a small quantity of gas still left and poured the balance into the tank of the generator.

Harry then walked two blocks over to Lee's Gas station where he always bought his gasoline, not only for his generator, but also for his Toyota. Walking up to the station, Harry saw that the owner, Lee, whom he had known for several years was working today. He also saw that Lee was in what appeared to be a heated argument with a customer, whose car was parked in one of the two fill lanes. Just as Harry approached the two dueling men he heard the customer say words that no businessman ever wants to hear, "Well, then, I'll *never* do business at this dump again....*never*....*never*." The irate customer jumped in his car and peeled out of the station, leaving a small cloud of exhaust fumes and burnt rubber.

Harry said, "Lee, sorry about that hot head. You can't please everybody, I guess." Holding out his gas can, Harry said, "I need to buy some gas for my generator. Never know when the power may go out. I expected quite a few cars would be here buying gas, what with the nuking on the coasts, and all."

"Oh, hi, Harry, yeah, well, we did have a run there for a while late yesterday, but it slowed down *considerably* once word spread in the area about our *new* policy."

"*Oh,* what policy is that, Lee?"

"No more cash or credit sales."

"Oh, okay....No, wait....I understand no credit sales. Who knows what's gonna' happen to credit cards, right? But, *cash? No cash sales?* What does that mean? How can you sell anything if you don't take cash or credit?"

"Barter."

"*Barter?*"

"Un-hunh. Barter only. I got the gas. Folks are going to need gas. I don't want their worthless dollars. Nobody else will be taking dollars, soon. Don't believe me? Try getting anybody in town to sell you anything of value for dollars. You own an appliance store, right Harry? Will you sell me a new refrigerator for worthless paper that's no good to buy anything anywhere? I didn't *think so.* If you want gas, I'll trade you for something that's actually *worth* something, you follow me?"

186

Harry couldn't get his breath he was so taken aback. When he tried to respond to what he had just heard, he couldn't get his words out. After wiping his forehead, he gulped twice, saying, "But, Lee, I've done business with you for years, *lots* of years. We're like....you know....*friends.*"

"Really? *Friends?* That's what the guy who just ripped out of here said when I told him his worthless money was no good here. You wanna' yell at me too, or do you have something you can *trade* for gas? What kind of watch is that you're wearing?"

"I'll pay you later, sign a note, whatever, but I'm not giving you my watch. *No way.*"

"Harry, Hunh?"

"Are you *nuts?* Do you think I'd trade in my generator for gas to use in the generator, that I'd just traded to you for the gas? *Get real,* Lee. Your gas fumes are going to your head. Just sayin'."

"OK, you're a businessman. A bargainer, I see that. You own a Toyota. I fill it for you every two weeks, give or take. It holds about sixteen gallons. I'll trade you a full tank of gas for the car in exchange for your generator. What do you say?"

"WHAT? Sixty bucks of gas for a four hundred dollar generator? As I just asked, are you *nuts,* Lee? Bonkers? *Who* would do that?"

"Lots of people, Harry. My repair bay over there is full of things I've traded to folks for gasoline. Harry, in case you haven't figured it out, they won't be making no more gasoline, no, not for a long time. Maybe *never*. You like walking, Harry? You wanna' walk two miles, ten miles? Places you don't think twice about driving to now. When your Toyota is empty Harry, how ya' gonna' get around? I'm your last hope Harry. I just stuck my tanks. I'm down to a quarter of my supply left. When that's gone, *it's gone*. What do ya say, Harry? Do we gotta' a deal?"

Harry studied the sky, thought about it and said, "*Two* tanks of gas for the Toyota."

"No. It'll be *gone* before you use up the first tank and come back for a fill up. Don't wanna' cheat ya, Harry," Lee said with a sardonic smile.

"Hum....*Fill* the Toyota....*plus* this gas can."

"*Done*....Bring the generator when you come back in your Toyota."

"Bandit. *Thief.*"

"Then *don't* come back. In tough times a man's gotta do what a man's gotta do....Harry, ya'll do what ya'll gotta do. *You'll see.*"

"I'll....be....*right*....back."

48

Columbia Food Distribution, Inc.

Columbia, Missouri

Thad Stevens was worried. His concerns weren't for his business, as he knew with nearly 100% assurance that his business was gone, over, done. With no diesel fuel he couldn't haul food products to his grocery store customers, nor could his suppliers bring food products to his warehouse. In addition to which he was about to find that when he flipped a light switch he would have no electricity.

Thad was worried that his warehouse would soon be overrun by hungry people who knew, or who learned, what his large aluminum building actually held. He looked out his interior window at the warehouse. Stacked on pallets for the length of the warehouse were hundreds of boxes of canned food. He pulled out the inventory of food products currently in-house. He calculated that in the warehouse he had at least thirty-two semi-trucks of food. He punched the inventory numbers into his hand calculator, concluding that what he had on hand was a normal nine to ten day supply. So, after about a week and a half his warehouse would be empty, that is if he were able to haul food to grocery store customers from Kansas City to St. Louis.

Thad couldn't decide what to do with the food he still held in his warehouse. He knew he could load it up in the eighteen semis at his docks and ship the food to his best customers, using what fuel he still held in the storage tanks behind the warehouse, and then bringing most of the trucks back, filling them with the balance of his supplies and delivering the last of the food to the closest customers, using what was left of his fuel. He could pay his employees with food to encourage them to come in to load and haul the food. His emerging plan struck Thad as the most humane way to dispose of his food supplies.

However, as he mulled it over he realized that even though he would be pushing food supplies out into Missouri grocery stores, the stores wouldn't really be benefitted by the food. Thad knew that marauding gangs would quickly grab the food, most likely without paying for it and probably before the semis could even be unloaded. So, he could help thieves, but not his good customers. Thad wasn't satisfied with his first plan, so he mulled over his other options.

Why not just open the front door and trade people cartons of food for silver coins, or gold jewelry or other tangible assets, he asked himself. He could then take the metals and other assets and....what....do what with them? Use it to buy fuel? There won't be any soon. Buy electricity? Same answer. Buy someone's house? Why? I have a house, so owning somebody else's house made no sense. Buy another car? Dumb thought. The only thing that would make any sense at all, he eventually concluded, would be to use the assets to buy....food.....Humh....Food is what I have *now*, so why should I get rid of it, and then *hope* I can get food later, trading for food with what I get from people who buy....my food? His circular reasoning made his head hurt.

Thad was not a religious person, but he finally came to the realization that he needed some divine wisdom. What to do with a warehouse three-quarters full of food? He whispered, *'God....I'm not on a first name basis with you....so you're probably wondering why I'm bothering you, but I've got a problem...I've got all this food out there....you know....out in the warehouse. But, because of the nuking of America it's pretty obvious that there won't be much food available to people....real soon. I don't know what to do with it....I can haul a few cases home in the car....But there's no way I can store enough to keep us fed for as long as it will take before food supplies are restored....I know the food biz....so I know that we're toast as a country....So, God, what should I do?*

While Thad's head was in his hands, a soft knock came on his office door. Wondering who it could be, Thad said, "Who's there? Come on in."

The door opened and Nick, one of the two employees who showed up for work this morning after The Day, opened the door slightly and stuck his head in, saying, "Sorry to bother you, boss, but I wondered if we could pray together?"

Thad wondered why Nick would even ask, as they had never discussed anything religious and he didn't know Nick all that well. But Thad was struck by what he thought was a coincidence that Nick would ask right after Thad finished stumbling through his prayer. "Uh, yeah, uh, Nick....have a seat. Uh....is Jim still here?....You want him to join us?....Uh....I guess prayer is a good idea....what with everything that's happened."

"Yeah, Boss. Jim went home, but I was in the break room praying....and....uh....you know I just felt like I should come up here and ask you if you were interested in praying together?"

"Funny you should ask, Nick. I'm not much into religion, but right before you knocked I was asking....you know....like....asking God....for *help.* We've got a warehouse out there mostly full of food, but I don't know what to do about it. We've got just enough fuel, I think, to get it all delivered. But....well....just to be honest with you, I was just thinking about trading the food out there to people who have silver coins or some gold or whatever."

"*Really?* How would that work? What would you *do* with the...."

"Already been there, Nick. Trading food for assets that could later best be used to trade for food is....kind of....not too smart. Once I figured that out I realized I needed help. *Wisdom.* You know. God and I aren't too tight....know what I mean? But I didn't know what else to do. I guess I didn't know you were a religious man."

"Oh, boss, I'm not....I'm not a religious man. Nope, I'm just a *Jesus* man."

"Hunh, Nick? I thought Jesus *was* a religion. What am I missing?"

"Jesus is my *savior.* He gave His life for a really good reason....to cover my sins....and everyone else who accepts Him as *their* savior."

"I'm not sure I'm getting what you're saying....Slow up a little bit. Why did you need....what did you call Jesus? A savior? Saved you....*from what?*"

Nick, realizing that he was sharing with a man who had almost no foundation in Biblical truth, took a deep breath and slowed up, saying, "OK, boss, here's the deal. When we're born we have a genetic flaw. We not only sin, we do things God doesn't want us to do, we also *want* to sin. It's in our nature. Adam and Eve. You know. The fall. We all have the nature now to sin. And, we're all going to die, someday. But, God had *a plan* to handle the sin problem and the death issue."

"*Really?* I've never heard any of this....at least....not like that. What's the *plan?*"

"God sent part of Himself, His son, Jesus, to the world. He came as a man, who was also God. He lived a sinless life. He did tons of miracles. All to *prove* who He was."

"OK, I get that, Nick....But how does that get rid of the sin and death problems you mentioned?"

"As you can imagine, His message went against the prevailing religious and political grain. He irritated the powers, to say the least. Neither the religious leaders or the Romans thought much of Him. Eventually, when it was time, God allowed the forces in control to *execute* the trouble-maker.

"I'm with you, now. I know that they....what's it called....they *crucified* Him?'

"Right. If that had been the end of it, then we wouldn't be having this discussion. But it wasn't the end of it. Jesus told His followers that He would be in the grave for three days, then He would come back to life....And He did it, *just* as He said. The proof of His divine nature was not only His many miracles, but also His resurrection. He walked the earth for several days after He had been killed and put in the tomb. *That's pretty impressive,* and frankly, boss, that's what led me to do it."

"Do *what?*"

"Oh, sorry, Jesus coming out of that tomb of death is what led me to ask Him to be my savior, to cover my sins and make sure that when I'm no longer walking around that I will be alive with Him, in heaven. That was a little over six years ago. It's been a much better life since I turned it over to Jesus, *I'll tell you that.*"

"Nick, you don't know how much I appreciate you telling me what you did. What would I have to do....to....you know....to do *the same thing?* I know I won't be around *forever*....what with the effect of the nukes and all....I don't know if *any* of us will be around a year from now?

"Boss, just pray with me. *Lord Jesus, I confess my sins. I know I need a savior. I thank you for dying on the cross for my sins. I invite you to come into my heart as my Lord and Savior. I thank you that no matter what happens in the days ahead, that I know that at the end of my life, I'll be with you in heaven. Thank you Jesus.* That's it, boss. From now on you'll find that you look at this world and what's in it a lot differently. Do you have a Bible?"

"Unh....probably....yeah, I think so. *Somewhere.* Pam'll know where it is."

"I suggest that you start in the book of John, that's in the New Testament, in the back part of the Bible. After you read John, then read the rest of the New Testament and then the whole Bible. If you're right about our not being around in a year," Nick said with a slight chuckle, "you might want to read several chapters a day."

Thad smiled, replying, "Probably a *good* idea. Thanks again Nick. You've been very helpful."

"One more thing boss. You said you were praying earlier for wisdom on what to do about the food in the warehouse. I've got an idea, since hauling it to stores isn't a real practical idea. Why not call in the employees, while the phones are still working, and *give each one* a few cases of food?"

Thad's eyes lit up as he saw an answer to his dilemma. He picked up his calculator again, punched in some numbers and said, "Nick, *great idea.* Let's give ten cases of food to each employee who's single. Twenty to each married employee and a couple cases for each child. Let's see, that will still leave us about forty percent of what's in the warehouse, that is if every employee shows up to pick up the food."

"They'll show up. Why not call some of the churches around this area and offer them a few cases each to help them with their church members who will soon run out of something to eat."

"Do you have any contacts with the local churches?"

"*Sure do,* boss, I'll give you a list of phone numbers."

"Nick, as soon as you get the list, come back in and help me call the employees and the churches. I want to get the food out of here before somebody figures out what we have here and they break in and loot the place. And....let's not forget our *own* families while we're passing out food. Be sure and get your cases, Nick. *Let's get to work.*"

49

Stone River Refinery

Roxana, Illinois

Frank Talbot was finally home asleep, well deserved after his several non-stop hours shutting down the refinery. He was so dead asleep that when his phone rang, he tried to integrate the incessant sound with what his mind was dreaming. By the fifth ring, however, the extraneous sound won over the fitful dream. Reluctantly, he reached his night stand to stop the noise. As he did he saw that the orange fluorescent numbers on his alarm clock showed 3:28 AM.

"Hello. *Who* is this?....What time is it? *What* the...."

"Is this Mister Talbot? *Frank Talbot?*"

"Yeah....who wants to know? Why are you calling *so early* in...."

"Sorry, Mister Talbot. This is Sheriff Bolton. Are you the Frank Talbot who is an officer at the refinery? Stone River? Your name is on our emergency contact list. That's *you*, right?"

"Yeah....Yeah. That's me. What's the emergency? If you guys need some gasoline for your cruisers, I can't help you. We're totally shut down. I can explain why, but we don't have fuel that we can give...."

"No, Mister Talbot, nothing to do with that. We've got a few gallons left in the supply tank down at the office. I'm calling to tell you that *the refinery's on fire.*"

Frank shot straight up in bed, his attention now fully on the early morning call. "Say that again, Sheriff. Did you say that the refinery's on fire? *When* did it....*how* did it...."

"Here's all I know, sir. Somebody, actually it looks like several somebodies, cut through the security fence on the back side of the refinery. Had to happen sometime in the last couple hours, maybe earlier, but after it got dark. It looks like they broke in to *steal fuel*, based on the two gas cans that they must have dropped when they started the fire."

"How did they start it? Does it look like arson?"

"No. Don't think so. They used some heavy metal tools to break the lock on the exit valve on a large fuel tank, at least that's the way it's marked. You'll have to tell us. They broke off the valve, but the sparks from slamming the tools against the metal valve set the fuel on fire. That's apparently when they dropped their gas cans and boogied out, leaving the fire to spread, which it *really has,* in spades. You better get over here, sir. Of course, with the fire department guys mostly not around since The Day, I don't know that there's much you can do."

"So the fire department is AWOL? Why are *you* still working? In Katrina the police almost all went home to protect their families giving up their law enforcement duties. Can't say as I blame 'em."

"That's what my wife keeps asking me. I'm the *only* one in the Sheriff's office that's still around. All the deputies are now off duty. That's what I like to call it, it sounds better, but in reality they're done. They won't be back to work....Sir, can you come down to the refinery? I'm sure that there a number of people in your operation that you will need to notify. I don't expect you to grab a fire extinguisher and start spraying, it's way too far gone, even if we had a fire department. It's gonna' burn *to the ground*, Mister Talbot, sorry to have to say."

"I hate to see it burn, but we were out of business, in any case. I'll explain why when I see you. We supply fuel for a 150 mile area in Illinois and Missouri. Better *save* whatever gas you have in that supply tank you mentioned at your office. There won't be anyone driving in this part of the world, very soon. I don't know if you have any food stored up, but you might want to go buy some."

"Are you *serious*? I guess you've been busy on other things, Mister Talbot, but every grocery store in Roxana has been cleaned out. Totally. Some people threw some money at the cashiers when they ran out with their carts or their arms full, but *most didn't*. They just took what they could. There's not a can of soup available anyplace in town. I truly don't know what folks are going to do in say a week or two. Winter's only a couple, three months away. We'll have a lot of starving people, *that's for sure.*"

"Sheriff, you're a good man...I'll be right over."

50

Home of Pastor Mick Kirkland

Sammamish, Washington

Pastor Kirkland's kitchen contained a comfortable amount of food, but since neighboring Seattle was nuked, he consumed only some soup and two crackers. His appetite was gone. He knew what would happen as soon as he Googled radiation poisoning. The Pastor managed to bottle up several containers of water on The Day, which turned out to be good timing, as his electricity went out that evening. With the termination of electric power went any further news from his television's snowy Vancouver channel. He had never met most of his neighbors, so none had come to his home to check on him.

Eventually his Church's Associate Pastor knocked on his door, inquiring as to his well-being. "Pastor Mick, are you *okay*? I couldn't call you, of course, so I walked over to see you. Can I come in?"

"Kerry, thanks for your thoughtfulness, but I'm *not* feeling well."

"I know, everybody's just *terrified* over the nukes, and we still don't know how many there were....or even really....who did this to us....I think that...."

"No, Kerry, I mean I am physically *sick*. I'm....umh...."

"Can I get you some medicine? We have all kinds of pills. Do you have the flu, or what do...."

201

"I was exposed to the fall out. I was outdoors, and the wind carried it. I was covered with the radioactive ash.....Kerry, *I'm a goner*....I won't make it to the end of the week.....I....won't...." Pastor Kirkland chocked up and couldn't continue speaking.

"Now, now, Pastor Mick, you don't know how long you have....*for sure*....we could walk over to the regional medical clinic and see what they have. They *must be* prepared for emergencies like this, don't you...."

"They'll be *overrun* with people in better shape than I am, whom they can actually *still help*....that is....if there's even anyone still there. Look, Kerry, look at my arms."

The Pastor pushed his screen door fully open, braced it with his foot and pulled back his long sleeves, baring his arms.

"Oh....oh *no....Holy*....yuck....you've....oh, Pastor Mick."

"I know, the skin was just red at first. But late yesterday I tried to wash my arms with some water I saved before the power went out....and....that's when the skin starting sloughing off. If I just touch the skin, it comes off. I've been bleeding like this *all day*. I'm wearing this Seahawk cap because most of my hair is gone, and the skin and the hair from my scalp is in the trash. Look here, Kerry, under the cap, look, it's *a bloody mess*....I just don't know how I can...."

Associate Pastor Kerry grabbed his mouth, couldn't hold it and wretched into the bushes in front of Pastor Mick's home.

At about 11 PM on the third day after The Day Pastor Mick was sitting in his reclining chair, slowly bleeding from his arms and head. He coughed twice, spitting up blood from his irradiated lungs, breathing his last breath. He then succumbed to the destructive effects of radiation on his human body.

51

Rancho McDonald

North of Durango, Colorado

Larry and Mary McDonald had first seen the light several years ago as they were watching television on a warm night at their home in western Ohio. Larry watched two back-to-back bank advertisements promoting home mortgages. The first ad said that new customers could borrow up to 110% of the cost of the home, Larry yelled at his TV, *"What?* You don't require *any* down payment and now you're loaning out *more* than the cost of the home? Are you kidding? That's voodoo economics. It's...."

"Now, *Larry,"* Mary said from the kitchen, "you're getting all steamed again. Calm down. It's just an ad.

"An ad? *Just* an ad? Don't you remember not so long ago we had to make a down payment of 20% in order to buy this house? Now, they *give* you 10% to sign up for a mortgage, 110% of the purchase price? That's *insane.* It's unsustainable....it's....wait, Mary look at that. There's another ad from a bank, pushing no down payment, up to 15% on top of the purchase price and *no* proof of income documents required. Have they *lost their minds?"*

Larry had previously worked in the finance industry and Mary was employed at a bank in western Ohio. They talked late into the night about what they had been seeing in America. Both knew that lending practices like what they had heard about and now seen with their own eyes would lead, inevitably, to widespread insolvency, mortgage foreclosures and bankruptcies, accelerating as soon as the bubble burst. The next morning they listed their home for sale. They priced it to sell, which it promptly did, allowing them to store their possessions and head west. Larry and Mary decided that when the bubble burst someday that they didn't want to be anywhere near an urban center.

Larry and Mary's search for a safe retreat led them to locate a forty acre abandoned farm north of Durango and near the San Juan National Forest. It looked to them to be about as remote and safe as one could expect, but still allowed them access to retail stores forty minutes away in Durango. They fixed up the old farmhouse and moved in with their son, Zach, their daughter, Melanie and two dogs. By the September, 2008 economic downturn, which Larry referred to as 'the beginning of the end', they had raised a barn, a stable, planted fruit trees and learned to raise animals. They also constructed an underground storage unit in which they regularly laid up canned goods, beans, rice and other food that would sustain them when, as Larry said, "things get really, really bad" Against that future day Larry had acquired three rifles, two shotguns and four pistols of varying makes. Before ammo supplies began to dry up, Larry purchased and hid away a considerable supply. Larry and Mary were ready for what they sensed would be coming bad days.

When the Lawrence McAlister Hate Speech and Hate Weapons Elimination Act became law Larry and Mary decided that they would rather face criminal charges than to give up their firearms, which the new law required. They told their children never to reveal to any of their friends in town that they retained their weapons. The McDonalds loved their remote 'prepper' home. They felt safe in a world which was becoming less so.

206

52

Oak Mountain State Park

Pelham, Alabama

Ten thousand acres of rolling Alabama woods would normally hold a wide variety of wildlife. By the time Scott, Tim and his son Tyler arrived at the area's largest state park they began to wonder if the popular forested area had been hunted out. They left their school safe house at 3 AM, hoping to be deep in the woods and up Oak Mountain before sunrise. They were delayed, however, when they bumped into two other small groups of armed men. The men in all three groups wore full beards, as all men were by now bearded. Electric and blade razors were no longer useable and few had access to long blade razors as used in the 19th century.

They saw the first band of hunters from a distance, both groups heading in the same direction along state road 119 towards the state park. Scott decided to hunker down and give the hunting party ahead of them fifteen minutes before they started hiking again. Just as they reached the eastern edge of Oak Mountain State Park Tyler spotted four armed men just entering the woods on the south side of Alabama 119. Tyler's yelp at seeing them was too loud, however, drawing the men to wheel around to locate the source of the sound. Scott raised his arms, stopping Tim and Tyler. The two armed bands of men stared at each other, about four hundred feet apart. No one spoke.

Finally, Scott took the initiative, "Greetings, men....we're just here *to hunt*....don't mean you or anyone else any harm."

The armed man with two rifles slung on his shoulders looked sidewise at his three armed companions. Seeing no reaction, he turned back, stared at Scott and said in a deep-toned, menacing voice, "Hey *pal*, get outta here....these here are our woods. *Got it?*....You come in this park you may find that a stray bullet will find its way into *your ugly face*....We'll let you live for now, but scat....*now*....leave this park alone. Any *questions*, hunter man?"

Scott whispered to Tim and Tyler, "We're leaving, but *don't* turn your back on them. Just move backwards up the slope until we're behind those cars we passed up there on 119." Slowly they shuffled back up the small rise to 119 until they were out of sight of the belligerents. Tim asked his dad, "Pops, what do we do *now*? We came all the way to Oak Mountain, hiked who knows how many miles? Are we gonna' let those *jerks* keep us out of the best hunting area in this part of Alabama?"

"We don't have any *choice*, Tim," his father replied. "The three of us have either got to fight these guys who have *more* weapons than we do, or we wait for a time, and then we head straight west and hopefully avoid meeting up with them."

Scott silently prayed for wisdom. Looking the situation over, he said, "Let's just move off the road on the north side, down in that ravine that leads into the park. We'll wait for a good half hour. By then it'll be dawn. Then we'll head straight west, since they went south. We can't take a chance of bumping into those guys. They looked pretty much like us, just hungry men out looking for game to feed their families, but we're out-manned and out-gunned."

By nine AM Scott, Tim and Tyler were deep into the park, climbing up Oak Mountain, staying away from trodden paths. Tim spotted a large oak tree growing near the side of a deep, heavily wooded ravine. By helping each other up to the lowest branches, the three hunters were able to climb into the heavy branch structure of the imposing tree. Once in position, as comfortable as possible, the hunting party waited for game to come by their position.

They waited....and waited. And waited. The closest they came to spotting an animal worth bagging before noon was a large rabbit hopping through the woods at the edge of the ravine beneath their perch. The angle was such that no one had a good shot. All three were praying for deer, but so far no deer were spotted.

As they waited in the oak tree, Tim whispered to his son, "Tyler, have you ever heard the story of Masada?"

"Masa....what? I don't think so. What is it?

"It happened a long time ago, in Israel." Tim spoke softly, so as not to scare off any game, though the last three hours of waiting had about convinced the hunting party that they were wasting their time. "The Romans who occupied Judah back in Bible times built a large fortress at the top of a quarter-mile high mountain named Masada, south of Jerusalem. They chose the site because it was almost impossible to scale the cliffs that surrounded the fortress. Several Jewish rebels against Roman rule took over the fortress on Masada in 70 AD. Three years later Rome laid siege to Masada. They built a siege ramp up the side of the mountain. Then they brought up a battering ram and hammered their way into the fortress. When they got in they found the dead bodies of 960 dead Jewish rebels, who took their own lives over destruction by the ferocious, blood-thirsty Romans.

"Interesting story, Dad, *why* did you tell it to me?"

"Oh, no particular reason, son....It's just....It's just that sometimes people do things to avoid a *bigger* harm....Umh....Do you know what I mean?"

"No, *not really*, Dad."

"It's probably time," Scott whispered, "that we head back to the school. We're not going to get any game today, guys."

53

Colonel James B. Irwin Elementary School

Birmingham, Alabama

"Hey, Mom, what's for dinner? I'm *really* hungry." Chris, twelve years old, was noted at the safe house for having an empty pit for a stomach. The unavoidable problem was that the twenty families had now been living for almost two months at the school named to honor one of America's astronauts who walked on the moon. The food the families brought to the school was dwindling. On the first day Scott's wife, Sally, along with Audrey, were designated responsible for meal planning. Soon after the families locked themselves into the school Sally and Audrey inventoried the available food. They found that about three fourths of the food was in the form of canned meat, vegetables and fruit. They also counted over thirty bags of rice and beans. Dried spaghetti filled out the food available to them. Within two days there was no more bread, fresh meat, nor fresh vegetables or fruit.

Once the inventory was completed, the forty adults met to plan how they would consume the available food. Scott, who was seen by the families as their informal leader, asked Sally and Audrey to give their report.

Sally listed for the group what the inventory showed, then said, "It's clear to me that we have only enough food on hand to feed eighty-seven people for no more than seven weeks, give or take."

Beau snorted and said, "*Hunh?* What about all those canned goods and bags of rice I saw when we moved stuff

211

into the school kitchen? We must be the *worst* preppers in the land."

Sally looked down at her hand-written list, looked up at Beau and softly replied, "Beau, *brother Beau*, don't forget that the number of people is eighty seven. Multiply that number times three meals a day and you need 1,827 meals a week. Beau, that's over *7,800 meals a month*. Unless we can pray up some miraculous expansion of the food in hand we will *barely make* it seven weeks."

Audrey added, "Here's *worse* news. What Sally and I concluded, after counting up the food supplies, is that we have to cut back to *two meals* a day, even to make it through seven weeks."

"*What?*" The heaviest set man in the room was having none of it. "I would *die* if I don't eat three meals a day. How can you *seriously....*"

Scott interrupted, "Look, we're not talking about running over to the super market and picking up a few bags of groceries for dinner. The stores, as we all know, are *totally* picked clean. We only have what we have, and what we can *scavenge* in the days ahead."

Beau said, "Scott's right. Think about how we get more food once what we have is all *gone*. It's late summer, so it's too late to plant gardens. If we make it through the winter, which I pray that we will, then next spring we can plant gardens in the inner court yard here of the school. In the meantime we have to find ways to supplement our diminishing food supply. We had some success hunting right after The Day, but since then we've come back almost empty-handed. It looks like the woods around here

212

have been *hunted out*. Too many hungry hunters it seems. I'm open to ideas."

Sally added, "There's a dairy farm a couple miles from here. It has a large number of dairy cows."

"That's not an easy solution," Scott replied, "We don't *own* those cows, they're the property of that farmer. I don't know if I'm totally comfortable with just *shooting* the man's cows."

"Scott," Beau said, "*get real*. It's either shoot the cows and *live*. Or don't harvest them, and then ....*just die*."

"But, we're not *savages*. Most people here are Christians. We don't *steal* other people's property. We have to...."

"You know, Scott, those are nice words....but, man, *we gotta' eat*. If it's us or *some farmer....I choose us*. Plus, man, if you don't think that somebody will eat those cows if we don't, you're living on another planet. We've been here now what, how many days?....I'm already losing track of time....I betcha' that most, if not all those dairy cows have already been slaughtered and have either been eaten or are being smoked and dried for eating later. There are a lot of hunters in this area, and they *all* like to eat, you agree?"

Sally asked her husband, "Scott, dear, isn't he right? I love you dearly, but he has a *good* point. If the cows aren't used for food, they're not going to be used for dairy farm purposes. How would the farmer get them milked with no electricity? No gasoline to haul the milk in tankers to a processing plant, which has no electricity to homogenize the milk in any case. I'm just saying that if we have some gold coins, or silver, why don't we offer to *buy* a cow or two or three?"

The heavy set member of the group responded to Sally's idea, "I have a small bag of pre 1964 silver coins. If we can have three meals a day, I'll throw in my coins to buy a cow, *alright?*" For the first time since the group had fled to the school, laughter filled the room. The group adjourned after accepting the offer and appointing a group of three men, headed by Beau, to come up with a plan to negotiate to buy a cow.

54

Rancho McDonald

North of Durango, Colorado

"Dad, there's someone down at the front gate," Zach yelled across the barn yard to his dad, Larry McDonald, Colorado farmer and prepper.

Larry's head snapped up as he looked at Zach and then at Rancho McDonald's front gate. In the five years the McDonalds had been living at their remote Colorado ranch he could count on one hand the number of people who had shown up uninvited. He reached behind his back to insure that his Glock was securely on his belt where he always kept it when he wasn't sleeping. At night it would be in a holster taped behind the headboard of his bed. What Larry saw didn't cause him any great joy. Two large men, both armed with long rifles, were standing at his gate. It was some time now since America was attacked with multiple nuclear devices. The nukes' EMP effect knocked out the use of the McDonalds' electronic devices, but their water was pumped by hand, they had plenty of cut firewood, their plentiful food and ammo stocks were secure and their 1952 Ford pick-up truck still worked.

Larry decided not to get too close to the gate. He stepped forward just a few feet, on the way whispering to Zach to get a rifle from the house.

Seeing Larry move slightly in their direction, the roughest looking of the visitors yelled, *"Hey, man,* come over here and talk to us."

Larry stopped, saying, "That's all right. I can hear you from here. What do you *want?*"

"Okay, pal, have it *your way.* We're just trying to be....like....like....*friendly.....*you know?"

"What do you *want?* I'm not asking again."

"*Cool it man,* that didn't sound *too friendly* to me. We just need a little food. You know, man, some foodstuffs. *We're hungry.*"

Larry considered how best to respond, finally deciding it was best to terminate the conversation and get rid of the uninvited intruders to Rancho McDonald. Out of the corner of his eye he saw Zach, his rifle up to his shoulder, standing several feet away from Larry, just as he had taught him. "We don't have any extra food. You'll have to move on. Try the churches in Durango. Now, *scat.* We've got work to do."

The visitor who had said nothing so far started to lift his rifle into firing position. Larry filled his hand with his Glock quicker than the intruder could fully raise his rifle, calmly saying, "*Stop right there,* Kemosabi. *Lower your* rifle, now....NOW....or you *won't* be walking out of here."

The visitor slowly complied. The verbal visitor, though, took everything to a new level, "So you think you're the *Lone Ranger,* right? Well, you're gonna' need a lot more than that pea shooter in your hand and the rifle in your teenager's quivering hands to stop us from eating. I *told you* that we're hungry. We know you're preppers. We know you've got food, probably *lots* of food. It didn't take long in town to find out where the preppers in this area are located. Did you think you could put away enough ammo and food to last you *forever*? Did you think you wouldn't have to *share* it?"

Larry, his Glock steadily trained on the men at his gate, his voice rising, replied, "I told you to scat. Now *scat*. Get out of here....and don't *even think* about coming back."

"Mister, you must think that nothing has changed in this country. Ya' been up here in your little enclave and you must *not know* how many people died with the nukes and the fallout. Ya' must *not know* how many preppers like you have been taken out by hungry folks, folks like us. Everybody knows somebody who's a prepper and where they live, so no one is safe, get my drift, pal? We don't mean you no harm, we just wanna' eat. But since *ya' don't wanna' share*, we'll leave. Sure enough, we'll leave ya' little rancho enclave. But, pal, you can count *on one thing....*we'll be back....*we'll be back....when you least expect it*. Adios, *Mister Lone Ranger*. Tell Mrs. Lone Ranger that we have *plans* for her."

55

Colonel Jim Irwin Elementary School

"Sally, we're out of rice," Audrey was shaking her head as she looked at the empty food storage container.

"I figured we were close to empty. How about the frijoles, the beans?"

"We've got enough to feed the kids today," Audrey replied, "but not enough for the adults. I *don't know* what we're going to do tomorrow." The ladies had stretched their food supplies to almost eight weeks, originally estimating that seven weeks was the maximum. Each person in the school/safe house had lost weight. For a few weeks they were able to provide meals, even though limited, three times a day. They had to eventually move to a two meal a day schedule, but had been on a once a day schedule for the last three weeks.

Sally asked the five ladies in the kitchen of the school, "Apart from prayer, what's our plan to feed everyone tomorrow?"

"Today's food scouting party isn't back yet. Maybe they'll come across some food in one of the nearby houses."

"Audrey, our food scouting guys haven't located any food in abandoned houses for at least two weeks. That's one reason we're where we are. We *keep eating*, but we *don't* keep finding food. Eventually....eventually....we're *totally* out of food. We've already voted, twice, that we won't take food away from anyone. We only take food that has been left in homes by people who are *dead*, or who knows what, but, nevertheless, are no longer in their homes."

Sally jumped in, "But, here's the *final* issue, what Scott would call the *real* bottom line. Abandoned food is nowhere to be found, now. We can't raise food until next spring, and then it will take the growing season before we can harvest and eat the food. No one in our hunting teams has found any game in weeks. We all have been praying, but we need to prioritize our praying....Girls, *we are facing starvation*. We especially need to pray that the guys' plan to buy a cow *will work*."

"Oh, how I *wish* we had listened to the Bible," Audrey sighed, "if we had fled, like Marty and Tom and Liz and Max, we wouldn't be watching our children wither away and die. God knew what He was doing when He warned us to flee."

Sally replied, "What's the verse? *The prudent see the evil coming and flee from it.* May God help us."

56

Colonel Jim Irwin Elementary School

Beau led the 'cow hunting party', as it was so labeled by Audrey, his wife. He picked as his fellow hunting party members Mark, an ex-veteran, and Quinn, a nineteen year old, reputed to be a skilled marksman. Beau had a small bag of silver coins in his back pack, along with extra ammo for the rifle which was slung over his shoulder. His strategy was to wake up and leave the school before dawn, at about 5 AM. His plan complied with his rule that no one be seen leaving the back door of the school during daylight hours. They planned to return from their mission after dark. The very last thing they wanted, Beau insisted on frequent occasion, was to be seen going out from or going into the school, as it would alert others to the possible presence of the most valuable item in America – something to eat.

The plan was to hike briskly from the school west across the no longer traveled state road to the Pleasant View Dairy Farm, estimated to be a two mile trek. Walking in the dark, with only a half moon to illuminate their path, the three man cow hunting party arrived at the farm just after 5:15, before sunrise. Though they didn't come to the farm to use their firearms, they were armed because there was a high likelihood that the farm would be well defended.

Beau assigned his two companions to spread out and carefully approach what appeared to be the farm house, as it was the only residential looking building on the sprawling farm. Having driven past the farm frequently, Beau knew the general layout. The two large dairy barns stood to the left of the house. Another low-standing aluminum farm building was behind the house, with three milk transport trucks parked nearby. Though no cows were seen in the pasture adjoining the first barn, Beau concluded that either the farmer had moved his herd further away from the road, to a distant pasture, or that the cows had already been slaughtered and taken by hungry neighbors. They would soon know.

Once the three men came within a hundred feet of the farmhouse, they began to crawl on their stomachs towards the residence. Beau used low bird-like sounds as his method to communicate. Now within twenty-five feet of the house, Beau gave a low two-twirp signal. As soon as he softly whistled, Beau heard a round being chambered and felt cold metal behind his left ear.

The holder of the firearm pointing at Beau's brain growled in a low voice, "Son, you better not move too fast, or you'll *never move again.* Get my meanin? Your two fellow crawlers *better not either.*"

Beau slowly turned his head towards Mark and Quinn. He saw that they also were under the barrels of rifles. Beau swallowed hard, then said, "Sir, we're not here to *cause any harm....*we have guns because we weren't sure what we would run into."

"*No harm, hunh?* So you're in my front yard, with two other men with guns? And you're not here to cause harm? What in the world kind of *stupid pills* do you think I take? You got *just seconds* to tell me anything you want to say before you meet your maker, *get it?*"

222

"Sir, we came here to buy a cow? *That's all.* Just to buy a cow."

"*What?*....Come on, sonny, we've had lotsa people come by here to steal a cow, some of whom have done it, a few of whom are lyin' out back. But, *buy a cow?* That's a new one. Anything else before you're no longer a burden to society?"

"*Wait,*" Beau pleaded, "Wait....Look in my back pack, we've brought the money. Silver coins. You know, *real* money....just look....I'm *not* lying to you. Don't shoot us."

"Just because you've got coins on you doesn't mean that you brought the money to buy one of my animals. Maybe you *stole the coins* from the last farmer whose house you *snuck up on?*"

"Mister, we're *Christians.* There are over eighty of us. We're almost *out of food*, just like probably everybody else. But, we knew about your dairy farm and we talked about taking a cow. Instead, since we don't believe in *stealing*, we voted to bring these coins here and buy a cow, so our wives and kids can live. *Please believe me.*"

The farmer didn't know what to say. Of all of the people he had accosted coming onto his property no one had said they were Christians. The farmer was himself a believer, so these words slowed him down in what he was about to do to protect his property and the lives of his family.

Finally, the farmer said, "I'll tell you what. Anybody can say *anything* they want, but how do I *know* what you're telling me is true?"

"Sir, you can open my pack back and...."

"No, I mean about being a Christian. Give me your personal testimony. Either that or give me at least *seven* of the ten commandments. Your choice. Make it quick."

Beau quickly counted up to four commandments. Stealing, adultery, idols, murder. *Humh.* Beau decided he'd better explain how he came to know Jesus. Otherwise, he would be *with Jesus* very soon. He started speaking with his voice shaking, "Mister, ten years ago I was like any other person, any other American, any other graduate of UAB."

With a half-smile, the farmer said, "Myself, I'm an Auburn fan, but I won't shoot you for being *a roll tide boy.*"

Beau also smiled, thinking for the first time since he felt the barrel of the rifle behind his ear that he might actually live. He went on, "But I was asked by my wife to attend a neighborhood Bible study. I didn't want to go. I didn't believe there was a God, or if there was one, that He couldn't be approached by somebody with *my* background of rampant sin....*big time sin.*"

"OK, so you were a sinner. *Big deal.* Got anything else to say? *Hurry it up now.*"

"*Yes, sir.* Well, I went with my wife to that Bible study. The guy who was teaching that night answered my

224

many questions, some of the questions being world class *stupid*. We stayed and talked till almost midnight. Hannah, that's whose house where the study was held, actually went on to bed. But by the end of the night *I was ready*. I understood what Jesus did for me and how foolish I would be *not* to accept His free gift of salvation."

"So, Jesus is your what? Your *buddy*? Your co-pilot?"

"No. *Jesus is my Lord and Savior*. That's it. Simple. If you put that bullet in my brain right now....well....then I'll be in *heaven*....you would be doing me *a favor*. My favorite verse is from Philippians. It says, 'for me to live is Christ, to die is *gain*."

The farmer motioned to his two sons. They took their guns off of Mark and Quinn. Withdrawing his own weapon he reached down to help Beau to his feet. "Sonny, either you are *really dumb* to crawl up my front yard with weapons, or you're incredibly hungry and desperate for food *for your family*. Either way, I *believe* your testimony of faith. As your brother, *I can't* kill you. Just so you'll know, we have killed some folks who came here to steal our cows and *kill us*. If you *ever* try anything like this again, anywhere else, don't *even think* about doing it like this.

"Now, about the cow. Before The Day I *saw* what was coming. As soon as I realized what America was going to do to Israel, I shipped our herd, all but one beef steer, to market. Converted the proceeds to gold, silver and ammo. The one steer is salted and dried and hidden. Sorry, but I *can't* share that. Wouldn't be enough for a crew as large as yours, anyway. Now, sonny, you take your buddies and get going. The sun's coming up and you don't want to be seen out in the open, especially with your weapons being so visible. We may not be able to give you any food, but *I promise* I'll pray for you. All of you."

57

The Woods Behind the

Colonel Jim Irwin Elementary School

Chris and his little brother Bobby, aged 12 and 10, were bored. They were also hungry. They had been cooped up inside the Colonel Jim Irwin Elementary School near Birmingham, Alabama for over two months. They knew that the rules inside the school were strict. No one could leave the school, otherwise, they had been warned repeatedly, someone might see them and figure out that there were people, with food, hidden inside the school. But, they didn't think that it was fair that the boys who were teenagers, 14 and up, were allowed to leave the school and go on hunting parties with the men, looking for animals for food. They reasoned that they were almost 14, so how much harm could it cause if they snuck out to play in the woods behind the school. They hoped to be able to catch a rabbit or maybe a squirrel for food to help feed the residents of the hideaway. The group was now down to just one meal a day, with a small, very small snack for the kids before bedtime.

Chris and Bobby knew that there was only one outside entrance/exit door that wasn't blocked with stacks of desks and chairs preventing access, a single metal door which accessed the utility room in the back of the school. The boys carefully watched the men who took turns guarding the door, to decide the best time to slip out of the school. They soon learned that two men watched the door during the night, which was assumed to be the time of greatest vulnerability to marauders. During the day only one man guarded the door. He had control of the air horn which would instantly alert everyone in the school of intruders. Chris and Bobby decided to play a board game down the hall from the door into the school from the utility room. That way they could watch and see when the assigned guard for the day took his rest room break, as the nearest facilities to the utility room were down the other hall.

At just past 11 AM the boys saw their opportunity to escape to go play in the woods. They watched as the guard sauntered down the hall towards the rest room, his rifle slung on his shoulder. The minute the door to the rest room closed, the boys ran as quietly as possible to the interior utility room door, through the room and out the back of the school into the trees.

The longer Chis and Bobby were in the woods, the more fun they had. Throwing rocks into the creek flowing through the several wooded acres, chasing small animals, unsuccessfully and having the best time they had enjoyed in months. They ran further away from the school.

Snake Head was dozing. His duty as the back guard was to sit on the rear patio of a three story house on a cul-de-sac which backed up to a large wooded area. The twenty-seven men who lived in the house moved into the abandoned residence soon after The Day. They were all inmates at Donaldson Correctional Facility, a maximum security prison northwest of Birmingham. It hadn't taken long for the guards of the 2,000 inmates to conclude after The Day that their services would no longer be required nor paid. The guards needed to get home to protect their families from what was coming. The prison emptied soon after. None of the men in the house were still married. All bore extensive tattoos. Each had a firearm and ammo. Each was in prison for committing a homicide.

Chris chased Bobby across a ravine, up the far side and up to the edge of the woods. While running the boys kicked up layers of dry leaves in the ravine, causing a noisy ruckus, loud enough to wake up Snake Head. Snake Head snapped up his head, looking for the source of the noise. He hadn't heard kids playing since The Day. What was this, he asked himself? He soon found what he was looking for, as two pre-teen boys ran to and then out of the edge of the woods behind the house he was guarding.

Snake Head jumped up out of his plastic deck chair, jumped off the deck and quickly grabbed the two playful invaders of his space. Chris continued to chase his giggling little brother, unmindful of the large man now just feet away from him, closing in fast. Too late the two boys looked up at the same time just as Snake Head grabbed their arms. They saw a tall man with a snake tattooed on his forehead. The snake's mouth was open, with dripping fangs and forked tongue, the snake's body tattooed down the side of his head and then coiled onto his chest.

Bobby immediately started crying, screaming to be let go, pleading for his older brother to help. Chris was so scared that he couldn't scream or cry. Snake Head yanked both boys up by their arms into the air, their feet suspended from the ground. He growled, *"Who are you kids? What are you doing here? Where are your parents?"*

Neither Chris or Bobby could say a word, not only from the pain of being held in the air, but also their increasing fear of their captor. Snake Head moved Bobby's arm over to his hand holding Chris, grabbing their two arms in one beefy hand. With his free hand he keyed the walkie-talkie clipped to his belt. Beep....Beep. "Hey....Snake here....We got some *visitors* back here...."

"Beep....*Repeat, Snake*....Didn't get that...."

"I got *two kids* here....small....probably ten or eleven years old. Better come back here....*now*...."

Snake Head dumped the boys on the deck, saying not to even think about moving. Chris wrapped his arms around Bobby, their chests heaving in paroxysms of tears.

As frightening as was Snake Head's tattooed face, the boys weren't prepared for what they saw next. The slider on the deck flew open and out walked an even larger man than Snake Head. On his face was tattooed a human death skull, with darkened eye sockets, a gaping tattooed toothless mouth around his blackened lips and blackened teeth and tattooed jaw bone hinges. On the top of his bald head were tattooed the words YOU'RE DEAD.

Death leaned over and stared into the eyes of the distraught boys on his back deck. He said nothing, just staring his blackened eyes into the wet eyes of Chris and Bobby. He continued to say nothing, knowing that the mere sight of his death skull face was enough to scare out of the young intruders what he desperately wanted to learn. Where had these boys been hiding since The Day?

58

Rancho McDonald

North of Durango, Colorado

It didn't take Larry long after his uninvited visitors left before he realized that one of the four members of his family would have to be awake standing guard at all times. Larry took the ten PM to six AM shift, with Zach on guard from six AM to 2 PM and Mary on guard between 2 PM and 10 PM, when Larry took over. Each was armed with a rifle and a hand gun, along with extra ammunition. For the first three weeks the McDonald family members were on high alert, suspecting that their unwanted visitors would soon return. Eventually, though, with day after day and boring hour after hour shifts with no one seen approaching their mountain enclave, the adrenalin slowed and caution waned. Zach was the first to suggest that it was time to 'stop being so hyper'. At first, Larry refused to change the guard schedule, but after hearing Melanie, Zach, and especially Mary, complain repeatedly, Larry finally agreed. The family stayed armed, but no longer posted a guard for eight hour shifts. Larry insisted, though, on sleeping on the farmhouse's front porch during the night.

Larry's front porch sleeping vigil proved to be the family's undoing. The unwanted visitors, now joined by a pack of three more similarly hungry and desperate men, kept their word. They came back to Rancho McDonald when the McDonald family least expected it. Using long-range binoculars the intruders watched the McDonald family for three days and nights to insure that they knew what to expect when they made their move.

Larry kissed his wife goodnight, hugged his daughter and prayed briefly with his son. He made sure he had his Glock, his rifle and extra ammunition. He unfolded his well-worn sleeping bag and stretched out on the lawn chair on the front porch. Having worked hard during the day chopping wood he was soon sleeping soundly. The intruders let him sleep for two hours and then silently moved across the Rancho's grounds. Grabbing Larry's hands, including his hand near the Glock, proved to be easy, as they were outside his sleeping bag. His rifle and ammo were snatched at the same time that his hands, mouth and eyes were tightly duct-taped.

The tallest of the invaders, who had been the outspoken one at the McDonald's gate almost a month before, leaned over and spate his words into Larry's ear, "I told you, *pal,* that we would *be back.* If you had shared your food with us then, maybe we wouldn't have to do what we're going to do to you now, you *stupid, selfish jerk.*"

Larry twisted his hands trying to free them from the tightly-bound tape, but to no avail. He tried to scream so that the family members inside the farmhouse would hear the ruckus and flee. Once he did so a crashing rifle butt to his temple shut him down. The invaders quietly moved into the simple farmhouse, easily finding the three small bedrooms. Zach was given a quick death as his throat was slashed, his blood soon filling his bed. Melanie was rousted rudely from her sleep, as her mouth was roughly covered by the hands of the invader assigned to find and silence her.

Whatever it was that woke Mary, either Larry's muffled screams, or the creaking floorboards of the old farmhouse, she awakened just before the door to her room opened. She reached over to the night table, grabbed her 38 revolver, with which she was now quite skilled, and started to get out of bed. Just then the door silently opened. She saw the dim outline of two men coming into her room, neither of whose shape or height matched that of Zach or Larry. She quickly stood, holding the revolver in front of her with both hands, while shouting, "*Stop....Don't* come any further. I'm armed....*I will shoot.* I will do...."

Both men pushed through the door going for her gun, but not quick enough to stop Mary from unloading six rounds, three into each man. They collapsed to the floor, dead on arrival. What followed was not as favorable, as the next man to come through the bedroom door, cast his flashlight on his dead comrades, saw the gun in Mary's hands and fired two rounds into her chest. Mary was on her way to heaven, along with her son. The three remaining invaders grabbed Melanie, rushing her out onto the front porch.

They ripped the duct tape off of Larry's eyes, excitedly saying, "Pal, your stupid wife just killed two of my men, but she paid for it. *She's dead.* Your idiot son is dead. It's now just *you* and this *cute little thing.* You've got *one* choice, pal. When I pull that tape off your slobbering mouth I only want to hear where you've got the food hidden....and the ammo....and any gold or silver you've got stashed. If you *don't* tell us....*everything*....this girlie here

233

will be our new take along plaything. If you tell us....all of it....we *might* consider just killing her. We'd have to *feed* her if we took her along, anyway. So, *your choice*, pal. What will it be?"

Larry's eyes were raging at the invaders on his porch, looking wildly over at Melanie, as he realized that they were most likely both about to die. His next thought was why did he think he could hide food and ammo away in the Colorado mountains and no one would bother them. His plan didn't prove to be a feasible long-term solution in a deteriorating country he finally realized, only fleeing offshore made sense. But, he knew those thoughts were way too late. What to do when they ripped the tape off his mouth? If he refused to talk, to tell them where their stuff was stored, they would likely shoot Melanie. As bad as that would be, wouldn't it be worse for her to be taken by these creeps and raped to death? Will Melanie talk if they kill me?

The tall invader reached over ripping the tape off of Larry's lips. "Talk, stupid. *Where's your stuff?*"

Larry studied the piercing eyes of the face now just inches from his. He said nothing for a few seconds, and then he spat the largest glob of spittle he could come up with straight into the glaring eyes, at the same time kicking his legs, which were not bound, straight into the invader's groin, knocking him back across the porch and onto the ground. Larry jumped up from his lawn chair, but he fell forward on the porch as his legs were caught in his sleeping bag. Larry's face was now just a few inches from the intruder whom he had just kicked off the porch to the ground. The tall invader, flat on his back, grabbed a pistol from his belt, looked in rage at Larry and fired a round into Larry's forehead. Just as he fired, Melanie broke free from her captor, throwing herself onto her father, catching the intruder's second bullet fired in anger, ending her young life.

Standing up, the tall intruder motioned to the bodies on the porch, and said to his two remaining murderers, "*Idiots*....Let's get rid of all these bodies....Then, we'll find the food and ammo. It *can't* be that hard....Boys, I think we've found ourselves a new home. A new fortress. *Such a deal.*"

59

Colonel Jim Irwin Elementary School

Beau immediately knew they had a problem....a major problem. With his military background, Beau had been selected to be responsible for security in their hideaway. Scott and Gary had taken to calling him 'Bolthole Beau', which Beau actually liked as a nickname. When Chris and Bobby didn't show up in the interior cafeteria room for dinner, everyone recognized that the boys had to be located. After a quick, but thorough search, neither were to be found in the school building.

Beau convened a meeting of the men, asking the women to calm the children who were upset about their missing friends and get them to bed. Beau started the meeting by asking Gary to pray.

"Father, we are in trouble, we know it....We're asking you to help us find Bobby and Chris....soon....before they are found by someone who may have evil plans in mind. *Help us*, we earnestly pray. In Christ's name. Amen."

Beau commenced the meeting, "Men, Gary just said it. We're in *real* trouble. The boys must have snuck out when John was in the 'john', so to speak. You've heard by now that two hours ago I sent out Gary and Charlie to comb the woods, which is undoubtedly where kids their age would go to play. No success. They saw some evidence of scuffed up leaves at the edge of the parking lot leading into the woods, but, they combed the woods and saw no boys. They stayed well back from the sub-division that borders the woods on the north end, about a mile or so from here."

Charlie, a member of the search party, asked, "Don't we need to go back out and *keep looking*? Those kids are too young to know how to survive outdoors very long, right?"

Beau hesitated, knowing what he was about to say would not likely be taken well. After examining the palms of his hands, he looked up and said, "Men. This is how it is. We know there are marauding gangs of men who are looking for food, ammo and women. If our two little guys are seen out by themselves it won't take the bad guys long to figure out that they're living in a safe house somewhere. It's been so long since The Day that they couldn't be out and alive on their own."

"So, Beau," Charlie replied, "What are you *saying*? Do we all go out tonight and try to find them or not?"

"OK, Charlie, you're the boys' dad, so you're *not* going to like what I say, but we have to face the facts. The facts are that it's been about five hours now since the boys left. That's *fact one*. Fact two is that even though the wooded area is good sized, it's not *that* large. The boys should be back here by now. Fact three is the *tough one*....more than likely the boys have been grabbed by somebody. Otherwise, they would be here by now."

Charlie, a catch in his throat, asked, "So, Beau, what are *we going to do*?"

Beau stood and walked over to Charlie, putting his arm around him, saying gently, "My brother, we *can't* go out tonight and search. We've *tried* that. The boys aren't in the woods, but they are almost surely in somebody's custody. Whoever's got them, they're interested in only *one* thing. They will do what they have to do to get Chris or Bobby to give up our location."

"But, the boys heard you explain why no one can reveal to anyone on the outside where we are, or we could all die. They heard you pound on that, Beau, they *heard* it."

"Charlie, they also heard me warn the kids, all of them, *not* to go outside the school, but they did it *anyway*. Everybody in the intelligence field knows that a prisoner will ultimately break. *Everyone breaks*, is the reality of life. How long do you think it will take a twelve year old, and how old is Bobby...?

"He's ten."

"Alright, he's just ten years old. How long will it take to get the boys to talk? They're *scared*. They know they messed up. Whoever grabbed them knows by now that they have been living in this school. We've been made. If we all go out tonight looking, again, for them, then that would leave our safe house with little to no security. The women and children would then be by themselves. We *can't do that*, guys. We have to assume the worst and get ready for an assault any time....*any time*. In fact, we need to get the women and kids into the secure room, without any further delay. If we get hit tonight it will most likely be in the early morning hours, but, like I said, it could happen *any* time....Are we in agreement?....Any

239

dissenters?....Charlie, I know this is *hard,* but do you understand why we need to hunker down and get ready?"

Charlie, his head bowed, a large tear running down his right cheek, murmured, "I guess....*I don't like it*....but....we don't have a choice....do we?"

"No, Charlie, *we don't*.....Okay, men, let's get the women and children safe, get all of your guns and ammo and we'll meet at the entry door. The boys will have told the bad guys that the utility room door is our entry point The bad guys will do their best to breach it. *Let's get ready.*"

60

Colonel Jim Irwin Elementary School

Shortly after moving into the Colonel Irwin School as their safe house the 87 occupants jointly decided that they would secure one interior room, with no windows, as the 'panic room' for the women and children to hide should they be discovered at the school. Though it was small, the best room in the school turned out to be the windowless sports equipment storage room off of the gym, used by the school to store basketballs and other sporting equipment. Once the room was chosen, the contents were stacked along the walls of the gym. The second part of the plan was to open a second entry to the room through lockers out in the hall on a wall adjoining the storage room. Two adjoining lockers were chosen. The concrete blocks in the wall behind the lockers were carefully removed, allowing the women and children seeking security to enter the room through the chosen lockers.

The removed blocks were then mortared into the space occupied by the original entry door off of the gym, using the closest substance that the men could devise to look like concrete. They located some old paint cans in the utility room, matched the paint in the gym and painted the wall, effectively covering the only previously visible entry door to the storage room, now re-named as the panic room.

Hannah's prime responsibility in the hideaway was to gather all of the women and all of the children younger than fourteen. Whenever Beau decided that the women and children were to go to safety in the panic room,

Hannah was to corral everyone through the locker door entrance to the secure room. She counted off each person as they squeezed through the lockers and into the room, "Twenty women, eight female teens and twenty-eight boys and girls. Though I really wish it were thirty. Chris and Bobby, *where are you*, my dear boys?"

Beau positioned his small citizens army in the hall outside the utility room, which was the only un-barricaded entry to the school, and half a school away from the panic room. His defense force consisted of the twenty married men and nine male teens. Strategically Beau concluded that they should not be inside the utility room, as any invading force would likely blow the door with explosives, killing or injuring the defenders in the room. Instead, they had pre-positioned teachers' heavy desks in the hallway, behind which they would be able to pick off anyone coming through the door into the hall from the utility room.

The men had three large flashlights which were only to be used during the armed defense of the school, carefully preserving their precious batteries. Beau's plan was to temporarily blind anyone coming through the utility room door and into the hall, lighting up the invaders to facilitate their shooting. They placed their sleeping bags and bedrolls behind the desks, planning to sleep in their defensive positions for the night.

Two men stood guard closest to the door, staying awake so they could sound the air horn should an attack commence on the school. The night wore on with nothing untoward happening. Two o'clock came and went. At three AM Beau awakened and walked the hall, checking on his men, many sleeping fitfully. Just as Beau went back to his position, hoping to catch some sleep, he heard a noise, not a very loud noise, coming from the other side of the school building, the front entrance area.

Since Beau was fully awake now, he decided to walk down his hall, turn at the cross hall, then walk the long hall to the main entrance to the school to see if he could determine the source of the noise. He used a small penlight to illuminate his path. Just as Beau turned to go down the long hall a deafening crashing sound came roaring down the hall. Beau fell to the floor, his rifle at the ready. What he saw turned his stomach to acid. A large, heavy truck, what appeared to be a dump truck, crashed through the locked front doors, smashing glass and metal in all directions, then shoving to the side the school desks stacked in front of the doors. The truck shifted gears and accelerated down the hall, heading straight for Beau, who was caught in the truck's headlights. As Beau jumped up to run back towards his men he thought he saw several tattooed men in the back of the truck now careening down the hall, all armed.

61

Colonel Jim Irwin Elementary School

Beau didn't even think about it. It was instinctive. Too late he realized that he should have run down a hall to a different location than where his men were located. By running toward his defense forces he led the careening truck and its armed men directly to his forces. The firefight that ensued was brief. Once the truck negotiated the corners, it crashed headlong into the desks outside the utility room door, running over and instantly killing most of the defense forces. Those who survived the crashing dump truck were shot dead by the tattooed invaders. Snake Head jumped off the truck and walked the hall shooting any survivors in the head.

Death walked the other way in the hall in the direction they had just driven, along with his armed men. He shouted, "OK, guys. We know what we have to do. Find the gym, that won't be too hard, then we locate lockers numbered 127 and 128. They'll be on a wall outside and just down from the gym. Those kids didn't *make up* those numbers. That's our entry to *the women,* and from them we'll find whatever food they have left. Both should be *yummy.*"

Inside the interior storage room Hannah was awakened by the sound of the truck, then its crashing into the desks in the nearby hall. It was followed by rapid gun fire. The gun fire went from rapid to sporadic. Then it stopped. Hannah concluded that either their men had taken out the invaders, or alternatively, they were taken out by them. She silently prayed as she woke up the women, leaving the children to sleep.

"Ladies," Hannah whispered, "Our safe house has been invaded. I heard *a lot* of shooting, but it's stopped. More than likely, someone will be coming through those locker doors....*soon*....so....it will either be one of our guys who will come to tell us that we're safe and the invaders are dead....or....well....*somebody else.*"

A distraught Audrey whispered back, not wanting to wake the children, "Hannah, if our men are dead....then....we all know what will happen *next*....right?"

"Audrey, dear Audrey. Yes, we do know what would happen. We've discussed this and we've planned for this. We *know* what we have to do. It's not about the food, of course, they can take all that....If our men are with the Lord....then....then....we *can't* defend ourselves. We never thought we could. They won't want the younger children, they'd just be more mouths to feed. They *will* want us....twenty eight women and teen-aged girls. But, Beau told us that his experience overseas confirms that they won't take *all* of us. Some they'll *just shoot*, some they'll take along with them if they leave here. Gary's opinion was that if marauders overwhelmed us they may use this as their new location, if it's a better location than where they came from. Beau told us, if you recall, that the survivors of The Day will kill and destroy, growing in size and power as they take over remaining safe houses."

Shots rang out, but only a short burst, then silence. Then the sound of men shouting. At first, all the women could hear was mens' voices, but they couldn't make out either the identity of the men nor their words. Then they heard, *"Down this way....Here's the gym....It's along the hall this way....the wall against....here....just follow the numbers....a hundred and fifty....the numbers go this way....a hundred forty two....Ah....here we are....one hundred and twenty seven and twenty eight. The kids better have been *right*."*

The locker doors were jerked open and Snake Head pushed through into the storage room first, followed by Death, then their tattooed men. The two candles and one dimming flashlight in the room revealed the horrific tattooed faces of the intruders and the frightened, sobbing faces of the women. The noise of their abrupt entry awakened some of the younger children.

Death said *"Well....well....well....*what *do* we have *here*?" Turning to Snake Head, Death said, "Just like I said Snake, *yummy....yummy.* Even some *young yummies."* Death walked over to a teen girl shaking in fear as she stared in horror at his death skull tattooed face. He licked the side of her face with his blackened tongue. "*Yup*, yummy."

Death nodded to the seven tattooed men who were with him in the room, giving them permission to do whatever they wanted with the frightened, sobbing women and children. They began to sort through the women, making their choices. Death turned and motioned to Snake Head to come with him as he went back out through the locker entrance to what was constructed to be a safe room.

Hannah stood in the shadows along the far wall of the storage room. She offered up her final prayer, reached behind her back and then pulled hard on a small steel cable which was tied to the ignition pins on six hand grenades.

III

A YEAR
AFTER
THE
DAY

"As God overthrew Sodom and Gomorrah along with their neighboring towns," declares the Lord, "so no one will live there (in the Daughter of Babylon); no man will dwell in it." (Jeremiah 50:40)

"It got to the point where the only thing we really thought about was food. How to find it. How we were going to survive if we didn't find food. It was terrible, not knowing if we would survive, whether we would starve." (The World at War, PBS Series on life in the Warsaw Ghetto in WWII)

62

BBC Studios – Broadcasting House

Central London, England

The studio floor director for WORLD IN REVIEW counted down for the evening newscast. "Five....four....three....two...." He then pointed to the male talking head seated at the long curved silver broadcast desk, behind which was the show's global logo and the network's three large letters. The studio's numerous overhead lights brightly lit the two newscasters.

Looking directly into the lens of studio camera one, the carefully coiffed newscaster, his full beard precisely trimmed, read the news from the scrolling teleprompter reflected in the one way mirror suspended over the lens.

"Good evening from BBC's London studios. Tonight we look at the subject of *America – One Year After The Day.* As virtually everyone on the planet knows, America was destroyed one year ago today by the detonation of several nuclear devices in ten American cities. At the outset, a disclaimer on what we are about to report. Though we believe that the contents of tonight's program are accurate, viewers will appreciate that obtaining news from what used to be America is a difficult task. There are no existing news services still reporting news in the U.S. Consequently, most of the news that we can report has come to us from the few short wave radio operators who are still alive in the devastated nation. Only those who had an independent electric power source, of course, are able to transmit their reports and updates out to the world.

251

There are no known American electric utilities still generating to customers.

"For our first special report on this important topic we'll go to Major General Archibald Raleigh, who joins us from the Permanent Joint Headquarters at Northwood, here in London. Major General, thank you for joining us this evening. Let me just throw up the first question, a question which many here have asked in the last year....Where is America's military? What happened to the armed forces of what some called the hammer of the whole earth? Can you enlighten us, Major General?"

The screen was then split between the newscaster and a mustachioed military officer, in full dress uniform, battle and service metals covering his left chest. Somewhat scowling into the camera, he said, "Why yes, Robert, excuse me, that is....yes....Rab, I think I can help your viewers in this regard. Not only was the American federal government decapitated with the nuclear explosions a year ago, but the US military command and control structure was almost *totally* destroyed. Once it became obvious to individual American forces in the field, those, that is, who survived the detonations, that there was no one, literally *no one*, in charge, the inevitable took place."

"The inevitable, Major General, and *that was*?"

"They scattered, they left their posts. Compare what happened with what took place in New Orleans in the U.S. a few years back after Hurricane Katrina struck. Virtually all of the city's police and law enforcement officials bolted from their assigned and routine duties in order to help

252

their individual families. What the Yanks call the 'thin blue line' totally dissolved. Within twenty-four hours *no policeman* could be found anywhere in New Orleans. It appears that each law enforcement officer made the conscious decision to leave and protect his own family as his highest priority. Personally, I can't say as I blame them....actually. But, I should hasten to add, that's not our *official* position, obviously."

"Is that what happened, Major General, did the American military *abandon* their stations in order to help their own families? And what about America's police officers, did they replicate what the New Orleans police did?"

"Essentially, Rab, that's *exactly* what happened. Most of what we learned in this regard we obtained before communications with the U.S. military went down, which I should say took at least a week to ten days for reasons that we can discuss, now or later, if you wish."

"Sure. Go ahead."

"Well, there was some limited flow of information from the underground Cheyenne headquarters in Colorado, at first, as I said, but over time it came to a halt. Initially, some of the ranked officers who were not killed in the nuking of America were still in place, but they had a problem. There was no command and control from Washington, DC, or anywhere else. Plus, with the troops very quickly drifting away to help their families, taking their firearms I should add, they had no one *to command*. So, with control gone from *the top* and troops gone from *the bottom*, these ranked officers, we understand, eventually saw the handwriting on the bunker wall, and themselves left to go help their own."

"And, Major General, what about the police forces in America after The Day?"

"Oh, yes, sorry. Our information regarding America's police forces is more sketchy, as we had no regular communication protocols with those officials. But, having said that, our intelligence services have gathered information from the short wave operators whom you mentioned at the top of the show. It appears that the police forces fled quite quickly in the large and medium sized cities, those not hit by nukes, of course. But we have a few scattered reports that in several small, actually very small, communities the local law enforcement officers continued to enforce the law and continued to do their jobs. Sadly, that didn't last for a lengthy time. We understand from these scattered reports, which we get on occasion, that with no pay and no support from missing governmental structures, those police officers who stayed on the job *eventually* gave into the inevitable."

"In this case, the inevitable was....?"

"Rab....that's the thing....You are well aware of Her Majesty's government's official estimate released just this week?"

"Our viewers have heard the report, naturally, but, Major General, why don't you cover the key points?"

"The calculation as to the death toll in America over the last year was derived by Her Majesty's government from a variety of sources. Our Royal Air Force planes were used, in part, for fly-overs. Relief agencies were understandably reluctant to send personnel into a radioactive environment. The airplanes were able to photograph metropolitan areas, largely. Counts were then made of dead bodies, those, that is, Rab, which were exposed and in the open. We were not able to count those who were deceased who were *indoors*, obviously. The persons who survived didn't stay that way by being out in the open where they could be seen by others, including by airplanes. The report cites a U.S. Congressional study of a few years back that estimated that if the country were to be hit by multiple nukes, EMP or any other major attack, that the American population would be reduced by 90%. Within the first year. Her Majesty's report concluded that the *actual* death rate in the last year has been between *92 to 93 percent. Very sad to say.*"

"That would make the attack on America, one year ago today, would it not, Major General, *the largest single loss of life in the history of the world?*"

"Let alone, Rab, the most *significant single man-made event* in world history - I should think."

63

Ambergris Caye, Belize

"Jack, you realize, I assume, that only God could have freed you and your family from the U.S.?" The question was posed by John Madison, Jack's father, who had been living in Belize, along with his wife, Debbie, for almost three years. Jack and Allison, with their two children, had managed to flee through Canada, eventually arriving by boat in Belize. At the time of their departure Jack was the pastor of a large church in Dallas. His final message was one of warning to his congregation explaining why he was fleeing the 'Daughter of Babylon' and suggesting that they consider doing the same.

"No question, Dad. We were definitely on the *'no fly list'*. Our only way out was the back door through Canada. Your suggestion that we use gold coins to buy passage here was spot on. Nobody wanted dollars even then. Now that the U.S. has been destroyed, the dollar has about as much value as moldy Confederate money. I'm sorry you had to go through more federal agent harassment. At least they didn't arrest you or Mom when they were looking for us."

"Jack, since we retired and fled by cruise boat to Belize I've tried to stay calm, keep the ticker from racing, you know. But when the two suits stood out on this porch and tried to intimidate me into giving you up, *I lost it.* I threatened to throw them off the porch."

"I wish I could have seen *that.* They're normally used to cowed compliance. Now that Washington DC is history, do you think there's any chance at all that they'll be back?"

"Not possible. Federal agents have to be paid, just like anybody else. There's no government left to pay them, so the likelihood of our ever hearing again from the feds is slim to none. However, Jack, even though that's no longer a concern, I do have what has become an emerging source of *worry*....oh wait....I'm talking to a pastor....*a source of interest.*"

"It's alright, Dad, as humans we *all* worry. The secret is knowing how to cast those worries on the Lord and let Him deal with them. What could you be worried about, though? You live in a tropical paradise? Health issues?"

"No. Your Mom and I are both in pretty good shape, all things considered. It's about Belize. A lot of this little country's income is based on American tourism. That's over, of course. We don't travel around Belize much, we stay pretty close to this rented condo, the beach, the boat and a couple of stores down the road. But what I'm hearing from other expats is that Belizeans are increasingly hurting, *financially.* No tourism income equals a loss of money to pay bills, to buy food, to live."

"Hunh. I guess I hadn't given that much thought. How *bad* is it? How will the Belizeans treat American expats?"

"*That,* my son, is the source of my concern. I've already heard about some expats who live in the mountains whose houses have been broken into."

"But isn't petty theft just a normal way of life? Even in the U.S. we...."

"True, but I'm not talking about petty theft, say of a laptop or TV. I've been hearing that when the houses were broken into whoever did it cleaned them out. Totally. All the food, all the clothes. Everything in the kitchen drawers. Appliances. *Everything* that could be carried out."

"Wow, Dad, that *doesn't* sound good."

"No, Jack, it doesn't, but yesterday I heard that an American expat was driving his pickup and stopped at a bridge where a car blocked it. He started to get out to help and three guys jumped him, hit him in the head and *slit* his throat."

"Slit his throat? OK, now I get why you're worried. What are you *thinking*?"

"I'm thinking that it won't be too many days, or weeks, before the folks who are hungry decide to boat over to Ambergris Caye and hit us. Actually, there are numerous Belizeans who live here who have been affected negatively by Babylon, excuse me, America being destroyed. So....I'm thinking we need to *boogie* while we still can. I know it sounds weird to consider fleeing from the safe place we originally fled to, but things have changed. So we need to change, too. Wherever we go we have to avoid countries with a significant Muslim population. The little news we still get here confirms that the Jihadists are on the attack to *take over* the governments in Europe, Africa and Asia, that is, that aren't already in Muslim hands."

259

"Allison will do whatever you guys think is best. She's frankly still *in shock*. Shock from moving out of the U.S. Shock at living in a different culture, even though we haven't been here very long. But her biggest shock....*our* biggest shock....is trying to adjust to the fact that America, as we knew it, *is gone*. Terminated. Annihilated. How can we *ever* get used to that? So many dead. So many dying. It didn't *have* to happen. I can't get that verse out of my mind....you know, in Jeremiah 51:9 where God says 'We would have healed her, but she is not healed'. We didn't *have to* turn away from God. We didn't *have to* betray Israel."

"I know....I know....but just thank God that He loved us enough to give us ten warnings to flee before the Daughter of Babylon would be destroyed. He didn't *have* to do that. But, He did. Now, we need to give prayerful thought to our next location. I did some research a couple months ago, once I realized how much the economy here is dependent on American tourism. What I concluded is that we need to either get to Australia or New Zealand or move far south in South America. Either Chile, Uruguay or Argentina. All three had very little U.S. tourism. Every nation's economy has been hit hard by the loss of the U.S. The Bible tells us in Revelation 18 that the merchants of the world look at the fall of Babylon and wail at their loss. But we need to move as far away as possible from folks who are *enraged at Americans* for their economic losses, their lack of food."

"I get it. What about Australia or New Zealand? Or even China, or...."

260

"China's out. It's guaranteed that they'll be in an economic depression. Not only won't we be shipping them billions of dollars from sales at China-Mart, excuse me, Wal-Mart, but the U.S. owed China 1.2 *Trillion* dollars. Nope. *Forget China.* Australia and New Zealand are possibilities. Very little U.S. tourism, but the question is *how to get there.* Almost every air flight from this part of the world to that part of the world went through the U.S. Or at least they used to. I could only find a flight or two out of Chile that used to fly direct. The other alternative is to fly from Panama to Europe and fly east across the globe to Australia or New Zealand. But, I'm not comfortable with even passing through a Muslimized Europe. We could drive from Belize to Panama, but we'd need to be armed, maybe even hire a couple guards to make sure we get to Panama."

"South America is *closer.* Which country is easiest to get to?"

"Either Chile or Uruguay. I ruled out Argentina."

"Yeah, the government there seems hell-bent on destroying their own economy. What are flights like now to Chile or Uruguay? "

261

64

Colonel Jim Irwin Elementary School

Death and Snake Head were happy, very happy. Not just because one year after The Day they were still alive. Not just because they uncovered that morning a cache of liquor hidden in an outbuilding behind a house in Pelham owned by a grocery store manager, who was long dead. Not just because they also found a large box of ammunition near the liquor stock. No, Death and Snake Head were overjoyed because they had been given the location of a small, supposedly well-provisioned gang hiding out a few miles to the east in Mountain Brook, formerly an upscale suburb of Birmingham. The expensive houses in the community had long ago either been looted or burnt. Prowling through the neighborhood streets during the year since The Day they had not seen anything to indicate that there was anything still left worth grabbing.

However, Snake Head had just persuaded a captured emaciated, obviously on the edge of starvation teen-ager, who was on a solo trek looking for food, to disclose where he had been living in the last few months, after The Day and through the biting months of winter. The shaking, sobbing teen finally revealed that he had slipped out late at night from a hideaway located in Mountain Brook. Before Snake Head took the young man's life, he forced the teen to draw a map of the location of the hideaway with enough detail for Snake Head to locate it without hauling along another hungry mouth to feed. The basement of Building Six at Bluemont Gardens in Mountain Brook. Bingo.

Snake Head reported his findings to Death. Death smiled, his blackened teeth showing through his tattooed skull mouth. He smoothed his bald head, on which was tattooed YOU'RE DEAD, with both hands. Death was pleased, very pleased, saying to his fellow gang leader, "Snake. Ya' done good. We be now up to eighty-six commandos, but we gotta' grow. If we don't add more shooters, the other gangs will, and then we be out-manned, out-gunned and we be dead."

Snake Head, the tattooed snake on his forehead glistening with sweat, smiled back, "*True that*, Death. So far, our little hidey-hole here at this school has escaped the attention of the gangs out there. The Bible thumpers done picked a good spot. Without more men and arms, though, one day it'll be discovered and they'll over-run us. I keep hearing about a gang that's well over a hundred and ten, at least that's what I hear. Supposed to be holed up at the UAB Hospital in Birmingham on 6th Avenue. If we don't add to our strength, that gang will head south down 280 and *take us out*. We've got to grow to at least as many shooters."

"Snake, how *many* did your dead snitch tell you are hiding in Mountain Brook?"

"He wasn't positive, but when I twisted him a little, he estimated between 20 and 24 men."

"Humh. But how many teen boys? They be our only possible new gang members, don'tcha know. Did he say how many women and teeny-bops?"

"He was sure on that number, Death. Twenty eight. Eighteen women and ten teen-age girls. About the same number of teen age-boys and some younger kids. I got him to tell me that three or four of the women folk were real lookers. He got all *weepy* on me when I pushed him on whether any of the females were related to him. "

"And?"

"His Mom and Dad are alive, and his sixteen year old sister is there. Or at least she was there."

"Meaning?"

"The kid said his sister told him that she was thinking either of running away or maybe killing herself. Said she was tired of worrying every day, every minute, that some gang of killers, you know, like us, I guess, would find their hiding place and she would be passed around by the men. You know, Death, the kind of *feminist clap-trap* we've heard from some of our women. They just don't *get it*."

65

BBC Studios – Broadcasting House

Central London, England

The co-host of WORLD IN REVIEW thanked Major General Archibald Raleigh for his contribution to the BBC's special report, *America – One Year After the Day.* He turned towards his female co-host, in what journalists call 'throwing' the newscast to her, "More than a ninety percent casualty rate. So, Jala, what do we know about the causes of such a high death rate? What led to these *astounding numbers* of dead Americans?"

"It's not a simple answer, Rab, as we learned in putting together tonight's special report. To help us understand what actually happened to our dearly departed cousins across the pond, we are joined by an American reporter who was not in the U.S. a year ago, as she was working here in London at the time as a foreign relations reporter for the New York Times. The newspaper is no longer published, thus Gretchen Rice is in studio with us as a private citizen. Thanks, Gretchen, for coming by to help us understand the result of the nuking of ten American cities. First, it is estimated that about fifty-five million died either on The Day or within a few days after as a direct result of the detonated nuclear devices. That's only about 17% of what was then the total population of about three hundred and fifteen million. So, how did the percentage of deaths grow from under 20% to *over 90%,* according to the British government report about which we just heard?"

Dressed modestly in a black business suit as befitted the occasion, Gretchen Rice looked down at the notes shaking slightly in her hands, then gazed into designated camera three, softly saying, "Jala, it was a combination of *many* factors. Let's first examine the most vulnerable. Hospitals and medical care clinics and facilities in America were *quickly overrun* as soon as people realized what had happened to their country. Patients in hospitals and residents of American nursing homes did not....well, let me just say that....they were among the *first to die*, apart from those who were vaporized by the heat and blast of the devices themselves, of course. The next persons who died quite quickly were those who were exposed to radiation from the blasts, generally those within three to five miles of the point of detonation. They didn't last much longer than *a few hours or days*, depending on how close they were to the nuclear detonations.

"Gretchen, we've read that American hospitals in or near the cities which were struck directly by nuclear devices were *overrun* and unable to provide any meaningful level of medical care to those who were near the detonations?"

"Yes. That's our understanding, again with the disclaimer that much of what we know came from unverified sources, but are believed to be accurate. An average hospital with say 100 to 300 beds couldn't even come close to treating *the thousands* of radiated persons knocking on their door. Pharmacies located in hospitals and general retail drug stores were quickly *cleaned out,* most by widespread looting. Pharmaceuticals available in the U.S. appear to have disappeared shortly after The Day.

268

Before we leave that subject, Jala, many further deaths occurred over the next several weeks and months as those who had previously survived on manufactured pharmaceuticals *didn't make it*, once they could no longer obtain their meds. That *alone* was a big factor in the exceedingly high death rate."

"Is it the case, Gretchen, that almost every store, food markets, clothing, hardware, all types of retail establishments, were, to use your phrase, 'cleaned out' and looted? If so, *how soon* did that happen after The Day?"

"Jala, my sources at the time, just under a year ago obviously, told me that the looting of retail stores in America was *almost instantaneous*. By that I understand that Americans who heard on the news that their country had been attacked with nuclear weapons wasted no time in rushing to the nearest mega-malls, strip malls and local stores. There were early scattered attempts by owners to ward off looters, but that apparently didn't last long. Within twenty-four to thirty-six hours of the detonations, as I understand it, virtually all retail establishments in America had either been blown up in the cities nuked or looted by those who survived the blasts."

"Gretchen, we mentioned at the top of the show that there do not appear to be any operating electric utilities in the U.S. Is that consistent with what you have been able to learn over the last year?"

"Yes....sad to say. Those electric utilities which operated on coal shut down early on, as it took diesel fuel for the trains which hauled the coal from the mines to the generating stations. As you may know, American oil refineries did not survive The Day for a variety of reasons. With no electric power, water systems couldn't function, which, of course, meant that sewage treatment systems ceased to function. Within hours of The Day, simply stated, America just *ceased to function.*"

"Can you tell us, Gretchen, what was the impact on everything you've just described to us of EMP weapons, those emitting an electro-magnetic pulse?"

"Well, Jala, there's not been a consensus on that subject. Normally a HEMP device, that is a High Altitude EMP device, is launched into the mid-stratosphere in order to have maximum effect over a wide area on the ground. Because the U.S. military was so hampered immediately after the attacks we were never able to confirm if any the cities hit by nuclear devices were by HEMP devices launched above the cities. It's possible, of course, that some of the nuclear devices which appear to have been land-based, in offices, or condo buildings, or in motor vehicles, were constructed with EMP emitting capability. That would explain why so many motor vehicles were disabled on American highways, clogging those roads to transit, more than would have just run out of fuel, I would think."

"Finally, Gretchen, a topic that I think most of us here in the UK would rather avoid, but many people are quite interested, particularly if they had family and friends, business associates and the like, in the U.S. What can you tell us about the status of the seven or eight percent of Americans who are still alive, who *didn't die* in the detonations, or since due to the devastating effects of a collapsed, non-functioning society?"

"All that we know, Jala, is what we have learned from the Royal Air Force fly-overs, by the Sentinel R-1s, and from the short wave broadcasts which we have discussed. Those who were able to flee America after The Day on available ships which were not destroyed in the blasts are not much help to us, from an information viewpoint. The last ship or plane to transit the Atlantic from the U.S. was many months ago. Our satellite systems of communication with the U.S. have been inoperable from almost day one, as the sending/receiving stations on the U.S. end of the system were either immediately taken out in the blasts, or ceased to function over time without power and with exhausted fuel for back-up generators."

"Given those limitations, Gretchen, what can you share that we *do* know?"

"It's not good. In fact, it's very, *very* bad. There were many Americans who saw that the nation was a target for future troubles. They were what were then called 'preppers', because they laid up substantial stores of food, weapons and other preparations for future survival. Some of the short wave transmissions that were received came from 'preppers'."

"That seems like a wise and prudent course of action. How are the 'preppers' in America faring?"

"Not well, Jala, not well *at all*. It seems that most 'preppers' knew other people who were *not* prepping, as they say. After the food supplies dried up, and there was no electric power, no gasoline, you know, then people who knew where they could find such vital items, that is from the 'preppers', located them and *took* what they wanted.*"

"But, Gretchen, didn't that lead to....*violence*? Were they willing to share what they had stored up?"

"We understand that *some* shared. At first, but when people get hungry they....well....let's just say that they lose some of their normal societal inhibitions....Then....they do what they have to do....to....*survive*. The end result over the last year has been that millions have died, either directly from starvation, or killed at the hands of starving people who wanted what people had stored up. Some of the things we have heard from short-wavers are *truly beyond belief*. In my opinion the percentage of Americans still alive is more like two to three percent, and that may be overly generous."

"Gretchen, without dwelling too much on the macabre, what does America look like *today* – a full twelve months, 365 days since The Day? We're about out of time, so I'll ask you to be concise, please."

"Imagine this scene. This is America one year after The Day. No houses or apartments are lit at night, not by electricity, of course, but also not by candles or oil lamps, as any light seen at night is an invitation to marauding bands of cutthroat killers anxious to find food and new prey. In the day time, no one with any sense goes out into the open, for the same reason. Spotters will alert the gangs and they will track and follow you back to your place of hiding, hoping to loot, rape and destroy.

"The result, as we understand it, is that what is left of America belongs to the armed gangs, many of whom were prisoners on The Day. They either escaped or were released from jails and prisons which weren't nuked. The U.S. had over two million prisoners incarcerated on The Day, the highest number in the world at that time. Estimates are that at least one million survived and are now in gangs. The gangs number from small, 15 or 20 killers, all the way up to what amount to armies, small armies, but with several hundred armed men, all safely hiding in tightly barricaded buildings, warehouses, office buildings. The type of building varies depending on the army. But, the critical aspect of their encampment is that have to be able to secure their bolt-hole location from entry by other gangs, or other armies who want to get what they may have."

"Wrapping up, Gretchen, you didn't mention how women and children are surviving in America in these perilous days."

"I didn't forget, Jala....I just didn't want to be the one who....well....the ....uh....gangs don't need youngsters, whom they would have to feed, or older women and certainly not any men who may have families and who need to try and protect them. It appears, Jala, that apart from teen-aged women and younger women who are allowed to live as....you know....as....sex slaves....sorry to say, *almost all* of the population still surviving and alive in the U.S. are men in gangs, in small armies. *I sincerely regret to report.*"

66

Carrasco Community Church

Carrasco, Uruguay

Pastor Jack Madison stood in front of the group assembled in a vacant storefront on Cambara Street. He smiled, swallowed hard, took a deep breath and began his first South American Sunday sermon, "Brothers and sisters, remember this day. The day when the Carrasco Community Church was born. Officially. What started two months ago with our Bible Study of five couples is now a church of thirty folks. If we are faithful to preach the Word, God will be faithful to increase our impact for Him in Uruguay. I've been asked why the Madisons chose Uruguay, since it is reportedly the *least* religious country in Latin America. Good question. Simple answer. We had a few choices of countries, but we wanted to be involved in a ministry where we could effectively spread the Gospel. Where better than in a country which *needs* evangelizing? Uruguay is our family's new mission field. We're very excited about it.

"Some of you know that I was a pastor in Dallas. It's a long way from Dallas to Carrasco, but anyone who knows the Bible understands that it records the many times that God moved His people from their comfort zones out into the world to share the Gospel. We pray daily for the dear people in the church that we left behind in our church in Dallas. Fortunately, Dallas wasn't one of the cities nuked, but with no gasoline or electricity, the result, as you know, was a scarcity of food, medical care and the basics of life. Communications being as poor as they are,

275

almost now non-existent, we have no word on how those whom we knew and loved are faring in a destroyed America. We *pray* for them, as I said, but there's precious little else anyone can do."

As he spoke, Jack looked at his wife, Allison, their two children and his mother and father, John and Debbie Madison. He reflected on how good God was to allow all of them to flee the Daughter of Babylon. He remembered briefly how his father had been indicted by the federal government for supposed hate speech in which he was charged with attacking the President in political speeches in Texas. John Madison had been set free, after a jury ridiculed the government's case in opening jury selection. Jack's memory flitted over the fact that, soon after, the federal government indicted Jack, also for hate speech violations, after he gave the Biblical view of traditional marriage in a Sunday sermon. Jack silently thanked the Lord, again, that he was tried and found innocent by the federal court jury, who took less than an hour to deliberate, not even enough time for the jury to order pizza. Now Jack's family members were gathered safely in a new place of divine adventure. God is good, Jack reminded himself.

"Most of us are Americans who chose to leave our native land. We've chosen to settle in this peaceful country for different reasons. One couple told me they were most attracted by Uruguay's rating as the freest nation in the world, with the fewest government laws and entangling regulations. Others moved here instead of nearer the equator because didn't like the heat. One couple has a child who came here as a missionary to the Uruguayan cowboys. Whatever the reasons for moving here, we have assembled ourselves together to see what God wants to do through us in our new home. I encourage each one of us to seek out a ministry in which you can be involved. I'm looking forward to a future Sunday, hopefully with even more expats who have joined with us, when we will share stories of *the Lord at work* through a bunch of re-located Yanks. What *a blessing* He has given to us."

67

Bluemont Gardens

Mountain Brook, Alabama

Mountain Brook's initial claim to fame was its Irondale Foundry, but it was destroyed by Yankee soldiers in the War of Northern Aggression, a/k/a the Civil War. Over time the area became famous for the several dairies located on its rolling and wooded hills. In the 1940's a local developer constructed Bluemont Gardens, an apartment complex with twenty high-ceilinged, wood floor buildings. In the mid to late twentieth century the area was extensively developed with expensive and imposing houses.

Mountain Brook after The Day was an immediate target for looters and hungry Alabamians who assumed that houses as large as those in Mountain Brook would have plentiful food and ammunition for the picking. Residents soon fled or tried, unsuccessfully and fatally, to defend their assets. Within just days every McMansion in Mountain Brook had its windows and doors smashed in, most razed by fire. The same thing happened to the twenty buildings in Bluemont Gardens. Because it was such an obviously looted and pawed over site, Darrell Wright, the group's leader, saw it as a perfect place to hide their several families who had come together from local homes and churches. Darrell was an engineer with a construction background. After some study he decided to select the basement of a large interior apartment building, one which from the outside looked totally ravaged. The windows and doors were all blown out. The ivy on the red brick exterior was burnt black from the fires that had been set in the complex. To any casual visitor coming through the apartment complex it looked just like the other destroyed buildings.

Death and Snake Head took their time. Once they figured out which building was number six they watched the hide-away from another building, though carefully hidden so they would not themselves be spotted. Death was the first to spot the armed, relatively tall man emerge from the burnt-out main door just after dusk, sneaking out so that in the fading light he wouldn't be seen. He carried an AK-47, with four ammo clips on his belt. He was followed by another armed man, with an AR-15, and two teen males, both carrying 22s. The four looked carefully around the apartment complex for unwanted visitors before they set off to hunt for game.

Death whispered to Snake Head, "Piece of cake. Your dead kid snitch was *right on.* It's a pretty good hideaway from a location viewpoint. Who would ever think anyone would be here? *What a dump.* But, from their defense standpoint, it stinks. It looks like they all go in and out of that entry door there. Inside there must be a stair down to their hidey-hole basement. Can't see any lights at all. Very good. Very good."

Snake was excited, as he could imagine fresh food, and armaments and women in his future. He was also apprehensive. He asked, "Death, what's *our* plan? We don't want to lose a bunch of guys to a bomb or to hand grenades, like back at the school."

"Don't remind me, Snake, if we hadn't stepped out when we did *we'd* have been blown apart like our buddies. No. My plan is simple. We quietly go into one of the first floor apartments, during the day when they're talking and making noise so they don't hear us. We hand drill a hole through one of the wood floors into the basement and pour a gallon or so of our remaining gasoline down the hole. They didn't use pre-stressed concrete floors to build apartments in the 40s. One match and we got a parking lot full of scared, suffocating people. As each one pops out of their little hidey-hole we wait by the entry door and disarm them. Like I said, Snake, *piece of cake.*"

68

BBC Studios – Broadcasting House

Central London, England

The co-host of WORLD IN REVIEW thanked Gretchen Rice for her contribution to the BBC's special report, *America – One Year After the Day*. She threw the newscast back to Rab, her male co-host, "Not a very cheery report, Rab, but, of course those of us living in the UK have known for almost a year how truly *devastating* was the collapse of what was then the world's remaining superpower. To wrap up our special tonight, Rab, what have we learned about the impact of the attacks last year on America's nuclear power industry?"

Rab smoothed his beard with one hand while gazing into camera one, carefully enunciating, "Well asked, Jala. This is really the other part of the story upon which we are reporting tonight. By now most persons on the planet know about the sneak attack on America, with an as of yet not totally known number of nuclear weapons, though it is known with precision that the bombs were all set off within ten American metropolitan areas. As we have reported, millions died immediately, estimated at around 55 to 60 million, with many millions more dying from radiation sickness, fallout health issues and the like. Once the initial nuclear device-caused deaths took place, the second large waves of deaths took place, from starvation, rioting, looting and the like. What has not been widely reported is that in the second wave of mass deaths, those that occurred well after The Day, there was a secondary cause of *additional* deaths. For the details on this story,

283

which the BBC is breaking for the first time publicly tonight, we go to Alastair Smyth, the recently retired Chairman of the Office for Nuclear Regulation. Thank you for joining us, Chairman Smyth."

The seventy three year old former British civil servant, looking every bit the part, replied, "Distinct pleasure to be with you, I'm sure."

"Chairman Smyth, we have only a very short time left in our newscast tonight, so I would appreciate if you could keep your responses brief. Let me just ask you, what have we in the UK learned about secondary causes of death in America that had been *largely unknown* until recently?"

"Humph....Humph....Well, let me just say that....Keep it brief, though, *right?* Certainly....Well....In brief, the one hundred or so nuclear reactors located at sixty five American nuclear power plants....well....they all experienced nuclear core meltdowns. Eventually....that is....*each one.*"

"Mister Chairman, can you explain to our younger viewers what that means? Nuclear core meltdown. Sounds quite *serious*, actually."

"It's much *worse* than serious. It's *catastrophic*, as we learned at Chernobyl and Fukushima, which took place 25 years apart. The results in Russia were epidemic cancers, what has come to be known as Chernobyl AIS, chronic fatigue, you name it. Genetically deformed and mutated human babies and animals. Horrible. Many innocent victims. The problem, Rab, is that about one third of all Americans lived within 50 miles of a nuclear power plant. So....humph....you can see the problem if the nuclear power plants all of them, uh, went into reactor core meltdown."

"Yes, Mister Chairman, you have explained what can happen when a nuclear plant, let alone over one hundred of them, go into core meltdown, but *why* did that happen, they weren't *all*, surely, within range of the nukes that were detonated?"

"Quite right. No, they weren't. A few were taken out by the nukes, of course, but most, we estimate at least three-fourths, were not destroyed by the nuclear detonations on The Day. The seventy to eighty that survived did not immediately go to core meltdown. What happened was caused by the Yanks making *two critical errors*, we now believe. They designed their nuclear power plants to be critically dependent upon maintaining connection to a functioning electric grid. Why? Well....humph....the electricity was *critical* to keeping the reactor cores *cooled* at any given point in time. Within two hours, give or take, after a failure to cool the reactor cores adequately the cores begin to *melt down,* throwing off massive amounts of radiation into the air, and into any nearby bodies of water."

"Surely, Mister Chairman, there were back-up generators at the nuclear plants should their electric grid power go down?"

"Well yes, Rab, of course. That was the second major error. The Yanks' Nuclear Regulatory Commission, which is very much like the agency I headed, that is, until recently, only mandated *a one week supply* of backup

285

generator fuel stored at each reactor site. Under normal circumstances, if a plant lost its electric grid power, it would go to backup generation, and if it saw a long term power outage it would be sure to start hauling in extra supplies of diesel fuel for the back-up generators, as much as would be needed."

"Ah, I see. *There was the rub*. America's electric grid went down with the nuclear attacks, as well as its *refineries*, so no new supplies of diesel fuel. The *result?*

"*Disasterous*. Truly catastrophic. It's almost as if those Yanks who lived through the initial blasts were then eventually felled by the radiation coming from eighty or so plus nuclear reactors, all in full meltdown mode, located all over the country. What an *unprecedented*....well, words fail me to describe what happened next. No electricity, no fuel. No cooling of the cores. *Full meltdown*. All over the country. Whichever way the winds would blow, radiation would soon follow, covering every square mile of the nation, eventually, with *high levels* of radiation, on top of what resulted from the nukes, of course."

"Mister Chairman, we have aired in this show the results of a British government study that 92 to 93 percent of the American population is no longer....this is difficult to say....but *no longer alive*. Before you came on the show we aired a segment from a former American newspaper reporter. Based on short wave transmissions and other sources, she opined that the number of Americans still alive could be even less. Do you have an opinion on this question of significant interest to many of our viewers?"

"Rab....humph....no one can be precise, naturally. But what I can say is this....however many Americans may still be alive, *very few*, if any will survive the next twelve to twenty-four months."

"Because of the *meltdowns?*"

"Because of the meltdowns and the radiation which has spread to every area of the nation. We are picking up increasing amounts of latent radiation in the jet stream here in the UK, as you may have heard. Incidentally, Rab, now that I have officially resigned as Chairman of the Office for Nuclear Regulation, I can confirm that all sixteen of the UK's reactors will be offline and eventually closed down within the next year, just as fast as they can be safely terminated as power sources."

"Well, breaking news here on the BBC. But Mister Chairman, what will that do to the UK's electric grid requirements? How can we survive without nuclear...."

"No, the question is how could we survive *with* nuclear power. The experience of the Yanks confirms that there are better ways to boil water and make electricity than nuclear radiation. We will suffer a great deal in the days ahead, not quite going back to the middle ages, though for many it will seem like it. We'll all....humph....*we'll just have to soldier on.*"

"Mister Chairman, thanks so much for joining us this evening, any parting words in the last few seconds?"

"Yes....actually. I'm not a religious man, certainly. But recently a nephew of mine, one of the funda....evangel....you know....*a Bible believer.* He showed me some verses. I don't know if I'm allowed to do this....now....that is....and I not yet sure as to what I believe, mind you....but...well, here.... I brought along a verse. Written by a chap named Jeremiah....let's see....50:40....whatever that means. It says *'As God overthrew Sodom and Gomorrah along with their neighboring towns, declares the Lord, so no one will live there; no man will dwell in it'...."*

The studio floor director tried to get the attention of the show's hosts, moving his hand across his throat in the universal cut sign, trying to terminate the guest's comments, but neither host was looking in his direction. The guest continued, "My nephew says this is in reference to America, which he says was the *Daughter of Babylon,* or maybe the Son....I'm not sure. I don't know how Sodom and Gomorrah were destroyed....or even if they were....but it sounds very much like nuclear radiation, since the *neighboring towns,* and their crops, were also affected. And the verses described darkened skin and stick-like legs and arms after the destruction....which sounds like radiation effects....But I will say that with the eighty nuclear core meltdowns across the pond I can easily see a totally devoid America, no population at all, none. Within just a few months. Humans can't tolerate that much radiation, not for very long anyway."

"With that parting note, Mister Chairman, thank you for being with us. Jala, will you close us out?"

Jala looked up at camera one through the narrow slit in her Burkha. "That's all the time we have tonight on WORLD IN REVIEW. Thanks to our distinguished guests and to our producers from Al Jazeera network. *Allahu Akbar, Barakallah* and good night."

The camera zeroed in on the large BBC Letters on the studio wall behind Rab and Jala. The letters were in two languages, British and Arabic. On the screen then appeared the slide which now ended all BBC programs:

THIS BBC/Al JAZEERA PROGRAM APPROVED BY

IMAM MAHDULA BAZARDI

Government Appointed Censor

The Islamic Republic of Great Britain and Northern Ireland

69

Carrasco Community Church

Carrasco, Uruguay

The Church had a problem. It now had more people attending the Sunday service than it had folding chairs to hold them. In just over a year attendance had grown to a hundred and thirty. To commemorate the Church's first year anniversary Pastor Jack Madison asked members to bring to the Sunday service stories of how they had seen God at work in their new home country.

After several spirited worship songs Pastor Jack Madison stood to lead the congregation in prayer. "Father, we *do* worship You....in spirit and in truth. Thank you for all that you are, *a great and magnificent God*. Thank you for bringing us here today to worship. Thank you for bringing us to Uruguay for Your good purposes. We don't take lightly Your guiding hand in bringing each one of us out of our home country. Use us here for Your good purposes. Open our eyes and ears as we see and hear the *many ways* in which You have been working through us in this pleasant land. In Jesus name we pray, amen."

Pastor Jack began their time by covering the Biblical imperative to share His Word with the world. He then opened up the service by asking those present to share their ministry experiences. A perky, smiling lady seated on the front row in the Church's storefront location quickly shot up her hand. "Yes, Sally, I thought you might be the first to share."

291

"Oh, Pastor, I've told this story to *many* here, but not everybody has heard how God worked....right here....in Uruguay. Several us here are involved in our Saturday morning kids club over in the park, two blocks from la Rambla. At first we just had four or five kids, but the word spread and now we play games, share Bible stories and give free rice and beans to nearly a hundred children....each Saturday. The first miracle I would like to share is that several of the Uruguayan kids have prayed to receive Christ. They'll be in the kingdom....They will...."

The congregation broke into applause interrupting Sally's narrative. Smiling back, she waited, then went on, "The second miracle that we've seen happened two weeks ago. We encourage the parents of the kids to bring them to the park where we play games and share the gospel. I noticed a shy young woman who had been there only once before, with her son, Juan, a cute ten year old. I could tell that she wanted to talk. My Española is un poco, but we were able to communicate, between us, in *Spanglish.*

"She had *quite a story* to tell. Her son had taken home the weekly small bags of rice and bean that we pass out each week. She had been out of work and had exhausted their supply of food. She told me that she had started to despair, in Spanish, *desesperacion.* Then she remembered that her son had brought the rice and beans home, which he had in his room. She cooked the rice and beans. They ate from the bowl each day. And the next day. And the next. And the next and the next. And the next, *for the whole week.* Get this. She asked me what we put in the rice and beans so that they *never get used up?*....Sorry....whenever I tell this I tear up....at *God's goodness.* Her story reminded me of Corrie Ten Boom's

292

World War II concentration camp miracle when God kept Corrie and her sister's small vitamin bottle from ever going empty. *What a God we have!*"

After the chorus of amens, praise and applause finally died down, Pastor Jack said, "Allie and I know that most of you in this room have become involved in ministries of various types. We've see great things happen in the Helpful Hope ministry to reach out to young girls in Montevideo who have been caught up into prostitution, to rescue them before they are swept up into sexual trafficking. Our Church has three Bible studies. One for men, another for women and a third for couples, which my Mom hosts and my Dad teaches. The men have a monthly prayer breakfast and the women, being better at organizing, have *a whole range* of luncheons and teas, and I don't know what else....too much for a mere man to understand," Pastor Jack said with a big grin. Allison was widely respected in the Church for her ability to organize.

"Our children's ministry teaches a whole roomful of our children and some from Uruguay each Sunday morning. I could go and on. We have actively sought God's will in what He would have us to do, and we're doing our best to obey and do what we are shown. Before we sing a concluding worship psalm, I've held off on asking Brad to share with us *his family's miracle* from last month. Many have heard, but even if you have, we can all hear it again, and again be blessed. Brad."

Brad, stood, all six foot two inches, with his surfer haircut and tats from his life before Christ. He started to speak, but realized that he had to get control of his emotions first. He opened his mouth, but couldn't talk. He knew if he did he would weep. The Pastor sensed the problem, walked over and put his arm up and around Brad's broad shoulders. "Let's pray for Brad. Lord, you did *a great miracle* in Brad's family. We ask that you allow Brad to gain control of his understandably strong emotions so that he can share with us what *You* did in his son's life. In Jesus' name we pray, amen."

Brad wiped his face, gripped his hands together and softly said, "God saved my son.....You all know our little boy, Joshua....he's now about two and a half. Not long ago....about a month now I think................Little Josh was....Well, let me start at the beginning. My wife, Sarah....you all know Sarah I think. She had to run to the store to pick up some things for the women's luncheon here at the Church. She told me to watch the boys. You know....we have three young boys. Well, the ten year old and the six year old were playing with Josh, out by the pool. I heard the phone ring in the kitchen, and I told the two oldest boys to watch Josh....that I would be *right back.*

"Well....the call took *longer* than I expected. A friend had a problem and needed some advice....Well....while I was talking.............After a few minutes......I noticed that the two oldest boys were wrestling in the family room, but I didn't see Josh. I told my friend that I had to go, I hung up and I ran out to the pool........And there was Josh..........*Floating face down in the water......*

"I jumped in and grabbed Josh. I pulled him out of the pool and immediately noticed that he was....blue....his face and arms and legs were just....blue....almost grayish in color.....I knew that *Josh was dead*..............He must have been without oxygen for.....I don't know how long......I carried him out into the front yard....some of you know our neighborhood....and I started screaming for help.....for somebody to *please help us*. The neighbors on both sides and across the street were all home....They heard me and ran over....One said 'Brad you know CPR....have you tried to....' As soon as he said that I instantly remembered that I used to teach CPR at the Y back home. I had just blanked it from my mind in my *panic* over seeing my dead son.

"I went right to work on Josh. I worked on him for I don't know how long, but he just got more blue.....not a breath....*nothing. Josh was dead.* No pulse. No Breath. *Dead.* My neighbor across the street is a nurse and a great prayer warrior. She's here so I won't embarrass her.... she asked me not to, but what she did was get down on her knees in my yard next to Joshua. She put her hands on his little cold body and she prayed....*Oh,* how she prayed....I've never heard such *fervent praying.* She approached the throne of God in a gentle, loving way just asking Him to glorify Himself by restoring life into Joshua's dead body....I don't know how long she prayed....joined by everyone standing in our yard.

"I prayed, but I *knew* that Josh was dead, that my negligence....had....killed Josh, so my faith that God would save Josh was *not* at a high level....just to be honest with you....If the miracle depended on my faith....which it didn't....it would have *never happened.* But.........God is good.......all the time......as Pastor Jack frequently reminds us. If Josh had gone on to heaven, God would still be good. I understand that....but in this case He saw fit to answer my sweet neighbor's fervent, effective prayers which availeth much. Josh coughed. HE COUGHED.

Praise the Lord, *he coughed*....Then he breathed..... His color came back within just a short time and he looked at us and....*he....smiled.*

"The nurse insisted that we take Josh to the hospital. She was very worried that oxygen deprivation would result in serious brain damage and mental or physical disability. We rushed him to the hospital where they tested Joshua for *almost two hours.* When we took him in and they heard how long he had been....well, they all had that real concerned look that's hard to hide. My faith *again* hit bottom....Josh was alive....But would he be a vegetable....Would he be permanently disabled because I *couldn't do my job* and watch him?

"The doctor came out to us. As he walked up I expected the worst news, but I was wrong. He said that he couldn't explain it, but Joshua had no evidence of *any* mental or physical damage, at all. None. He said Josh was a normal healthy, precocious little boy....and that we should take our precious gift from God home and *just love on him*....And also buy him some chocolate ice cream which he had begging for...........Well, Church....*that's my Uruguay miracle. Praise the Lord.*"

Brad was quickly surrounded by the tearful congregation as they patted his back, shook his hand and praised the Lord with him. Pastor Jack wiped the tears from his face and dismissed the service in thankful prayer for His mighty works using Americans He had transplanted overseas.

70

Bluemont Gardens

Mountain Brook, Alabama

Death took his time. Along with Snake Head, Death watched building six for three more days and nights. Though they never did see any of the adult women, for obvious security reasons, they did spot two of the teen-aged girls who carried in buckets of water from a nearby stream early each morning. Apparently fetching water was considered to be women's work. Young women's work. Death liked what he saw. Snake Head told Death that the pony-tailed blonde was his. Death smiled.

At 10 AM, a time during which none of the inhabitants of building six had previously been seen outside of the building, Death sent in a two man team with a large two inch auger and hand drill found in a barn they had previously rifled. The team also carried a two and a half gallon red plastic gasoline container, with rare combustible petroleum sloshing inside. The team walked slowly and carefully into the first apartment they came to on the first floor. The hole was slowly and quietly drilled through. So far so good they thought, as no discernible noise of discovery was heard from below or from the hall leading to the basement stairs. They screwed the yellow spout on the end of the gasoline container and undid the air escape hole on the other end. Lifting the container gingerly, they stuck the spout into the newly-drilled hole. They pushed in on the sides of the container to make it flow rapidly down into the basement below. After about half of the gasoline had been poured into the basement a long wooden match was struck and dropped down into the hole. With a loud WHOOSH a lick of flame shot up through the hole, confirming that the gasoline and the match had met.

The two men ran from the apartment building out onto the adjoining parking lot, waving their thumbs up signal of success to Death and the men who were stationed just outside the door of building six. Immediately after, the first fleeing inhabitant ran from the building, followed by three more, then a steady stream of men, women, teens and smaller children. Though most did not appear to be hurt by the explosion and fire, a few were aflame, and rolled on the ground to extinguish their burning clothing. All were coughing and wheezing at the effects of the gasoline and ensuing fire. As each man or male teen holding firearms emerged from the building, Death and Snake Head's men, standing hidden next to the exit door, slammed them to the ground, seizing their weapons. Within less than a minute all seventy one people were out of their hiding place, coughing and trying to clear their lungs. Each looked haggard and emaciated, as if they could not lose another pound without expiring. Knowing the approximate number of people he would be dealing with, Death had brought all but five of his men for the operation, with those remaining guarding their school hideaway.

Snake Head's job was to separate the captives into manageable groups. Using their rifles as prods, Snake Head and his tattooed, armed marauders waded into the collected and now un-armed crowd, most standing, but some sitting or lying on the pavement. Snake quickly pulled the younger women and female teens to the side.

He then separated the male teens into a second group, a few feet away. He forced both groups to sit on the parking lot pavement. He nodded to ten of his armed men who herded the older women and the younger children into a group and out of the parking lot. Darrell Wright, wiping blackened soot from his face, shouted at the men, *"Hey, where are you taking them? You can't...."*

Death was ready for the outburst. He used the butt of his AR-15 to smash Darrell in the back of the head and neck, splaying him unconscious onto the ground. The group of younger women and female teens broke into tears, sobbing and pleading for him not to hurt Darrell any further. Death snarled back, "If I had wanted to kill him I woulda just shot him. So shut up. *Shut up!* We just trying to help ya out here. Look at ya selves, ya're starving. Look at us, we ain't fat, but we eat at least one good meal a day, sometimes more. Y'all look like ya haven't eaten in days. We here to have ya join up with us. We'll be sure that ya eat a lot better than ya have been, by the way y'all look. But, ya gotta shut up. We got work to do."

By now the older women and children were gone from the parking lot. Snake nodded at another ten of their men who circled the men into a group. There was some mild pushing and shoving back, but no one wanted to be rifle butted in the back of the head, so for the most part they stayed quiet, waiting to see what would happen next. They were prepared, each of them to fight, if the opportunity presented itself. The nineteen men, absent Darrell who was still splayed on the pavement, were marched at rifle point out of the area. Death's plan was to take them to building twelve, which was on the other side of the apartment complex.

With the men gone, along with the older women and children, that left two groups now sitting in the parking lot. The younger women and the female teens were quietly sobbing. The male teens, seated a few feet away were not visibly crying, but were obviously shaken by what was happening. Death waited a few minutes to let it all sink in, as he had earlier told his men, for better crowd control. Death rolled a cigarette, lit it and walked over to Snake Head, who was studying the group of twenty three young women. "Snake, whatcha think?"

Snake Head couldn't take his eyes off of the women, replying to Death from the side of his mouth, but not loud enough that they could hear, "*Yummy*. Pony-tail is mine. You pick yours, then we'd best get out here so the boys can....*clean....up*. Know what I mean?"

Death leered at the thirtyish redhead sitting with her arm around a teen whose hair matched hers. Death whispered to Snake Head, "I'll take the two carrot tops. Both of 'em....Now, let's scat. We got a long walk back to the school. The boys won't shoot the men in building twelve until we're out of earshot. Don't wanta start no *rebellion* from the teen boys. They be our only shooter recruits, so we gotta convince 'em later that we sent their dads and the older moms, and the kids a course, to another camp. Better food and treatment at the other camp, dont'cha know? Over time, we can convince some of the teen guys to join us....*or die*. Simple choice."

"That's good, Death. Another camp....kinda true I guess....an underground camp. Get it? *An underground camp....*"

"Yeah, Snake. I *get* it. Six foot underground....'cept, we don't bury anybody anymore. Too much trouble," said Death, leering at his choices from the assembled women. "Two Teeth and the boys know what to do with the old women and the kids, once we be outta here, right?"

"Covered, Death. They'll herd 'em all back into the basement of building six. Shove them in the room with the hole in the ceiling. Nail the doors shut. Empty the gas container through the hole from above. *Whoosh.* No more useless eaters."

Death smiled. Then Death laughed.

71

BBC Studios – Broadcasting House

Central London, England

Following the evening presentation of WORLD IN REVIEW, the BBC studio director pointed to the BBC employee who was tasked with switching from a live studio feed to a pre-recorded segment. Under applicable Sharia Law requirements instituted of late, the pre-recorded segment was required to be aired nightly, in prime time. The mandatory segment began with an Islamic call to prayer, the Adhan. While the call was being recited the screen carried these words:

"Islam is not a normal religion like the other religions in the world, and Muslim nations are not like normal nations. Muslim nations are very special because they have a command from Allah to rule the entire world and to be over every nation in the world....Islam is a revolutionary faith that comes to destroy any government made by man....The goal of Islam is to rule the entire world and submit all of mankind to the faith of Islam. Any nation or power in this world that tries to get in the way of that goal, Islam will fight and destroy." (Mawlana Abul Ala Mawdudi - Founder of Pakistan's fundamentalist Muslim movement)

The screen then cut to a color picture of the Kaaba in Mecca, Islam's holiest site. Superimposed on the still picture on the screen were these words:

TRANSCRIPT OF TELEPHONE CONVERSATION BETWEEN PRIME MINISTER ROBERT RUSSELL AND THE MAHDI ON SEPTEMBER 15th (Approved for Broadcast by Imam Mahdula Bazardi)

303

RUSSELL: "Is he....is he....on the line? You *said* that he would be...."

MAHDI: "Prime Minister Russell? Are you there?"

RUSSELL: "Why, yes it is I. May I know your name, I've only been told your title....that is.....if you don't mind."

MAHDI: (NO RESPONSE)

RUSSELL: "Hello? Are you there?....Would someone please see if I've been dis-conn...."

MAHDI: "Mister Russell, I am here. My name is not relevant to this conversation. You say you know my title....that is....more than sufficient for your purposes....I am calling you as the Mahdi. The Guided One. The successor to the Prophet Mohammad, blessed be he. I have come to rule before the Day of Judgment and to rid the world of evil."

RUSSELL: "Alright....well....so....you have called me....what can I do for you?"

MAHDI: "We have graced you with this call in order to inform you that the United Kingdom of Great Britain and Northern Ireland will be honored to be the first nation in the newly created European Islamic Union. Your country will...."

RUSSELL: "Wait....Wait....The European Islamic what? What do...."

304

MAHDI: "Listen carefully, Mister Russell. We will...."

RUSSELL: "If you don't mind, my title is Prime Minister, and I deserve to be addressed as...."

MAHDI: "Mister Russell, you're *not* listening. Now listen to my words. I won't repeat them. We will allow you to formally change the name of your country to the United Islamic Kingdom of Great Britain and Northern Ireland. Within thirty-six hours. No extensions. Then you will...."

RUSSELL: "Impossible. Who do you think you are? We have been a united kingdom since 1707. We are a sovereign nation of over sixty million citizens, only a few of whom are Muslim. We won't...."

MAHDI: "I promised I would not repeat myself. After you change the nation's name, formally, by act of Parliament, then you will join me at Number Ten Downing on Wednesday to sign over to me your title and duties, also as approved formally by Parliament and your Queen. I will expect you and your family to be gone from Number Ten Downing by Wednesday, no later than five PM."

RUSSELL: (NO RESPONSE)

MAHDI: (NO RESPONSE)

RUSSELL: "Well, do you have any other demands? I can safely say that this bizarre conversation is over, so if you don't...."

MAHDI: "Anything else, you ask? Yes, Mister Russell. There is one other thing. We have two nuclear weapons in Central London, one from our friends in Iran, the other from Pakistan. Ten megatons each. That is the only thing I will repeat. Two nukes in London. Not far from you, actually."

RUSSELL: "You wouldn't....you...."

MAHDI: "Really? You doubt our ability? You question our resolve? Did you not see what we did to the Great Satan, to America? A much more important country than your little island? Test me, Mister Russell. Try us. If our demands are not met in the times that I just outlined, then London will be no more, Great Britain will be no more. You, *sir*, will definitely be no more."

RUSSELL: (NO RESPONSE)

MAHDI: "I will be at Number Ten Downing at noon on Wednesday. If our demands are not met, in detail, by and at that time, then London will be history by close of business, Wednesday evening. *Allahu Akbar.*"

The BBC broadcast segment ended with these words on screen:

306

ON SEPTEMBER 17TH PRIME MINISTER RUSSELL
HANDED OVER HIS OFFICE TO THE MAHDI,
WITH APPROVAL BY PARLIAMENT AND THE QUEEN,
WHO ALSO FORMALLY CHANGED THE NATIONAL
NAME TO THE UNITED ISLAMIC KINGDOM
OF GREAT BRITAIN AND NORTHERN IRELAND
AND AUTHORIZED ITS MEMBERSHIP IN THE
EUROPEAN ISLAMIC UNION
ALLAHU AKBAR

THE END

Author's Note to Reader

I wrote the Second Term Trilogy (SECOND TERM, THE WARNING and THE DAY) for a singular purpose – not to entertain, but instead to share with readers the truth of Biblical prophecies describing the future fate of America. The three novels are based on the 223 verses written by OT and NT prophets describing what will ultimately happen to a rich, powerful and influential nation in the last days. The books, though fiction, have as their foundation the truths contained in the Bible as analyzed in the non-fiction book, THE END OF AMERICA.

Of the three novels, this book proved to the most difficult to write. It's one thing to write about events happening in the future of a nation, but quite another to write about the termination, the destruction, the annihilation of that nation. THE DAY is replete with tears, from those who face death and who die during the Ezekiel 38/39 invasion of Israel, from those who don't flee from America before it's destruction (and who knew better) and from those men, women and children whose lives end with the fall of a nation which not only turned its back on Israel, but also on God Almighty. Also included are tears from Christians who moved offshore and who watched God working in miraculous ways through them in their new ministries. I wept more than once during the writing of THE DAY at the enormity of what is soon to happen, in Israel, in America and the world.

Post-apocalyptic literature varies greatly as to what authors speculate will happen. One such book popular in the 1960's was based on a family after a nuclear attack living comfortably on a river, raising fruits and harvesting *pecan trees. Needless to say, as long as there are large numbers of hungry people, those with food will not be living comfortably. In THE DAY I attempted to describe what life will really be like once Russia and Iran (Gog and the Medes) are allowed by God to attack America, after it betrays Israel. It's not a pretty picture. A Congressional study cited in the book postulated that 90% of Americans would die within one year of a major nuclear/EMP attack. That figure long-term might actually be too low when one considers the impact of the meltdown of the nation's many nuclear power plants, once they have neither electricity, nor diesel fuel for generators, to cool reactor rods. The scenario discussed on the fictional BBC newscast is all too real in light of the deficiencies in planning for long-term electric grid outages and petroleum product unavailability.*

I know and respect many who are "preppers". Though they have seen the danger and are trying to prepare for it, I fear they've missed part of the following verse regarding what to do, i.e., seek a safe place. "Wise people see danger and go to a safe place. But childish people keep on going and suffer for it." (Proverbs 27:12, NIRV).*America will not be a safe place. THE DAY describes what life would be like in a nation in which food is not available. Once any other person knows that a prepper has food, the prepper and his/her family will be in grave danger. No one can lay aside enough prepper food to last forever, nor enough ammunition to defend it indefinitely.*

Let's face it, when God warned ten times that Christians and Jewish residents of the Daughter of Babylon should "flee", He had good reasons. He didn't say "hide in Babylon" or "lay up stores of food and ammo in Babylon". "Flee" can only have one meaning. Flee. He said to flee

Babylon "so that you will not share in her sins" *(Revelation 18:14)*. He also said to flee so you will "not be destroyed". *(Jeremiah 51:6)*. Jeremiah warns *(51:29)* "no one will live there" (in destroyed Babylon). *If you are a prepper, pray and ask God for wisdom in regard to this critical decision.*

Readers who are interested in a non-fiction study of Biblical prophecies regarding the Daughter of Babylon/ Babylon the Great may be interested in reading THE END OF AMERICA. The book is available on Amazon and also on Kindle (for 99 cents so that all may have access). A Study Guide is also available. Only America fulfills the thirty clues written by Old and New Testament Prophets as to the identity of "Mystery Babylon". Study the thirty Biblical clues for yourself and decide which nation is Mystery Babylon. If you conclude that Mystery Babylon is America, then pray about heeding God's warnings to flee. The author prays that readers of THE END OF AMERICA will study, research, pray and obey the Bible's warnings to flee from The Daughter of Babylon. The ten warnings to Christians and Jewish residents of the Daughter of Babylon to flee are set forth below in an edited version of Chapter Thirteen from THE END OF AMERICA. Articles on the subject may be found at www.endofamericabook.com. Communication with the author is available through the website.

God bless,

John Price

April 1, 2014
Central America

Chapter Thirteen

GOD'S WARNINGS TO LEAVE

THE DAUGHTER OF BABYLON

If God states once in his Word to take an action the command obviously has great importance. How much more so if He says two or three times to do the same thing? Because God loves His people He has graciously provided through several different writers of the Bible the same identical message, stating it ten times.

TEN SEPARATE WARNINGS TO FLEE

The prophet Jeremiah, along with Zechariah, Isaiah, and the apostle John gave these ten specific warnings to God's people to flee the Daughter of Babylon. The first seven of the ten warnings are:

"Flee out of Babylon; leave the land of the Babylonians, and be like the goats that lead the flock." (Jeremiah 50:8)

"Let everyone flee to his own land." (Jeremiah 50: 16)

"Flee from Babylon! Run for your lives! Do not be destroyed because of her sins. It is time for the Lord's vengeance; he will pay her what she deserves." (Jeremiah 51:6)

"We would have healed Babylon, but she cannot be healed; let us leave her and each go to his own land, for her judgment reaches to the skies, it rises as high as the clouds." (Jeremiah 51:9)

"Come out of her, my people! Run for your lives! Run from the fierce anger of the Lord." (Jeremiah 51:45)

"You who have escaped the sword, leave and do not linger! Remember the Lord in a distant land, and think on Jerusalem." (Jeremiah 51:50)

"Then I heard another voice from heaven say: "Come out of her, my people, so that you will not share in her sins, so you will not receive any of her plagues." (Revelation 18:14)

These seven specific warnings all appear to be addressed to God's people - the Church, made up of believers in the Lord Jesus Christ. God also warns His Jewish people through these three prophets:

"Oh Zion! Escape, you who live in the Daughter of Babylon." (Zechariah 2:7)

"Leave Babylon, flee from the Babylonians! Announce this with shouts of joy and proclaim it. Send it out to the ends of the earth; say, 'The Lord has redeemed his servant Jacob.'" (Isaiah 48:20)

"They will ask the way to Jerusalem and will start back home again. They will bind themselves to the LORD with an eternal covenant that will never be forgotten." (Jeremiah 50:5)

Most Jewish people know they are Jewish, some are Orthodox and some adhere to more liberal branches of Judaism. But they know who they are. In these verses they are warned not to continue residing in the Daughter of Babylon. Moving to Israel is, of course, an option, but

314

one to be seriously studied before such a move, in light of the coming Russian-Muslim invasion, and accompanying blood to be shed in Israel.

Thus, the Lord warns believers in the Lord Jesus Christ seven times, and three times He warns Jewish residents of the Daughter of Babylon, to FLEE from this great end times nation. No other warning in scripture is recorded ten separate times. These multiple warnings to Christians and to Jewish residents of the Daughter of Babylon dramatically confirm that He has emphatically warned His people to flee the coming disaster that He knew from the beginning of time would occur.

God doesn't waste His words. We've just read that Christians are warned seven times to flee. God evidently wants to be sure that His people get the message, which leads to an obvious question: *Are you one of God's people?* How can you know, for sure? For the first few years of my life I thought I was a Christian. I was active in our church's youth group–I bought the cider and donuts every other Saturday night. If someone had asked me in high school if I was a Christian (which no one ever did) I would have said, 'sure, I'm not a Buddhist or a Hindu.' Then in college, I married a girl, my dear wife now of 53 years, who knew exactly what she believed – she was an avowed agnostic. We had some interesting discussions in those early married years. I remember driving back to college late one evening. I was listening to Billy Graham on the car radio. My wife soon tired of the message and told me to "turn that stuff off." I said, "Hey, do you want lightning to strike this car?" So you can see we had an elevated theological tone to our discussions.

After law school, we moved to a traditional suburb of Indianapolis to raise our children. After we were in our neighborhood for a short time I came home one night and my wife asked me "guess what I did today?" I didn't have a clue, but she soon told me that she had been invited to attend a neighborhood women's Bible study. I admitted that I was surprised, but after I thought about it I thought it was a good idea, so she could "meet our neighbors." I didn't hear any more about the Bible Study for a few weeks, then one night she asked the same question again, "guess what I did today?" Before I could guess, she told me that she heard a speaker at the Bible Study that she had been attending every week (I didn't know she had become a regular). She said the speaker, the wife of a dentist, "told us that to know God personally we need to accept His Son, Jesus Christ, as our own personal Lord and Savior. So, I did it."

My reply? "You did what?" She said, "I accepted Jesus as my Lord and Savior." My response? Not so good – particularly since before this time I was the 'religious one' in the family. I said, "that sounds like something you hear on your car radio driving through the Bible Belt."

Needless to say, that comment, and my increasing resistance to my wife's continued use of her growing knowledge of scripture, led to a running, and not always harmonious debate. Even though I had been on my college debate team, I was soon losing the debate, because my wife was acquiring her debate points from scripture and the Christian books that soon began to fill our house. After several months of ongoing debate, I was leaving for a business trip to California. On the way out the door, not having a book to read on the long flights, I picked up a

316

book my wife had (conveniently) left lying around for me to notice. It was Hal Lindsey's *"The Late Great Planet Earth"*, which eventually became the 1970's biggest seller.

On the red eye coming back from California I couldn't sleep, so I decided to see what my wife had been reading. Lindsey focused on Israel, in which I had some interest as a political science major. Lindsey wrote that God had written in the Bible, through the prophets, that the people of Israel would go into dispersion around the world, for centuries, but would in some future day be re-gathered back in the nation of Israel, in the same location of its original home. I knew that no nation in the history of the world had gone out of existence, been scattered widely into other nations and then 2,000 or so years later, been re-gathered into the same location. I can take a Jewish person to lunch, but I can't take a Chaldean or an Assyrian to lunch, as they've been dispersed and disappeared over time.

Lindsey then said that the Bible contains hundreds of prophecies about a coming Messiah, all of which were fulfilled in the life of one man, Jesus of Nazareth. He said that the mathematical chances of that just happening were so high that it would be the equivalent of tossing a marked silver dollar into the State of Texas, filled with four feet of silver dollars, stirring them up, and then finding the marked silver dollar on the first try. I was convinced. Lindsey also said what my wife's Bible Study speaker had said – that I needed to know Jesus personally as my own Lord and Savior. Because Jesus was resurrected after His death on the cross, if I know Him, I could be sure of life after the death of my earthly body. He gave a simple prayer to start the process of knowing Jesus.

When I came to the prayer I thought, briefly, 'hum, my wife's going to win our argument,' but I went ahead anyway, bowed my head on the airplane, and prayed a prayer like this: "Jesus, I don't really know you. But I want to, so I'm asking you to come into my heart as my Lord and Savior. Help me in the days ahead to understand what this is all about and what you want me to learn from the Bible. Amen." I didn't see any fireworks, but within a relatively short time I knew things had changed. I had changed. Over time, I lost interest in things I used to pursue, and I developed an interest in things I didn't previously care about. I soon developed a peace about why I was on the earth and what God expected me to do while I was here. And, by the way, losing that debate to my wife was the best thing I ever did.

If you are pondering the content of this admittedly frightening book, you may wonder if you are a Christian or not. If you can't say that a point in your life came, in which you placed your faith and trust in Jesus and came to know that He is the Lord of your life, you may wish to pray a similar prayer. If you seek Him, you will find Him. Once that issue is settled, you can move on to other warnings God has given to His people in His Word.

THOSE WHO FLED THEIR HOMELAND BEFORE US

The thought of leaving America to live in a foreign land, at first, naturally, seems unthinkable. But, it should be seen in an historical context, a Christian and a Biblical historical context. The history of Christians and Jews fleeing from persecution is well documented. The Bible contains many instances of God taking an action in the Old Testament that He mirrors in the New Testament. For example, the sacrifice of a spotless innocent lamb was a picture or foreshadow of the physical sacrificial death of Christ. Similarly, we find in this section of Jeremiah God's warnings to His people at the time of Jeremiah to leave their home city of Jerusalem in the nation of Judah. When they obeyed His warnings to leave, given through Jeremiah, they lived, they *"escape(d) with (their) life, (they) will live"* (Jeremiah 42). The warnings also given to Jeremiah (chapters 50 and 51) and to the Apostle John (Revelation 18) to flee from the Daughter of Babylon have the same result–if we flee-we live, if we don't-we die. It's a simple concept. It's doing it that's tough.

The Lord warned the Jewish inhabitants of Jerusalem and the cities of Judah well before Nebuchadnezzar's invasion that they should flee from Jerusalem and not try to remain as residents. Jeremiah warned Jewish residents that the Lord had told him Jerusalem and the cities of Judah would become a *"desolation without an inhabitant."* (Jeremiah 34:22) Those who heeded His words were safely secured in Babylonian captivity for seventy years. *"This is what the LORD says: 'Whoever stays in this city will die by the sword, famine or plague, but whoever goes over to the Babylonians will live. He will escape with his life; he will live.'"* (Jeremiah 38:2) *"Do not be afraid of the king of Babylon, whom you now fear. Do not be afraid of him, declares the Lord, for I am with you and will save you and deliver you from his hands. I will show you compassion so that he will have compassion on you and restore you to your land."* (Jeremiah 42:11-12)

Our nation was settled and populated by Christians who could not abide persecution. Shipload after shipload of our Christian ancestors, for decade after decade, chose to move from their homeland in Europe immigrating to a land known for its religious freedom. Their decision to leave their own nation, leaving most of their family members and lifelong friends, in almost all cases to never see them in this world again, had to be gut-wrenching and tearful. They left their nation because the level of religious persecution they were experiencing was not tolerable.

In the last century, in the 1930's and 1940's, Jewish residents of central and eastern Europe were increasingly alarmed that they were being targeted for extinction by the growing Fascist movement. Russia's Czar instituted pogroms to exterminate Jews in Russia. As a consequence, many Russian Jews moved to Germany, only to be confronted not long after with Adolph Hitler's "Final Solution." Those who moved to Poland and Austria had similar problems, as Hitler expanded the reach of the Third Reich.

As more Jews were taken into captivity and their assets seized, increasing numbers began to realize that fleeing Europe was a rational, life-saving option. France rounded up and deported 76,000 Jews (including 11,000 children) to concentration camps. Only 3,000 returned alive. Prior to deportation, across Europe, tens of thousands fled to freedom, most with only the clothes on their back and a suitcase. Millions who chose not to flee were killed in Hitler's Holocaust, "Hitler's Final Solution." Nazi Germany purposefully and deliberately slaughtered millions of men, women, and children, with bullets and nerve gas, solely because they were of Jewish descent. (A&E series – The World at War). By the time they had been rounded up and detained, it was too late to flee. 25%

died within ten days of being taken captive. Six million who didn't flee eventually died. Confirming God's demand for an accounting of shed blood, Germany, which led the slaughter throughout conquered Europe, suffered over seven million deaths. One million Jewish residents of the Soviet Union died, but over time one million Jewish residents of Russia immigrated to Israel. Those who saw the danger and fled from it lived; with many still alive even today. It is estimated that about 500,000 Jewish émigrés left Germany fleeing to freedom, before Hitler closed the borders to Jewish emigration. Most left with nothing. No future job. Little assets. But they lived.

A common denominator of the Christians and Jews fleeing for their lives over the last two hundred years was that they trusted God to provide for their needs as He promised and as He did. We find no reports of emigrants who fled to America dying from lack of food. *"Where He guides, He provides."* But what of those Christians and Jews who didn't flee Europe when life was threatened? Jeremiah told his fellow countrymen: *"Whoever stays in this city will die by the sword, famine or plague."* (Jeremiah 38:2[a]).

In the same sections of scripture which contain the prophecies warning of what will happen to the Daughter of Babylon, it is also stated that in the Daughter of Babylon will be found *"the blood of the...saints."* Once Americans who are active in church, Bible studies and various ministries are arrested, hauled away, sent to prison or worse, God's warnings to flee will become a lot more urgent. As unlikely as this may seem, any review of the news over the last few years confirms that there is a growing anti-Christian, anti-religion sentiment in America.

321

BUT WHERE SHOULD WE FLEE?

God has warned the residents of the Daughter of Babylon to flee their native land before its destruction, but where should we go? Jeremiah suggests that the residents of the Daughter of Babylon may want to go to their own land (50:16). That observation fits a 'melting pot' nation of mixed peoples described in Jeremiah 50:37. For many people that will mean moving to countries in which they have relatives. For those who don't have any known relatives in foreign nations, they may be surprised how many people they know who do have family in other nations. For others it may mean immigrating to other parts of the world in which they may have some connection. Fortunately, God's people who have been engaged in missionary activities, even short term, will have contacts in other nations who will facilitate immigrating. For many, however, it will mean locating in a new land, with little or no prior connections.

No one, least of all our Lord, would suggest that leaving the land of one's birth is an easy task. When Jeremiah warned the residents of Jerusalem to leave Judah going into captivity in Babylon their first reaction was to accuse Jeremiah of treason: *"But when he reached the Benjamin Gate, the captain of the guard...arrested him and said, "You are deserting to the Babylonians!"* (Jeremiah 37:13). The leaders of Judah then had Jeremiah flogged and thrown into a prison dungeon, where he *"remained there many days"* (Jeremiah 37:16). Shortly after, *"Then the officials said to the king, 'This man should be put to death. He is discouraging the soldiers who are left in this city, as well as all the people, by the things he is saying to them. This man is not seeking the good of these people but their ruin"* (Jeremiah 38:4).

What happened to the warned residents of Jerusalem? Many listened to God's warnings, given through Jeremiah, then they fled Jerusalem and lived relatively comfortably in ancient Babylon. They wept for home *"by the rivers of Babylon"* (Psalm 137:1), but they were alive to weep. After their time in Babylon, along with their families who grew during their time in relative safety, they returned to Jerusalem, following the prophesied period of seventy years. Those who refused to heed God's warnings were either slain in Jerusalem, or died after fleeing to Egypt, a nation that God specifically warned them against. (Jeremiah 42:13-22)

There is a distinguishing characteristic between Jeremiah's warnings to the residents of Jerusalem of his time to flee and his warnings to the future residents of the Daughter of Babylon to flee. God told the residents of Jerusalem at the time of Jeremiah that they would *come back home* after seventy years (Jeremiah 25:11; 29:10). The promise was fulfilled. Jeremiah's warnings to God's people who would someday live in the nation called the Daughter of Babylon never, not once, tell them that they will return home after the destruction of their home nation. On the contrary, Jeremiah, Isaiah, Psalm 137, and John all specifically, and unequivocally, say that the Daughter of Babylon will be destroyed and desecrated. *"The land trembles and writhes, for the Lord's purposes against Babylon stand—to lay waste the land of Babylon so that no one will live there"* (Jeremiah 51:29). Thus, there will be no return of those who flee to go back to the Daughter of Babylon, unlike the residents of Jerusalem at the time of Jeremiah who did return home after seventy years, as He said they would.

As God's people examine the difficult decision as to where they should emigrate, it will be evident that European nations will not offer an acceptable relocation venue. The nations of the European Union, after the fall of the world's only superpower, could be re-named the European Islamic Union, or a similar name will be chosen conveying the new Muslim identity of the continent. Muslims have tried over the centuries, unsuccessfully, to conquer Europe. Therefore, moving to a European nation before the Daughter of Babylon falls could result in living in the "belly of the beast" and would be highly dangerous for a Christian or a Jewish immigrant. Recall that Daniel warned that the Antichrist will be *"a king of fierce countenance"* (Daniel 8:11) and *"He will cause astounding devastation...He will destroy ...the holy people"* (Daniel 8:24). The prophesied Antichrist will rule the conquered nations of the world with an iron fist. Fleeing to Europe would be an unwise move.

Likewise, most of the Middle Eastern, many African nations and many Asian nations, would be poor relocation choices due to current significant Muslim domination of the government and population of those nations. They also have high levels of abortion, inviting God's justice. Islands of the world aren't ideal as potential places to move, due to the potential of being 'trapped' on an island, with no escape, if things go bad politically or in any other way. Riots over food prices and against "elites" broke out on two Caribbean islands in February, 2009, with tens of thousands in the streets.

So where does one move? This clearly is a matter for much prayer and seeking God's face. In doing so, two factors should be taken into account: a.) does the potential location for immigration allow abortion; and b.) what is the level of Muslim population? The remaining nations of the world that today prohibit or severely restrict abortion and that have low levels of Muslim population are mostly in Central and South American, nations that, therefore, may offer an appropriate refuge. So what would be a good move? Pick a nation with: a.) no or extremely limited abortion, and also b.) a nation with no or extremely low numbers of resident Muslims. (For more detail on nation choices, see pages 240-246 of THE END OF AMERICA.)

LIVING CHEAPER

Living in Central and South American countries is generally cheaper than a comparable lifestyle in America. Food, housing, entertainment, medical care, utilities and taxes are generally lower, but of course, vary nation by nation, and region-by- region, within the nation. Some Americans living abroad write that two people can live comfortably on $1,000 to $1,500 per month, though expenses related to automobile transportation tend to raise that level of spending. This fact of economic life has attracted many American "expats," purely on financial grounds.

Good resources for more research include International Living, (www.InternationalLiving.com), which publishes guidebooks on individual countries and sends daily e-mail newsletters detailing how to live abroad. Other resources:

www.liveandinvestoverseas.com

www.escapeartist.com.

Some claim that over 300,000 Americans emigrate from America every year. That's a sizeable number, which goes against the conventional wisdom that the entire world wants to immigrate to the U.S. Apparently, for many reasons, large numbers of Americans have decided to live in a nation other than their native land.

The internet provides millions of pages of information about the nations of the world and allows one to engage in e-chats about specific overseas locations. Let what you learn help guide your decision, after much prayer and fasting. [Set forth below are seven practical suggestions for those who preparing to flee from the Daughter of Babylon/America.]

FORSAKE NOT THE ASSEMBLY OF BELIEVERS

In planning to emigrate, God's people should remember the importance of assembling together with other believers. *"Not forsaking the assembling of ourselves together, as the manner of some is."*(Hebrews 10:25). We are commanded to associate with, pray and worship with fellow believers, plus it's medically indicated. Neuroscientist John Cacioppo concluded that people who don't associate regularly with other people are more prone to illness, obesity and feelings of helplessness. (*Loneliness: Human Nature and the Need for Social Connection*).

Those who decide to emigrate will find that the many tasks involved in doing so are best accomplished when shared with others, such as those in one's small group, Sunday school, Bible study or church. The Pilgrims who immigrated to America didn't arrange their moving plans separately, but as a group of believers, committed to a common goal. Think of it as an adventure, a Godly venture into the next chapter of our walk with Him, as He leads us to step out in faith, in obedience to His Word. (The ministry events described in THE DAY occurring in Uruguay are based on true stories, though they happened in a different nation.).

As a future safety consideration, arranging housing in locations not clustered together could be advisable. Networking in common church activities could still be easily arranged, just without the obvious "American Christian Compound" potential as a target. That's how we live today, scattered in various neighborhoods and gathering to meet, worship and fellowship as the body of Christ. Most believers will seek new opportunities for ministry in their new homes overseas. Following the lead of Biblical Christians, we will naturally desire to spread the Gospel to those whom the Lord brings into our lives in our new homes. It is exciting to see the Lord at work in our lives, as we make a difference for the Kingdom of Jesus Christ. Being used by God to help change eternity, in an offshore adventure, is no small job assignment.

(THE END OF AMERICA, Christian House Publishing, Inc. 2013, © John Price)

SEVEN THINGS YOU SHOULD DO IF YOU ARE MOVING OFFSHORE FROM THE DAUGHTER OF BABYLON/AMERICA

1.   PRAY – I know, that sounds elementary. But, no major move should ever be attempted without a solid, prolonged foundation of prayer, seeking God's will through His wisdom. It's not wise to just read a book, even THE END OF AMERICA, and then start packing. Be sure that you believe that God has called you to emigrate out of the US before actually moving. Yes, He tells us ten times in His Word to flee (seven times to Christians, three to Jewish residents) the Daughter of Babylon/Babylon the Great. So, it would seem almost automatic to do so, in obedience. I'm only suggesting that you lay a basis in prayer before doing anything else preparatory to emigrating.

2.   RESEARCH – Google, Google, Google. At your fingertips are literally millions of pages of material on all the nations on the globe. Try to narrow your search to just a few nations, maybe three or four. Look not only for socioeconomic facts, climate, currency, government stability, etc., but also for churches, ministries and Americans in the area. Search for reader forums where you can dig deeper and ask questions of people who are already there. You can, of course, also search for rentals and real estate for purchase (more on this below). Try to select the top two countries that appeal to you based on your research. Don't forget to ask family and friends if they know anyone in the countries you have preliminarily chosen. We visited several countries before moving to Central America. Good candidates are New Zealand,

Ecuador, Costa Rica, Uruguay, Chile, Belize and Panama. You may find others that appeal to you.

3. RECONNAISANCE VISIT – Once your search is narrowed, buy a ticket for a 2-3 week visit. Stay in hotels/B&B, etc. while you are looking. We learned a lot from the B&B owners we stayed with while in New Zealand Ask about local evangelical churches, if there are any in the area, people there will know about them. Talk to American Christian and Jewish residents, anyone who can tell you anything about what it's like to live in the nation you are visiting. Try and visit the two or three most popular/most visited communities in the nation you are visiting. Hook up with a local English-speaking Realtor, who can show you what rentals in your price range look like. Unless you are mega-wealthy (or maybe even if you are), don't look for real estate to buy. Maybe later, but not at this stage, nor the next. The main purpose of this trip is the same as the Israeli spy party, as God told Israel to go in and spy out the land (Numbers 13:17-20):

"Moses sent them to spy out the land of Canaan and said to them, "Go up into the Negev and go up into the hill country, and see what the land is, and whether the people who dwell in it are strong or weak, whether they are few or many, and whether the land that they dwell in is good or bad, and whether the cities that they dwell in are camps or strongholds, and whether the land is rich or poor, and whether there are trees in it or not. Be of good courage and bring some of the fruit of the land." Now the time was the season of the first ripe grapes."

The spy party spied out the land, bringing back a cluster of grapes so large it took two men to carry it on a pole, along with pomegranates and grapes. The minority of the spy party saw a good land and told Israel to go up at once and possess it. The majority lacked faith, gave a bad report and led Israel into the sin of doubting God's Word. I mention this because a good prayer is that God show you what you are seeing with His eyes, so you get a good idea of what you are seeing. If you encounter a nasty taxi driver, does that mean everyone in that city is nasty? Obviously not, but be careful about seeing the 'giants' of the land (Numbers 13:32-33) and not seeing the land for what it really is.

4.   TIME TO DECIDE – Once you have visited one, two, maybe three or more countries, and you're back home, it's time to decide. Don't decide while you are visiting. Realtors offshore call people who do this 'Margarita Buyers', referring to visitors who are wowed by the sunsets and beaches, after too much libation and who then buy real estate without really knowing what they're getting into. Again, pray, make sure that you and your spouse are in agreement. What do the kids who may be moving with you think? Do a budget. What will it cost to rent an acceptable housing unit, cell, cable and internet costs, car and food expenses, travel to visit relatives, etc.? Once you know what it will cost to live in your chosen location, you will need to decide if you have the income/assets to make it work. We know Americans who supplement their social security/pension/savings income by managing properties for absentee owners, handling rentals, etc. Lots of people make money on the internet. There are books and courses available on how to do so. Pray and make your final decision.

5.   SELL IT OR SHIP IT? – Assuming you have decided to move you will need to decide what you are going to sell and what you are going to ship. We've seen it done both ways. Some Americans arrive with a few suitcases, having sold everything else. Some arrive with steel containers full of furniture, furnishings, even cars. A middle position is to load a pallet, which is combined with others in a container. Generally, a container will cost about $10,000 + - to ship, with a pallet being in the $3,000 range. How much do you like your 'stuff'? Frankly, some folks really need to bring it because it's what they have grown accustomed to having around them. Others enjoy getting rid of almost everything, feeling a sense of freedom when it's gone. Needless to say, furniture and furnishings are sold in foreign countries.

6.   TRY IT OUT – Next, move to your chosen location. Pre-arrange for up to a 3 month lease/rental of an acceptable housing unit near where you may end up on a longer term basis. Concentrate on getting to know local Christians (Americans and locals), your neighbors, a good doctor and local clinic, a good attorney for residency application, a good fruit stand, a skilled mechanic (if you eventually buy a car) and your local church. By the end of the 3 months you'll know if this area and these people in this country are for you. If so, look for a 12 month lease/rental and settle in. If not, leave and try your second choice for a country in which to live. You will probably need a car, though it's cheaper not to have one. Buying a used car is expensive in most foreign countries. If you can buy from a trusted person who is selling because they are moving, that may be your best option, but it's not guaranteed. Cars are machines – they break. Budget for it.

7.   REMEMBER, IT"S THEIR COUNTRY – Here are a few tips we've learned after 18 months living abroad: A.) There is NO perfect country, including the US, so when you get frustrated over something (local rules, slow responses, misleading time estimates, excessive heat, high electric or gasoline costs, etc.), just remember that it's their country, you're just visiting. B.) After a few months we decided to stop asking: "Why Do They_____". The answer is because they can and….it's their country. C.) Look for opportunities to share the gospel. People outside the US are much more open to hearing about Jesus. D.) Develop relationships with Americans. Go to dinner. Play cards. Watch movies. All of these inter-personal actions help in the adjustment from leaving home in the US. E.) Praise the Lord for allowing you to safely settle in a secure area which is not a police state, is open to the gospel, not saturated with sin and provides a home for you. God bless you as you heed and flee!

ABOUT THE AUTHOR

John Price was for forty years an Indianapolis attorney who was active in political and governmental matters. He now devotes his time to his wife, his grandchildren and to writing. He and his wife live in Central America. The author may be contacted at:

john@endofamericabook.com

Published Books by the Author

AMERICA AT THE CROSSROADS
Repentance or Repression

Christian House Publishing, Inc. 1976

AMERICA AT THE CROSSROADS

Tyndale House, 1979

THE END OF AMERICA

4th Edition, 2013

The Second Term Trilogy

SECOND TERM

THE WARNING

THE DAY

www.endofamericabook.com

CPSIA information can be obtained at www.ICGtesting.com
Printed in the USA
LVOW06s1550200715

446912LV00017B/1135/P